T0274445

# WISH YOU WEREN'T HERE

### ERIN BALDWIN

VIKING

VIKING

An imprint of Penguin Random House LLC, New York

First published in the United States of America by Viking,
an imprint of Penguin Random House LLC, 2024

Visit us online at PenguinRandomHouse.com.

Library of Congress Cataloging-in-Publication Data is available.

ISBN 9780593622698

1st Printing

Printed in the United States of America

LSCH

Edited by Aneeka Kalia
Design by Lucia Baez

Text set in Quire Sans Pro

Hold on, do you mind if I take a moment to tell you about the Glue? The Glue is a term my friends Sarah and Shelby came up with to describe the invisible connection between people who didn't get the childhood they deserved.

This book—its tireless whimsy, its unconditional joy, the fireflies over the lake, the predictability of Pat asking, "S'more what?"—is for everyone with the Glue.

But this book is not for Sarah, who made me pay for my own almonds one time in 2017 and for that I will never forgive her.

# PRIYATOPIA

The day I started second grade, my teacher told me that Juliette Barrera-Wright was much too difficult a name for such a little girl.

"What about Julie? That's pretty," he said, probably smug and condescending, though I can't picture him anymore.

Most of the memory has slipped through my fingers, but a part still lives in me, vivid enough to feel even now: the smallness.

I shrank, like Alice after eating the mushroom. Everyone was watching, waiting for me to agree with this adult just because he was an adult. Even though it was *my* name. And the longer they stared, the smaller I got. I was drowning in my desk, surrounded by all these giants with easy names. Despite ten years of distance from that classroom, my hands still sweat.

When I think of it, my chest still tightens.

Right as I began to taste the acceptance of "Julie" on the tip of my tongue, a girl I'd never met before said, "There's no such thing as too-complicated names. My mama says only lazy people say that."

Arthur pulling the sword from the stone. Gandalf and the Rohirrim arriving at Helm's Deep. The little crowd in my brain goes wild.

There was no more discussion after that. Everyone's called me Juliette since.

That is the one and only reason I don't hate Priya Pendley.

Even after she told Milo DeMontes she thought I was obnoxious. Even after I begged for a different science fair partner because she was annoying and bossy. Even after I beat her in the spelling bee and she said it didn't count because "of course Juliette can spell *argumentative*."

Out of respect for our seven-year-old selves, I come to her ridiculous birthday party every year.

The first Priyatopia was very normal—store-bought decorations and everything. After that, it escalated quickly. Carnival rides for her tenth. Mirror mazes and art installations at thirteen. Last year, Hozier performed a song he'd written specifically for Priya. *Seventeen* did a feature on this year's party titled "Birthday Queen Turns Seventeen (We Ask Social Media Darling Priya Pendley How She Invented the Next Coachella)." Priya's glossy glamour shot took up two pages.

Oh, wait. Sorry. Before we move on, can we talk about how she calls it *Priyatopia*? It's plastered everywhere. I have a theory that if a guest stands still for more than two minutes, Priya herself comes over and spray-paints her name across their body. In white or gold, obviously.

And she had the nerve to call me obnoxious.

I feel distinctly impoverished as I pull through the Pendleys' gates into their winding driveway, already lined with luxury cars on both sides. I maneuver my crappy old Honda Civic between a Mercedes and a BMW and begin the hike up to the house.

The Pendley Mansion sits on an ungodly large parcel of land. Impeccably manicured, but you already knew that. The house itself is a gleaming stone and glass monstrosity that I've spent entirely too much time in over the course of my sixteen short years, which is how I know to follow the path around back, past clusters of networking C-list celebrities.

Usually, I love this time of year—the liminal space between final exams and the start of camp. Warm breezes linger after nightfall, and they always smell like a trip to the state fair. Well, minus the post-Gravitron corn dog vomit. I fear that one day I'll begin associating this weather not with campfires and kayaking but with thumping dubstep and this gaudy arch of white and gold balloons spelling out PRIYATOPIA.

I step under the arch in question, led by the scent of barbecue to a row of trendy food trucks. While trying to decide between Burrito Boys and Holy Crepe, I'm swept into a warm hug that smells like vanilla and spice.

Before I turn, I know I'll find Priya's mom, Deepika, looking up at me with her big brown eyes. She's an adorably short Indian woman with wavy hair, radiant dark skin, and the kind of carefree beauty only money can buy.

Unfortunately, I love Deepika. She isn't just Priya's mom; she's everyone's mom. When we were growing up, she chaperoned every class field trip and helped serve lunch when cafeteria workers called out sick. If anyone in town needs a place to stay, a meal to eat, or a shoulder to cry on, they can always turn to Deepika.

It's almost unbelievable that Priya is her daughter and not her evil twin.

Deepika yells to be heard over the music, "Juliette, you're more beautiful than ever! I bet you have to beat the boys off with a stick, hmm?"

I bite back a snicker. In this nosy town? After I spent years making it clear a romantic relationship is at the rock bottom of my priority list? Nobody is pursuing me, let alone "the boys," and I like it that way.

"I wouldn't say that."

Deepika frowns prettily, glowing in an embroidered yellow kurta. "No need to be modest, my love." She flexes, but her twinkling eyes betray any chance she has of looking fierce. "A girl as gorgeous and smart as you should own it. Priya tells me you're going to Yale, too!"

I cock my head. "I'm *applying* to Yale? But I won't hear back for a while." Neither of us will, but, unsurprisingly, the Pendleys are already counting their privileged chickens.

She swats at the air, as if the Yale admissions committee is a fly that simply needs to be redirected out of the house. "My darling, if they don't take you, they're out of their minds." Her voice drops to a conspiratorial whisper then, and she says, "And I'll have Jack put in a good word with his golf buddies. They have connections everywhere."

"Thank you," I grit out, trying desperately to be grateful instead of bitter.

Deepika beams. "Of course! We'll help however we can. Now, tell me about your summer plans. I didn't realize so many of you kids were doing these special programs. I have to find something for this one"—she jerks her chin at an ice sculpture of Priya—"to do also."

"No programs for me," I say. "It's my last summer at camp." The words catch in my throat, and I realize it's the first time I've said it out loud. Wow. Last summer.

She nods, chewing absently at her lower lip. "Frogbridge."

Trying not to snort, I enunciate, "Fog. Ridge."

"Ah, yes. That's right. Fogridge." Her brow furrows. "Why camp? Wouldn't something academic look better to colleges?" she asks, like she didn't just tell me I'm a shoo-in at Yale.

I've had this conversation with countless adults, and it's infuriating every time. Why do teenagers always need to be reaching for someone else's goal? At what age am I allowed to do things solely because they're fun and I enjoy them?

Whatever age that is, it's not sixteen, apparently.

"I love it" isn't enough, so I give Deepika the kind of answer she wants. "Like you said, everyone's in academic programs. Wilderness camp sets me apart. It makes me well rounded." I form a circle with my hands.

"Hmm. I suppose so." She looks ready to ask me something else, but then her thoughtful gaze snags on someone and she shouts, "Neha! You came!" Patting my shoulder, she whispers, "Excuse me, my love. It's so much responsibility being the life of the party. Priya's by the pool."

She disappears in a whirlwind of Gujarati, leaving me alone on the lawn.

The waits for both Burrito Boys and Holy Crepe have become absurdly long, so I amble over to Lotsa Tots-a. The line moves quickly and soon I'm at the front, reaching for my wallet.

The cashier stops me with a raised hand. "Everything is free on Priyatopia," he recites.

I fail to suppress a surprised "Jesus."

"I know, right?" He hands me a paper boat of tots. "Happy Priyatopia!"

"Happy Priyatopia," I repeat under my breath, heading for the nearby pool gate.

Strangers, like a school of fish, whorl around me the second I step onto the concrete deck. I become Marlin protecting Nemo, tightening my grip on the container of tots and crouching my upper body over them. My precious boys.

As I circle the pool, seeking a refuge in which to eat my sons, I scan the crowd for a familiar face. I spot Alison, my favorite of the friends that Priya and I share, at the same time she spots me.

"Juliette!" She stands from her chaise and rushes in, leaving wet footprints on the ground.

I hold my tots out to the side, steeling myself for the hug that soaks my clothes. Alison makes every hello feel like a return home from a decades-long war. We just saw each other in school last week, but I find myself choking back tears at her welcome.

"You look like a model," I say, gesturing at her curvy body, perfect in the retro one-piece except the areas where her white skin has started to pinken and burn ever so slightly.

Alison holds out a palm like she's about to impart some vital wisdom, but then says, "I've been rewatching all of *ANTM*. I just got to the pinup episode in cycle five. You know, the season with the *lesbian*, Kim?" She cups her hands around her mouth when she whispers *lesbian*, as if she's an offended Midwestern aunt and not a woman who loves women herself.

"I haven't seen that one," I admit, chuckling lightly.

"Oh, you should watch it. It's unhinged." Her eyes go to the blue envelope I pull from my back pocket. "Trying to find Priya?"

At my nod, she looks pointedly behind me.

I turn, sighting Priya's unmistakable hair moving smoothly through the heart of a crowd. Her angled lob is black, but about halfway down her back, it transitions to a pure snow white. The rest of her outfit—a sequined crop top and fringed bell-bottoms—is also in her signature all-white. I'm so focused on this bizarre pool party attire, it isn't until my double take that I register she's casually gliding about in a pair of white roller skates.

Huh.

It really makes you think: If Priya isn't the center of attention at every moment, will she cease to exist?

I roll my eyes before I can help it. Apparently this summons her, because she heads in our direction, sailing over so gracefully that she appears nearly motionless, like the world decided it would move so she didn't have to.

She coasts to a stop, the fringe on her pants billowing in a self-made breeze, and smiles. Like me, she's biracial, but where my mom's white side dominates my features, Priya's face is a carbon copy of Deepika's. Right down to that unethically charming smile.

"Juliette Barrera-Wright." My name tumbles from Priya's mouth with a slow ease that curls my upper lip. "Welcome."

"Yeah, happy Priyatopia." I extend the envelope robotically.

A few years ago, I forgot her present and had to stop at a Starbucks to pick up a gift card. The only one they had left was a rainbow Pride Month design that said YOU'RE MY HERO!

On my birthday, I found the same gift card in my locker, with the exclamation point turned into a question mark. Since then, we've traded the YOU'RE MY HERO? card back and forth for every gift-giving holiday. Like much of our relationship, it feels like a weird inside joke, a secret understanding between two people who understand nothing else about each other.

That's an exaggeration. I do understand some things about Priya. Too much, in fact. She's a kiss-ass, for one. Pleasant to a fault. She treats her haters like they're stans she just hasn't had a chance to win over yet. She's so good at bending over backward, you'd think she's the one who does high jump, not me.

And she's *on* constantly. It's exhausting, to be honest. But don't go thinking this disdain is one-sided. God knows Priya would pay money to keep me from standing up for myself. She cringes every time I rock the boat even a little.

Despite our polar-opposite personalities, she and I have an uneasy truce because, in some cosmic joke, we can't seem to escape each other. We end up in the same friend groups, the same clubs, the same classes. I go out to eat, there's Priya. I show up for yearbook committee, so does Priya. She's everywhere. It's creepy.

No matter how Priya-free I try to make my life, our paths stay inextricably linked. Two planets, forever intertwined, wildly orbiting the same sun. Narrowly avoiding collision.

She's *fine.*

*I'm* fine.

Our lives aren't a nineties teen drama. There are no catfights. No love triangles. No betrayal. Instead, we find ourselves in the Tenth Circle of Hell: Cooperation.

In photos, we stand on opposite sides so we can crop each other out. We don't vent to shared friends. On group projects, we turn in A+ work with nary a physical fight. And twice a year, we hand the same gift card back and forth like a ritual.

Priya takes the envelope by the edge, fingertips as far from mine as possible. "Thanks."

Even with two arm lengths separating us, I still get a whiff of her fancy lemongrass shampoo.

I'm feeling just awkward enough to start shoveling my swiftly cooling tots into my mouth when Priya says, "Barry brought a *drink,* if you want some."

Barry, Priya's dopey boyfriend, materializes beside her, surprising me. He sports (pun absolutely intended) his varsity jacket over shark-themed swim trunks. One of his hands squeezes Priya's shoulder and the other holds a large water bottle.

I've always liked Barry. He's my track captain, runs cross-country, and is always the first to cheer on a team member. I'm pretty sure he started the chant when I broke my record at state championships sophomore year. A nice enough guy, even if he is a few clowns short of a circus.

I consider the bottle. I'm not opposed to drinking; in fact, it'd probably make Priyatopia bearable. But do I want to drink half the school's warm, apple Bacardi backwash? Pass, actually.

I shake my head. "I'm good. Thanks, though."

Ever supportive, Barry gives me an enthusiastic thumbs-up. "Let me know if you change your mind, dude," he says. Then, he trots off to spectate a game of nonalcoholic beer pong, leaving Priya staring after him.

They're weird together. Don't get me wrong, Barry is white-jock handsome: strong jaw, lean muscles, dimples that are visible from the Hubble. Something about them just doesn't fit, but mentally dissecting my hatred for the Prarry power couple always gives me a migraine.

As an act of self-kindness, I sigh and say, "Well, that's enough of this conversation."

Priya nods at a group of our classmates forming in front of a live plant wall with 'Priyatopia' spelled out in roses. "Wait," she says. "Pictures first?"

I sigh, looking down at my food. "My tots are getting soggy."

"Come on. It's my birthday," Priya complains.

"You'll have another one." At her pout, I continue, "Do I have to?" *Just so you can crop me out?*

The group by the wall beckons for their queen as she looks between me and them anxiously. I would be flattered by her hesitation if it were actually about me. But it's not.

It's about them: the fans and friends watching. It's about Priya's image, and her need to be liked by all those people who might judge her if she lets me walk away instead of forcing me to be included. And I know firsthand that fighting Priya Pendley's people-pleasing is a losing battle, so I set my tots down—we weren't meant to be—and gesture for her to lead the way.

There's nothing more telling than the strata of a group photo.

Because it's her birthday, the unwritten Pendley/Barrera-Wright Accords allow Priya a rare spot in the middle of the photo, with her inner circle. The second tier is a mix of close friends and social butterflies, thrown across the foreground in deep squats and swimsuit model sprawls. Casual friends make up the third group. The fourth consists of blood relatives, mostly.

And finally, there's the loneliest, most distant layer of stratum, where I "cheese" with Gabe Rosario. In the Land of the Crop-Outable. I knew what I was getting into, but it still sucks.

I smile the same practiced portrait smile for each photo: the serious ones, the happy ones, and "now one silly one!" I don't hand my phone over to the partygoer they've recruited to take pictures. If I were on the season of *America's Next Top Model* that Alison is watching, Tyra would eliminate me for being dead behind the eyes.

When the photo shoot is over, I find myself a shady lounge chair. In minutes, my phone pings with a notification from the Camp Clowns 🐨⛺☀ group chat.

> **itsgiapham**
> The ✂ queen strikes again

> **juliettethehumanperson**
> probably don't call her that????

I click the link to p.r.i.y.a's post. The photo is slightly oversaturated and already liked by over a thousand people. My eyes go straight to the edge. I don't know what I was expecting.

> **juliettethehumanperson**
> no, im in this
> if you zoom you can see my hand on
> that guy's shoulder

> **lucygooseyy**
> 🙄 wow you get more
> visible each year
> things I hate: priya
> pendley, "scissor queen"

Gia sends a picture of us three, arms around each other. Lucy blocks the sun by resting a hand against her copper hair. Gia's as handsome as ever with his crooked grin and dangling silver cross earrings. Between them, laughing, not dead behind the eyes, is me. I hadn't learned how to manage my curls, so they're half-wavy, half-straight, and all-frizzy. I love this picture.

I double-tap it. A heart appears in the lower corner right before I'm startled by a loud scraping sound, a splash, and a bloodcurdling shriek. The phone slips from my hold and hits the ground hard, bouncing several times on the concrete and settling face down.

The source of the sound is immediately apparent. Priya, thrown off balance by a cannonballing guest, teeters precariously on the edge of the pool. Her face is frozen—eyes wide, mouth gaping. If not for Barry's arm around her waist, she'd be upside down in the deep end.

Her shock dissolves into relieved laughter. She presses a hand over her heart as Barry easily hauls her back from the water. Twirling, she wraps him in a hug. Ugh.

I reach for my phone, closing my fingers around the rough ridges of the freshly shattered screen. Ignoring the spiderweb of cracks, I open the group chat again.

**juliettethehumanperson**

i miss yall

**itsgiapham**
Miss you too! One week!
**lucygooseyy**

literally dying every day that I don't get
to spend with Papa Pat.

itsgiapham
Not papa pat 💀

It should make me feel better. But there's a heaviness that tethers my laughter deep inside me. Lately, it feels like it's been tethering all of me down.

Running my thumb over the screen, I think about how much I wish I could fast-forward my life. How much I want to be at camp. How much I *don't* want to be at Priyatopia, watching Priya somehow manage to lead the Cupid Shuffle, even the "now kick" part, in roller skates.

The palm trees sway gently overhead. I study them, breathing in the smell of chlorine and sun-warmed skin. And time, that bastard, continues to pass at an agonizing 1x speed.

# THE SOUND AND THE FURY

On the winding stretch of road that becomes Main Street, the trees grow so thick that we have to turn on our headlights in the daytime. Old-fashioned streetlamps line the sidewalks, guiding tourists by the warm glow of an interdimensional portal to a simpler time. It's a carefully cultivated part of Woodland Park's postcard-town charm. Like the city council thinks people wouldn't visit if they knew we had access to tree trimmers.

The cozy, historical aesthetic fades the farther I get from Main, until the pastel Victorians and ornate hedges give way to scattered street hockey supplies and imperfect paint jobs. It looks like any other suburb.

The only difference is that this particular neighborhood has the ability to make me irrationally angry. Because, once again, the spot in front of the house—my spot; the parking spot that's always gone to the oldest Barrera-Wright child living at home; the spot I earned by waiting for not one, not two, but *three* of my siblings to move out—is occupied by my younger sister Eloise's hatchback.

I don't crash into her car (because then how would I get to camp next week?). I find a spot two blocks away and trek home, carrying the bag Deepika handed me on my way out of the party. *You always leave before the cake,* she'd said. *So I asked the caterers to cut a piece early.*

It was thoughtful. But as I walk, the iconic gold Priyatopia gift bag becomes a beacon for busybodies. When I pass his porch, Mr. Gossy tells me Priya is a "lovely girl." Mr. Freedman jogs by, pulling out his headphones to pepper me with questions. Little Luke Reyes hops off his bike and asks if he can have one of my presents. His mom gives me an apologetic smile, but when she bends to scoop up her son, she angles her head to peek inside the bag.

Even on my own street, I am forced to endure Priya Pendley's existence.

Is nothing sacred?

They say no man is an island. I guess that's true. After all, I don't really feel like an island. I feel more like a dinghy with a hole in it, slowly capsizing off the coast of Priya Nation as onlookers shout about how lucky I was to even get this close to her.

*Priya could drown my family, and I'd thank her. She's so beautiful and nice and—*

That's the worst part. She *is* nice. She could so easily tell our mutual friends that she doesn't like me, and they'd pick her. Yet, since our truce, she hasn't said anything about me. Not one bad word. Not a moment of whispered frustration. Nothing.

I mean, I'm glad for that, but I won't prostrate myself just because she's not malicious. Why should I idolize her? Get on my knees and worship her for . . . what? Being rich? Gorgeous? Knowing celebrities? Having too much self-confidence?

Please.

The bar is so low.

Juggling my car keys, the bag, and my constant lingering guilt for hating Saint Pendley, I reach over and release the latch into my front yard.

Rocket launches. Building demolitions. BTS stans when Jungkook flashes his abs.

These are a few things calmer than my house when I return from Priyatopia.

Drumming shakes the entire structure. I toe off my shoes in the mudroom, inviting the vibrations to travel out of the floorboards, into my bones, and up to my brain, where, with any luck, they'll rattle loose my memory of Priya doing the Wobble.

However badly I want to go mope in the privacy of my room, I can't. When I look up the stairs, I find Lizette, my youngest sibling, with her head stuck between two banister poles. She bawls as Eloise tries to extract her. Forcefully.

"You'll break her neck!" I scream, dropping my bag and racing up the steps.

Eloise's mouth moves, but I can't hear her. I barely hear myself over the drumming.

I push her aside, probably harder than necessary, and check that Lizette is safe from major injuries. Stabbing a finger toward the basement door, I shout, "Tell Henry to stop!"

My baby sister, who is six and not a baby, shuts her eyes tightly. Though tears still pour from them at a concerning rate.

The drumming comes to an abrupt halt, but the noise doesn't. The music's absence is filled with Lizette's sobs and a chorus of howls, our dogs begging to be released from behind their prison bars (the dog gate).

The basement door swings open, and Henry barrels toward us. My ten-year-old brother stops opposite me, drumsticks in hand. He's talented, started drumming before he could even talk. His first word was *paradiddle*. That's a drum joke.

Seeing Eloise emerge from the basement stairwell, I clap a hand over Lizette's mouth and ask, "Where the hell are Mom and Dad?"

Eloise rears back, scrunching up her face. "Hospital."

I meant it rhetorically, a reminder that I am nobody's parent. It was a way of saying, "This isn't supposed to be my problem." But, of course, Eloise thinks I'm so useless that I literally can't guess where our workaholic doctor parents might be.

"What'd you get me?" She snatches the cake bag from where I left it and sets it down on the coffee table, peering inside.

"Nothing. Don't touch that," I say, peeling my hand back from Lizette's face. A line of snot trails behind. I gag, which makes Eloise gag and Henry laugh and Lizette cry even *harder.*

I wrap my hands around Lizette's head and wiggle it from side to side, wishing it was Eloise's neck.

"This frosting is good," Eloise says, licking her finger and reaching back into the bag.

I don't even know what flavor it is. She's eating my cake and I haven't even tasted it.

"Can I try some?" Henry asks.

"No."

At the same time, Eloise says, "Sure!" She glares at my answer, holding the bag out to Henry, who takes it greedily. "Can you be nice?"

I try to calm my breathing. It does nothing.

"I saw a happy birthday post to Priya from that actor," Eloise announces. "The hot one. I mean, they're all hot, but, like . . . *the* hot one." She pauses to take the bag from Henry, since he's done smearing half my cake across his face. "From that new CW show? *The Trainwreck* or whatever? Long black hair?"

"I have no i—Don't!" I raise a hand to stop my brother, poised with a stick in each fist, from drumming on the front door. He skulks away, daggers in his eyes.

After ten minutes of micro position shifts and Eloise's incessant Priyatopia chatter, I free Lizette's head. My back hits the wall with a thunk.

"Thankth, Juliette!" Lizette lisps, flashing a gap-toothed smile.

"You're welcome, buddy," I sigh.

She skips away, hair sticking straight up in clumps like one of her paintbrushes' bristles after she's chewed on it. That's Lizette's thing. She paints. Henry drums. And, when she's not too busy being insufferable, Eloise codes.

I used to sing. I won a big contest once. For a long time, everything was about my singing—what my family ate, what shows we watched, what music we played in the car. But all that stopped when it became clear I wasn't *good*—just good *for a kid*.

Come hell or high water, the doctors Barrera-Wright are determined to raise a prodigy. When they realized I wasn't that prodigy, they shifted my share of their attention down the line. Just like they had with Arthur, Laurent, and Ariadne.

Like they will with Eloise, but somehow she hasn't realized that yet.

"Did you really even go to Priyatopia?" Eloise asks.

I don't answer. I know she's trying to get a rise out of me, because that's what my family does when they're bored.

"You aren't in her post." Her voice is sharpened, pointed, and aimed right at my heart.

We may live in the same house, but we aren't friends. My siblings were always more competitors than confidants. By the time I realized I couldn't compete anymore—when my mom canceled my vocal lessons and I cried under the bed for hours—it was too late to change that. What's more, I don't want to. Between those of us so close in age, there's been too much cruelty to forget.

Eloise waits for a fight, but I'm not in the mood.

Crashes echo from the kitchen. I don't care. I'm done parenting my siblings for the night. I just want to go pack for camp and bury my rage under a thick layer of nostalgia.

By the time I register the slide of nails on hardwood, I've missed my opportunity to stop the puppies from barreling into the coffee table. Our pit bulls, Dr. Blueberry and Salem, gobble up the rest of my cake. Powdered sugar clouds scatter as Eloise's wide eyes dart to me.

I sigh. I didn't even know it had powdered sugar.

Last year's Fogridge T-shirt is a garish shade of orange, covered in signatures, like a walking yearbook. I skim the messages.

*So proud of you, NORTH STAR!!!!! I'm lucky to know you. See you next summer!*

There's no name, but I know who wrote it—Flagstaff, one of my favorite counselors and a Fogridge constant. A bittersweet wave of yearning rocks me.

Another, from a senior named Karina, who isn't back this year, says:

*You deserve all the good things. Enjoy that tree house!*

Every square inch contains an inside joke, a doodle, a name of someone I love. I ball it up and squeeze it against my chest, like a heart I can put back inside myself.

I'd made a neat list, intending to check off each item as I pack it. Instead, I gather all my camp shirts and read them over and over again until I fall asleep on the floor.

# THE VICTORY TOUR

An antsy two-hour drive deposits me at the bottom of Fogridge's steep driveway. I exhale in relief at the sight, the warmth of the sun, and the rush of the river that runs the edge of camp. Part of me wants to pull over and bask in this lightness I've missed so fiercely. A bigger part of me itches to *go*.

So, I go.

The tires crunch at my overzealous acceleration, slipping a little where the gravel has worn away. I slow and soon crest the hill into camp proper. The dirt road widens to a forest clearing, filled with staff in red-and-white shirts enthusiastically greeting campers.

Familiar faces beam at my arrival. A sports specialist gestures for me to stop. As he circles around to my open window, Strat—one of the counselors whose messages turned me into a sobbing mess last week—hip-checks him out of the way.

"I got this one, DC," she declares with a puff of her chest, and he backs away, laughing.

Then she launches up onto my hood, seating herself on the passenger side. Flinging a hand toward an open wooden gate, she commands, "To the parking lot!"

I guffaw. "Strat, get down! You'll fall."

"I will not. I have impeccable balance."

When it becomes clear she won't budge, I inch the car along, not wanting to decommission one of camp's best counselors before the first bonfire. She chortles, waving regally as we pass people who don't bat an eye at her antics.

Halfway into an empty spot, a white man in a long-sleeved shirt and a bucket hat strides toward us, shouting, "Strat! Get down from there!" His frown holds the hint of a smile. "The summer camp industry is dying. I cannot afford workers' comp."

Pat Zimmerman is in the fourth generation of Zimmermans to own Fogridge, and the only staff member who goes by his actual name. About ten years ago, to keep campers from finding their counselors on social media, management began enforcing the use of "nonsense names" instead of real names. But a lot of the staff like their nonsense names so much that they end up using them all year round, which kind of defeats the purpose. Strat once told me even her parents call her Strat, a name she only chose because of a joke about board game strategy.

She leaps off my hood after I finish pulling in, her messy lavender bun waggling gleefully atop her head. Pat gives her hair a reproachful look.

"Sorry, I'm just excited about baby Juliette's last year." She throws my door open and tugs me out by my cheeks, pinching them hard. "Can you believe it? They grow up so fast."

"Stop that!" I groan, pushing out of her hold. I rub my sore face with open palms.

Strat attempts to casually lean her elbow on Pat's shoulder, but he's at least a foot taller and thirty years older, and he frowns deeply at where her arm touches him.

"I prefer to think of it as a victory lap," he says, lifting his chin.

My cheeks heat. I duck my head. "I like that."

Pat shakes Strat off and begins strolling away. Flashing one last self-satisfied grin over his shoulder, he says, "Plus, it's not your last summer. You'll be back to work for me next year."

"You'll need more money to pay Juliette what she's worth," Strat singsongs after him.

He gives no indication of having heard.

"Typical. He doesn't pay me what I'm worth, either," she jokes, rounding the car. "Pop the trunk. Let me help you bring your bags in."

"I'm okay," I insist, shoving her lightly. "Go help a newbie. I don't have a lot to carry."

"Oh, I get it." Strat drapes a forearm over her eyes, drifting away dramatically. "You don't need me anymore." She fake-sobs through the chorus of "Sunrise, Sunset" from *Fiddler* until she reaches the parking lot exit and launches into a cartwheel, cackling demonically.

I adjust the straps over my shoulders, swallow thickly, blink back tears. It's not that I—

It's silly.

My whole life, I've been told I was too intense.

By talking too loudly, wearing my thoughts on my face, and acting upset when I feel upset, I make people uncomfortable. I've been asked, "Are you mad at me?" more times than I can count. I've been told to relax even more often than that.

I don't wake up with Priya's charm or Barry's eagerness. It's hard work for me to be likable, and sometimes I don't want to work.

But then I come to camp, where there aren't expectations or deadlines. The goal isn't to be the best at having fun. Nobody tells you to dial your personality down. I don't have to pretend to relax here, among the Strats of the world, the people who are A Lot anywhere else.

I guess . . . I'm just really, really glad to be home.


Fogridge is shaped like a diamond and divided by an X into four symmetrical sections, which we call quads. The top point touches the parking lot. The bottom touches the lake. Quad 1, closest to the parking lot, holds the cabins, the mess hall, and the main office. Quad 2, to the east, houses the art departments, theater, gymnastics, and other indoor activities.

On the west end of camp, Quad 3's outdoorsy activities stretch into the forest while sports fields take up most of its in-camp area. The fire pit where we roast marshmallows sits between them, right at the border of the woods. The last quad is rarely called Quad 4; more often, people call it "the lakefront." That's self-explanatory. In the center of camp, where the X crosses, is the pavilion, where meetings are held.

There's more than a little spring in my step as I bypass the cabin assignment board at the very top of Quad 1. We're sorted into cabins by age, living with anywhere from six to twenty campers and a counselor. Normally, I would join the long line of luggage-laden losers, but this year is different.

At the end of every summer, the staff votes for a North Star, an MVP. The North Star's reward is a private cabin, called Polaris, shared with their assigned mentee. Last year, I was chosen. It's not clear if there are criteria for voting or if it's a popularity contest. Lucy used to call it the Narc Award before I won, but she's been strangely supportive since. Either way, who am I to question a semiprivate bathroom and a little trophy that someone clearly cobbled together in Woodshop the night before the awards ceremony?

Unlike all the other plain log cabins, Polaris is a small split-level tree house nestled in a massive oak tree at a fork in the main path. I've spent every summer of my life staring up at the twin rocking chairs on the porch, wondering what it was like inside.

After years of fantasizing, it's surreal to finally climb the steps to the cabin's door.

I lean into the railing and savor my final moments of not knowing, demurely ignoring stares from younger campers. I pretend I'm so swept up in the beauty of Fogridge and the rustle of the leaves that I couldn't possibly be bothered to notice anything else.

When the anticipation becomes too great, I open the cabin door and inhale deeply, bracing myself for the smell of cedar and freshly vacuumed carpet that's always marked the beginning of camp. But it doesn't come.

I furrow my brow and survey the space before me. Stairs to the loft level branch off to the right. The loft overlooks the main floor, which has already been claimed by my mentee. Their bed is neatly made, a fluffy cloud of white sheets. Four enormous suitcases huddle in the corner. Meticulously organized cosmetics line the desk, which has been turned into a vanity with an oversize gilded mirror and several expensive-looking organizers.

A vase of baby-pink roses sits on the open windowsill, wafting sweet bursts of air through the cabin with every breeze. The first floor's dusty blinds have been traded for billowing drapes, and I feel like I've stepped into a French perfume ad. As beautiful as it is, something within me sours because it's just not camp.

Behind the closed bathroom door, the shower is running. I'm glad my roommate isn't sitting on their bed, excited to show me the work they've put into their space. I can't muster my inner North Star right now.

A small weight lifts off my shoulders when I enter the loft and it still smells faintly like the camp I know. A wave of first-day memories hits me the moment I set my duffel bags down on the shiny blue mattress. Faces of long-gone counselors and campers flash through my mind, and I smile.

It takes all of ten seconds to dump my clothes unceremoniously into the dresser. I unpack the last few items—bed linens, toiletries, a book, a metal water bottle—and stuff the empty bags under the bed frame.

Leaning into the railing that overlooks the main floor, I study my mentee's room again. I try to see past their weird glamping situation and remember why I was so excited to live with a brand-new camper.

I have friends. But I feel like I'm still trying to find my person—someone who just gets me, a kindred spirit. Someone who doesn't think I'm too intense. A deep part of me holds out hope that this roommate will be my person.

And the exact moment I have that thought, in what can only be described as a divine prank, the bathroom door opens.

A thick cloud of lemongrass nearly knocks me over.

That smell turns a key in my brain. No. White luggage. White linens. White shoes.

Oh no.

As if in a movie, the shower steam disperses and reveals the one face I don't want to see right now. The one face I hoped had taken a summer program in England or New Zealand or . . . anywhere but Fogridge Sleepaway Camp.

Priya goddamn Pendley.

# GALAHAD AND THE KNIGHTS
# OF THE ROUND TABLE

Priya barely looks up as she unwinds her hair from a towel. "Hey," she says, as if the world didn't just flip inside out.

I can't conceal my shock. Several times, my mouth opens to form a question, but the words get stuck in my throat and I'm left gawking.

"You good?" she asks, draping her wet towel over the footboard.

Her nonchalance is forced. It has to be. I can't imagine a world where being my roommate for five weeks warrants such a casual response.

"What . . . the hell?"

Priya watches me calmly. "What?"

I sputter and gesture frantically at her, at the bathroom, at the bed. "You! Here! No!"

"Why are you acting surprised? Didn't you see my name on the board?"

"No," I say emphatically. "I didn't look at the board because I knew this was *my* cabin. I won this cabin. I won it! This is my cabin!"

"Well, if you'd looked, you would have seen my name right

under yours, roomie." She speaks with a resigned acceptance.

I'm surprised she was able to cycle through all the other stages of grief so fast. I, myself, am going to need at least a few days to conquer denial.

Priya reclines on her bed, retrieving her phone from her pocket.

Watching her scroll nauseates me. I all but whine, "You can't use your phone here."

She gives me a knowing look. "Juliette, relax."

That's it. I'm gonna kill her. "Why are *you* . . . *here?*"

"Same reason *you* . . . *are.*" She emphasizes the words haltingly, clearly mocking me. Waving a hand ambiguously, she says, "Build a fire, look at sticks. Connect with nature."

"Couldn't you connect with nature in Ibiza or something?"

Priya smiles sweetly up at me and slaps a hand on her bed. "Oh, gee. I would have loved that, but someone convinced my mom that camp would be the best thing for my college applications." Her green eyes flicker between me and her phone screen. "I believe the words 'well rounded' were mentioned."

Deepika! Damn that woman for being so friendly and nice.

My hands clench into fists. "But you don't *need* college app help. You're a legacy."

She rises to her forearms and shakes her head at me. "Please. Plenty of people are legacies, dude. It's competitive out there. Why are you so anti-camp all of a sudden? You're always going on and on about this place on social media."

I'm in such a state of shock that I don't even question her

following my accounts with enough regularity to know what I "go on and on about."

It's all I can do to tear my eyes away from her, plop down on my bed, and try to ignore the pounding behind my eyes. Priya Pendley is a human migraine.

This is my senior year at Fogridge. The Encore. The Victory Tour.

She has the whole year. School. Priyatopia. Great parents. Probably Yale. Even my friends like her more than they like me. But I get Fogridge. It's the only thing that's mine, and this is the last time it's going to be mine.

So, of course, here she is. Eclipsing me once again.

I shake, fighting the urge to scream. Luckily, the camp's speaker system booms to life before I have the chance to commit a crime.

"Hey, Fogridge," rolls Pat's deep voice.

I hesitate, then get angry with myself for feeling self-conscious about this thing I love just because Priya Pendley's in the room. I call, "Hey, Pat!"

There's a distant echo of surrounding cabins doing the same.

"Come on down to the pavilion for All-Camp," Pat sings into the mic.

I almost walk out alone, but when I reach the door, I'm torn by my sense of duty. For years, the Zimmermans have drilled "KARE" into us. Kindness And Respect for Everyone. It's an acronym to keep kids from tearing each other apart over sandbox toys, but I've recited the words at every assembly

I can remember. It's finally wormed its way into my monkey brain.

Kindness And Respect for Everyone. Even Priya. Because she's not just Priya Pendley here. She's also my mentee. Gross.

"Come on." I gesture to the door. "It's an All-Camp assembly."

She side-eyes my change of heart but pulls on a pair of white tennis shoes—nondescript in a way that suggests that they were exorbitantly expensive—and follows.

We join the fray of campers heading deeper into camp. Despite the tension settling into the pit of my stomach, I can't help but smile as I take in the familiar sights. Wildflowers grow with abandon alongside the walkway, swaying in the breeze that blows off the lake.

We pass a couple of other seniors who sweep me up into rib-crunching hugs and laugh in my ear, simply because they're happy we're here together. They make me want to slip back into friendly, chatty Camp Juliette, but I'll have time for that later. After Priya has been sufficiently oriented, I can desert her without guilt.

"That's Medical." I gesture toward the low cabin with the white-and-blue awning. "It's the only building with air-conditioning."

Priya's eyebrows rise. "Wait, our cabin doesn't have air-conditioning?"

I laugh at her joke before realizing it isn't one.

Her face scrunches up. "What do we do when it gets hot?"

Shooting her a withering look, I say, "Be hot."

I point out the trailheads for the paths to Quads 2 and 3, explaining what activities can be found in each area. Fogridge has never been boring to me before, but even my eyes are glazing over as I talk.

My lackluster tour is interrupted when a tall Black counselor in an orange body suit gently headbutts me in the shoulder. "Jules!"

"Flagstaff!" I shout, clapping his back. I ignore the look Priya shoots me when I don't correct him on my name. If anyone in the world is allowed to call me Jules, it's Flagstaff. "How was your year?"

"Same old. Missed my happy place, of course." He gestures widely around. "But, hey! I landed a full-time phys ed position. I start in September," he says, pumping a fist in the air.

"Yes! Congrats." Finally. He's been substitute teaching since graduating a few years ago. I can't believe it took him so long to get hired; he has such obvious gym-teacher energy.

I raise my hands above my head, and he meets them in a double high five, beaming.

"Thanks. It's elementary school, so I took a younger group thi—" His eyes flash when he spots his campers, a group of boys who look about eight, and he takes off running. His feet kick up dirt from the path as he screams, "Sam! Sam, do not put that worm in your mouth! No!"

I smile after Flagstaff, who remains one of my favorite staff members just on the strength of how many extra popsicles he snuck my group when I was his camper.

"You're a celebrity," Priya remarks.

I startle, having forgotten about her for a blissful second. She sidesteps the path traffic, watching Flagstaff wrap his arms around a young boy in an attempt to softly Heimlich worms out of his mouth.

"BNOC," I correct and motion for us to continue walking. "Big Name on Camp. It's what they call the people who have been here for a long time."

The crowd thickens as we near the domed gazebo sitting at the heart of camp.

"That's our counselor," Priya says, pointing to a white woman who seems to be tallying a group of seated seniors. She's young, probably still in college, with short brunette hair and a tie-dyed staff shirt. "She's new this year. Galahad."

I shiver, a visceral reaction to Priya trying to teach me anything about Fogridge. Pretending I haven't heard, I march up to my counselor and look her right in the clipboard.

"Are you Galahad?" I ask.

"I am." She lowers the clipboard and smiles down at me, a feat considering I'm five nine. "Are you Juliette?"

"Yup." Not allowing myself space to think, I plow forward. "And I actually wanted to ask you something."

Galahad cocks her head, her eyes straying to Priya somewhere behind me. I glance back to make sure we're far enough away that the enemy won't overhear, and I catch the tail end of her giving Galahad a brownnosing wave. "Okay, go ahead."

I wince, stepping into her line of vision, hopefully obscuring

Priya. "You might know that I'm the North Star this year. Did they . . . tell you about that in staff training?"

"They did," she says slowly.

"I've been going to—coming to Fogridge for a really long time, and . . . I . . ." I feel like such a child. "My roommate, in Polaris, we aren't—we don't get along."

She frowns but doesn't say anything.

"So, I guess I was wondering . . . if you could move her? To a different cabin?" My pitch rises as Galahad's frown deepens.

"You want me to move your roommate?" Her eyes flick to my forehead, like she can see through my skull to the golden child behind me.

"No, I mean . . . yes, but you don't understand. She's really—I was here . . . first," I finish weakly.

Galahad's mood sours. She kisses her teeth. "I actually helped your roommate move in this morning, so I know that's not true."

My mouth drops open. "No, not, like, here first. Like, *here* first."

I can tell that my counselor doesn't note the distinction. To her, it probably seems like I'm just trying to backpedal, but I really did mean camp as a whole, not just today.

Any warmth in her eyes is gone as she says, "Please take a seat. I will not be removing your roommate. If *you* decide you'd like to switch cabins, you can let me know. Otherwise, the housing decisions are final."

"But I—"

She leans around me and says, "Priya, if you need help with

anything these first few days, please let me know."

Embarrassment floods me at the brush-off. In an attempt to stop the rising heat in my cheeks, I only dig the hole deeper. "And if you need help with anything, Galahad, you can let *me* know." I force a smile, despite my immediate regret.

Galahad doesn't smile back. "I think I'll be okay."

*Let it go*, I tell myself. *Let it go, let it go, let it*—"I don't know; camp can be pretty complicated for newbies."

Galahad fixes me with a contemptuous stare. "Take a seat, Juliette."

# 5

# BIGGER FISH

"First of all, I want to say welcome back to my Fogridge family," Pat says. A cheer rises from the gathered crowd. "I hope you all had a fantastic school year and that you're ready for an even better summer."

I wrap my arms around my knees, tuck my head, and survey the nearby campers. I recognize most of them, but Lucy and Gia are nowhere in sight. I wish they were here.

"Tried to get me kicked out?" Priya whispers from her spot behind me.

I shush her without looking up from my all-important task of pulling up the grass and shredding it into tiny pieces.

Galahad hasn't so much as glanced in my direction since I slunk away in shame, though she has reprimanded several campers around me, including ones she isn't in charge of.

"—at the campfire," Pat is saying. "Does anyone want to guess what's for dessert?"

"S'mores!" the crowd cheers.

"S'more what?"

Pat makes that same joke every summer, but the crowd still groans like it's brand new. There's a comforting familiarity in it, a song we all know the words to. The world outside Fogridge goes on, but in a hundred years, Pat will still be here on the first day of camp asking, "S'more what?"

But I can't sink into that comfort because I *feel* Galahad disliking me.

"I knew you'd be weird about sharing a cabin," Priya goads. "When I was putting out my makeup, I knew you would hate it. You're weird about anything feminine."

My eyes narrow. This cannot be real. "I am not," I grumble, earning myself a disdainful warning glance from Galahad.

Like a mosquito, Priya buzzes in my ear, "You are. You always have been. You hate women."

"I do not. I do not hate women. I am a women!"

"Woman," Priya corrects unnecessarily.

"I know!" I snap, too loudly.

Galahad makes a sharp noise, looking between me and Priya with accusation in her eyes. Great.

"Relax," Priya says, lowering her voice.

"Don't tell me to relax. I was relaxed," I hiss into my shoulder. "I'm not having this conversation."

"Because you know I'm right." I can picture the way she nods sagely. Unquestionable.

An exasperated sigh escapes me, but Galahad looks ready to duct-tape my mouth shut if I speak again.

What a ridiculous thing to say.

I don't hate women. I do traditionally feminine things! I wear dresses! I—

How do you prove that you don't hate women? Why do I feel like I have to?

My original plan was to look for Lucy and Gia after the assembly, but now that's out the window. I have bigger fish to fry.

Much as we love Pat, everybody knows he's not the Zimmerman you go to for advice. Most of the time, he's wise, insightful, and empathetic. But sometimes, he acts exactly like what he is: a middle-aged white man who spends 80 percent of the year alone in the woods. His elusive wife, Delta, isn't much better.

Thank goodness Fogridge has TK, Pat and Delta's eldest daughter. Whereas TK's siblings aged out of camp and didn't look back, she never left. Well into her thirties, she has always been here to fill the role of Fogridge Older Sister for staff and campers alike.

She also runs the Mini Camp, a day program for kids younger than third grade. She shuttles them from activity to activity on a little train, the kind you find at zoos or amusement parks. It makes finding TK convenient whenever you're having an emotional breakdown.

I stand up the second Pat dismisses us, leaving Priya and Galahad in the dust as I traipse my way up to the Mini bunk, eyes open for a little red-and-green caboose.

TK pats the bed beside her, smiling gently.

She takes after Delta's Irish side more than Pat's Airheads-White-Mystery-Flavor, with thin, red hair pulled back in a frizzy ponytail. Freckles dot the bridge of her nose, creating a shadow underneath her tortoiseshell glasses. She says, "I'm so glad to see you back, Juliette. How was your year?"

I take the offered seat and shrug, finding myself shrinking

just the tiniest bit—something I rarely do at camp. It doesn't escape TK's notice.

"It was fine. Couldn't wait to get back here, as always," I say.

The conversation pauses as we watch the Minis unpack their belongings. They don't sleep here, but they do keep extra clothes and toys. They even have their own bunk beds for nap time.

"Do you like working with the little kids?" I ask as one camper runs up and begs TK to braid her hair.

TK gestures for the camper to stand in front of her and begins skillfully working brown strands of hair into a French braid. "I love it. They're so fun at this age. Right, Ella?"

The girl being braided nods carefully. "Yes!"

"Ella is really funny, too. Tell her one of your jokes, kiddo."

Ella cranes her head toward me as much as she can without disturbing TK's work. She pushes her lips together in thought, squints her big brown eyes, and then says, "Hmm. Okay. Wha . . . ? Who? If . . . ?" Ella glances up at the ceiling, drawing the words out slowly while TK disguises a laugh with a cough. "Wh-what if . . . if when there—If when you were playing racing, and . . . Mario was a different color than red, then—?" She furrows her brow, seeming to just now realize that she doesn't have an ending in mind.

When she looks back to her counselor for guidance, TK shoots me a smile and bends down to whisper in the little girl's ear.

"Oh, yeah!" Ella shouts, lighting up. She bonks herself on the forehead with a little fist, as if trying to hammer the information into her brain. "Knock, knock."

I let out a barking laugh. "Who's there?"

"Interrupting cow."

I smile. This joke resurrects every summer. I answer slowly. "Interrupting co—"

"MOOOO!" Ella says, jumping up. TK has to raise her hand to avoid pulling the girl's hair while she ties it off with a cheetah-print scrunchie.

I genuinely laugh at Ella's enthusiasm. "Wow, that was really good!"

"Ella's a genius," TK says soberly. "She's our little goofball." She leans down and pats Ella's hand. "All done."

"I'm not a goofball!" Ella protests, playing with her new braid.

"You're right. You're too kid-shaped to be a ball. You're just a goof."

Ella laughs and runs away screaming, "I am not a goof! You're a goof!"

Because I have terrible timing, I choose this moment—the one where we are surrounded by screaming children, the one where TK's attention is being pulled in a million different directions—to ask, "Do I hate women?"

In classic TK fashion, she is entirely unperturbed. Picking invisible lint off the bedspread, she asks, "I don't know, do you?"

"TK!" I give her a swift whack on the shoulder.

"Hey, it may look like I know everything, but I don't know what goes on in your brain. Where is this coming from?"

I sigh and cross my arms. "A girl from school is my roommate in Polaris this year—"

"Oh, yeah! I forgot that you're our North Star. Well deserved!"

"Thanks. Well, this girl, she's . . ." I pause, considering how to move forward. To her credit, TK doesn't rush me. She just watches her campers, occasionally calling out instructions on sharing. "I'm not the same person at school as I am here. And she's . . ." I stop, frustrated with my inability to explain.

TK shakes her head. "Everyone lives in several ponds. In camp, you're a big fish. In school, she's a big fish?"

I nod.

"That's life, Juliette. Did your roommate say that you hate women?"

I nod again, feeling like one of her young campers.

"Do you hate women?"

"No! But she puts these things in my head. I don't want to live with her, and I told my counselor and she acted like I, I don't know, was being unreasonable."

TK looks thoughtful for a second. "Would you like me to tell you what I think or not?"

I actually don't want TK to tell me all the reasons I'm wrong, but if she doesn't, nobody will. So I say, "Sure."

She pushes an escaped strand of hair behind her left ear. "You are a great kid. And you love camp, but sometimes that can be a little . . ." she trails off with a conciliatory grimace.

A lot. Intense. It hurts without her even saying it. I protest, "But nobody is 'too much' at camp! Strat rode the hood of my car into the parking lot this morning!"

TK laughs and clutches her hands to her chest like a Disney princess. "Oh, I love Strat. And that's true, but both these people are new here, right? They're not used to the big emotions of Fogridge. And maybe this girl, your roommate, isn't used to you being a big fish, so she's making some connections that just aren't there. I don't think you hate women, kiddo. But I do think you and this girl have some things to work through." She finishes with a definitive nod.

I run my hands through my hair. "I don't want to work through things with her. She never tried to work through things with me when she was the big fish."

"But she wasn't the North Star, was she? The time comes for everything, Juliette. Even nap time." She waves her hand around the bunk.

I take this as my cue to leave, but first I give TK a big hug. "You always have the best advice."

"I learn from them," TK replies, gesturing toward the Minis. "Right, Ella?" she calls.

Ella, whose braid is already half-undone, is much too far away to have heard anything we just said, but she still stops dead in her tracks and nods with her whole body. "Right!"

TK says, "Maybe your roommate won't be so bad once you understand each other."

I try not to roll my eyes.

And fail.

# 6

# HOT TAKE

After the talk with TK, I avoid Polaris, deciding to track down Lucy and Gia instead and finding them in the playground of Quad 1. Gia pumps his legs back and forth on the swing set. His thick black hair, usually painstakingly styled to feature a single swooping lock across his forehead, is pushed back with a dark sweatband. It catches the air and fluffs up as he swings, revealing a flashy new piercing in his left ear.

He's a hottie now, but Lucy and I befriended him back when he still had an unflattering bowl cut and a baby face. The summer he came back to camp looking like he'd gone through the puberty machine, Lucy and I were stunned. Between his appearance and his carefully cultivated air of mystery, there isn't a girl in the universe Gia Pham couldn't pull. The worst part is, he knows it.

Lucy sits cross-legged on the ground, pegging wood chips at him when the swing brings him close. She's drowning in a stiff, oversized denim jacket that has WHEN HELL FREEZES OVER, I'LL SKI THERE, TOO! embroidered on the back. Two summers ago, Pat told her it wasn't camp appropriate and asked her to take it off. She just said, "No thanks," and that was the end of it.

Lucy spots me first and immediately puts a finger to the

side of her head, as if she's listening to an earpiece. I raise my index finger to my ear before Gia can. A second later, he realizes what's happened and has the good sense to bring the swing to a stop by digging in his heels.

Lucy and I exchange a smirk and tackle him to the ground, simultaneously shouting, "Get down, Mr. President!"

We face-plant in the wood chips, laughing as Gia thanks Lucy and me for our commitment to the country. I try for a gracious acceptance but catch a mouthful of my own hair and momentarily choke on it. Of course this causes us to dissolve into puddles of crying laughter.

This.

This is what camp is. Not arguing with Priya. Not asking TK about whether I hate women. Not Galahad's disapproving looks. This. Wood chips down my shirt and tears running down my cheeks from hysteria. Playing Get Down, Mr. President in ill-advised places and impaling myself on Gia's bony knees.

I wipe my face and pull them each into a hug. "I missed you bozos."

Lucy pats my head like I'm her pet. "We stopped by Polaris after the assembly. Where were you?"

"Oh my God, yeah," says Gia, eyes growing wide. "Your roommate has money, huh?"

My body suddenly feels very heavy. I flop onto my back dramatically, hands tucked behind my neck, trying not to wince at the pointy wood chips now digging into my spine. "You're not going to believe this. It's Priya Pendley."

"No!" Lucy gasps down at me. "You're kidding."

I shake my head, scratching my knuckles against the wood chips. "Remember when I texted you about Priyatopia? I talked to Deepika that day and . . . I guess I accidentally put the idea in her head that Fogridge was a great place to spend the summer."

"Deepika, no!" Gia throws his arms wide. "We trusted you!"

"You must've flipped when you found out," Lucy says.

"If Pat hadn't called a meeting at the exact moment he did, I might have." And then I tell them everything; I recount the morning from Strat's joyride to Galahad to the conversation on TK's bed.

"I can't live with her," I finish. "I just can't."

With his brows knit together in concern, Gia places a hand on my ankle. "You have to. Polaris? You can't leave Polaris."

"I know!"

"Maybe you can kill her with kindness," Lucy suggests hopefully.

"Maybe I could just kill her," I deadpan back.

"Well, there you go!" Gia chimes in, his voice coated in mock cheer. "At least you have options."

The heady spice of woodsmoke and pine trees almost convinces me to leave without Priya. But, as tempting as the thought of her animal-ravaged carcass is, I'd probably be blamed if she got lost in the dark and eaten. So, I wait by the door, checking my watch every two minutes until she's satisfied with the fluffiness of her space buns.

To top it all off, I can't say anything about how absurd it is to do your hair for an event where nobody's going to be able to see it. It doesn't take a psychic to predict what Priya would say about my take on her wearing lip gloss to eat goddamn s'mores in the dark.

Finally, finally, she finishes, and I lead us to the grassy trails of Quad 3. The glow of our flashlights only illuminates a small enough circle to keep us from tripping over roots. Normally, there'd be plenty of light as other groups head to the campfire, but we're running late.

As we get closer, my steps fall in time to the Taylor Swift song blasting from the speaker system. It thrums through my chest like a heartbeat, immediately lifting my mood. I survey the crowd, and when I spot Galahad's group, I point, making sure Priya sees before I summarily abandon her for the marshmallow line.

The counselor in front of me in line shuffles deftly to the music, her rainbow light-up sneakers blurring into colorful streaks. A group of boys who are clearly her campers chant her name, Seafoam, in their hoarse, prepubescent voices. Her smile is almost as bright as her shoes.

By the time we reach the front of the line, Seafoam is doubled over, gasping for breath dramatically. The boys try to climb all over her as she pants out threats about never dancing again if they hurt each other with their sticks. The girl is going to be a Fogridge lifer, I can tell.

"Here you are, Juliette," Pat says, handing me a long stick, the pointy end already coated in marshmallow guts. I accept it and harpoon my own jumbo Jet-Puffed, shoving it right into the heart of the campfire and letting it catch.

This is the trick to a perfect s'more: you have to burn the marshmallow.

Controversial, I know. Everybody wants the golden brown. Some people at camp even pride themselves on their perfect marshmallow technique, but a perfect marshmallow does not a perfect s'more make. The crispy char from the burn is the key to the ideal texture.

I sandwich the blackened cube between chocolate and graham crackers and take a bite. The marshmallow is crunchy and gooey. The chocolate is semisolid enough to bite through but melts quickly in my mouth. I nod to myself—I'm a genius—and hand the stick back to Pat on my way out of the fire ring.

Groups of returning campers gather on the soccer field at the edge of the campfire's glow. I make my way over, instinctually catching and releasing fireflies as I walk.

The groups are midconversation, but, unlike at Priyatopia, I comfortably insert myself into all of them. I crouch next to old friends and talk about school, dance competitions, and academic awards, about friendship breakups. I see Lucy and Gia flitting around, but we don't talk. I don't need to. I fit into this crowd without clinging to the safety of my friends' shadows.

I feel normal again as I join a group sitting in one of the soccer goals. Kuya, a new specialist in Fogridge's international work exchange program, motions me over as if we're old friends. He's telling me about his childhood in the Philippines when a pair of hands slips under my arms and yanks me up.

I spin to find Strat, joyfully snapping off beat to the opening chords of "Sweet Caroline."

"When it begins, I can begin to sew it," she yowls over the music, tugging at me to join her in the center of the field.

"Those aren't the words," I yell back. We sing this song infinite times a summer and Strat gets it wrong every time.

"Wasn't a thing and spring decayed to summer. Who'd a believe a blah, blah, blah! Han—Let's go, we're gonna miss it," she whines. "Leeching out . . . C'mon, Juliette!"

One look at her frantic expression and I give in, just in time for the chorus, letting her drag me to the center of the soccer field

"Sweet Caroline!" Fogridge shouts in unison.

I have to do high knees to avoid a minefield of metal bottles as I bounce to the *bum bum bum*s. Arms flail. Pitchy voices transcend the need for musical keys. I shout echoes of the chorus, something I've done for so many summers that I forget it isn't actually part of the song.

I join the counselors in pointing at seated campers, inviting them up to dance. On my third "so good" I turn to my left and find myself pointing directly at Priya, propped against a tree just past the sideline. Most of the crowd is cast in silhouette, but she stands at such an angle that I see her clearly—her crooked smile, her curious amusement. In her fluttering dress and styled hair, she becomes an ethereal nymph escaped from the deepest parts of the woods.

I falter.

The firelight sparkles in her lip gloss as she mouths, *So good*, but doesn't make any move to uncross her ankles and partici- pate.

With horror, I realize she's eating a marshmallow. Just a single, uncooked marshmallow by itself. Not whole, either. She's straight up taking *bites* out of a raw marshmallow. Unhinged.

Before I can react, Strat grabs my hands and leads me in a faux polka. Plastering on a huge smile, I fight off my humiliation. I've never been embarrassed doing camp stuff before. I·hate Priya Pendley for bringing that part of me here.

The song ends to thunderous applause, and Strat leaves me with a proud, "Excellent North Star–ing!"

If I love camp. If I love Strat. If I love goofy dancing and "Sweet Caroline" and being the North Star.

Then why do I feel so un-excellent?

# 7

# AN EXTREMELY PRIYA-DICTABLE OUTCOME

I wake up the next morning to a bugle playing over the loud-speakers and the sound of the shower running.

*How many showers does this girl take?* I grumble internally, trying to make peace with smelling like campfire smoke all day.

When Priya deigns to exit the bathroom, I slide past her before she can lock me out again. It's steamy, a warm fog of lemongrass engulfing me the moment I step onto the white tile. I clear a small section of the mirror with my forearm and run the water.

"Why do you always look like the personification of the nineties?" Priya asks, watching me spit toothpaste into the sink.

How she got nineties from my outfit—athletic shorts; a faded green, signature-covered Fogridge shirt; and a *Leave No Trace* cap over my unwashed curls—I have no clue.

I scan her reflection as I rinse, then ask, "Why do you always look like a cult leader?"

Priya smiles, smoothing down her white romper, plain except for a neat row of wooden buttons down the front. "I'm going for the sacrificial virgin aesthetic. Bible-core."

I side-eye her. "You're really gonna wear white every day for five weeks?"

She adjusts her high ponytail, repositioning the two seem-ingly useless white butterfly clips near her hairline. "Yep."

I snort a laugh and brush past her, making for the front door. "You better have thirty-five outfits then, because they're all going to get ruined."

"Don't worry your pretty little head about that, Juliette. I have thirty-six."

Apple juice with ice in it always transports me to a splinter-laden table in the Fogridge mess hall. However, as I sip it now, I wish it would transport me out of the mess hall.

Priya sticks out like a sore thumb. Of course, other people here get dressed up and do their makeup, too. I mean, Flag-staff's campers walked in this morning each proudly sporting cow-print tutus. Flagstaff himself also wears matching cow ears.

But there's something about the way Priya dresses that just makes you want to keep an eye on her. Just in case she falls into a mud puddle. It seems almost inevitable, and I have tickets for the front row. Right in the splash zone.

Campers and counselors alike make excuses to walk by and pretend to ignore her. I'd be able to convince myself it's more of a day at the zoo than an adoring crowd of fans if some of them didn't circle back around to tell her how much they like her content.

I've seen Priya's videos. She talks to the camera like it's her best friend. I can see why she has such a devoted following, being likable and relatable and gorgeous. But I can't imagine letting the whole world act like they know me when they don't.

I've spent years observing the surface of Planet Pendley and she's still a mystery.

Priya grills Lucy about the sandwich bag of gorp—that's trail mix, for the uninitiated—she's constructing. Lucy says she hates raisins as she pours in a handful, and Priya reacts like it's a nature documentary.

If you hate them, then why are you adding raisins? Because they're part of the family. So, you'll eat them? Absolutely not. You'll just pick them out? Right. Does it change the flavor of the surrounding nuts and chocolate if you just don't put them in? I don't know. Now, is this a normal behavior in the community?

Lucy answers, squinting at the bag's contents. She adds one more heap of peanut butter chips and seals it. With Priya's interest free, Gia jumps in.

"So," he starts, spearing a piece of French toast with a fork, "have you decided which programs you're going to choose week one?"

Her eyes are fixed on Gia's food as she answers. He pauses, his fork hovering outside his mouth, waiting for her reply. Teardrops of maple syrup threaten to drip onto his lap. Gia doesn't seem to notice or care, but Priya tenses up like it's her own pristine outfit at risk.

"Yeah," she says distractedly. "My mom overnighted them the day I signed up. Didn't you have to send in your weekly forms, like, a month ago?"

Lucy, Gia, and I burst into laughter, clawing indiscriminately at each other's arms in an attempt to ground our hysterics.

"What's so funny?" Priya asks, eyeing us suspiciously.

"Oh, you sweet summer child," Lucy says. "Never send your camp forms in early."

Priya leans back. "But the website . . . ?"

"Oh, never go by the website," Gia scolds, waving his fork around haphazardly, Priya's eyes anxiously tracking it.

Lucy speaks for all of us when she says, "I guarantee you, they lost it."

Priya crosses her arms, saying, "Well, it's a good thing I remember my choices. This place is a shambles." Like she's making fun of herself.

My brow furrows. I've never seen her do that.

"Can I guess what you picked?" Gia asks, raising his hand like we're in school.

Scheduling at Fogridge for seniors is simple. Hour breakfast. Two ninety-minute activity blocks. Hour lunch. Two ninety-minute activity blocks. Hour free. Hour dinner. Head count at nine. Lights out at ten. Weekends are mainly free time.

For each of the five weeks, a senior camper chooses activities for the four blocks. They do those activities for the whole week, choosing new activities every Sunday.

Whether or not you get your choice depends entirely upon the whims of the Fogridge gods. Once, I was assigned Photography, Weight Room, Paper Crafts, and something called "Cairns with Cornball." I'd asked for Volleyball, Mountain Biking, Kayaking, and Gymnastics.

"Go ahead, guess," Priya says.

Gia leans forward to scrutinize her. She stares back, poker-faced.

"Okay. I'll start with an art. Sculpture," he declares, pointing at her.

She shakes her head, wrinkling her nose prettily. "Sculpture's not really for me."

"Great, more clay for me. Okay, then, Dance. Soccer. And . . ." he draws the word out, squinting into the distance, like the answer is written just beyond his field of vision. "Archery."

"No, no, and yes, actually." Priya swirls her glass of water, clinking the ice cubes together. "I'm requesting Theater all five weeks."

Some activities, like Ceramics, run projects that require more than a week, so a camper is locked in for longer. Theater requires three hours a day for three weeks. One cast does mornings weeks one to three, and another cast does afternoons weeks three to five. Although, they're often the exact same cast. Theater kids.

Priya continues, "For the open two blocks, I just want to try new things."

Lucy knits her brows together, giving a swift tilt of her head. "Couldn't be me." She lives all five weeks firmly in Quad 3, Hiking, Riding Horses, and Rock Climbing. I've seen her in many a heated discussion with Pat over being placed in Cooking or Swim. If there's one thing to be said about Lucy, it's that she stands her ground. It's just that her ground frequently happens to be forty feet in the air.

"And the last activity?" I ask. Not that I'm interested, I'm just making sure our choices don't overlap.

To my annoyance, she says, "Wilderness Adventure."

"Juliette, weren't you—Ow!"

I shoot Gia a frustrated look and decide I should have kicked him in the shin harder.

The look on her face tells me Priya knows exactly what just happened under the table. She leans her chin into her hand and faces me. "Guess we're stuck together again."

I sip my apple juice vacantly. "We're not both gonna get it," I say, already thinking about what activity to pick instead.

"The North Star and a newbie? Of course you'll both ge—Ow! Are you kidding me?"

"Bro." Lucy breathes out a laugh, dropping her forehead into her hand. "Read the room."

"How did you even win this North Star thing anyway?" Priya asks me. "Something heroic? Put out a fire?"

"That's ridiculous," I deadpan. "You have to put out at least two fires *and* rescue a baby before they'll even consider you."

She snorts.

"Our Juliette was a shoo-in," Lucy brags, reaching across the table to pat my hand. "She's a legend. Everyone loves her."

I don't look at Priya. I'd rather not see the surprise on her face.

"Did your brother go here?" Priya asks.

I shake my head. Does she think that's the only way people would like me?

"None of her siblings did. Or do. Or . . . will?" Gia's eyes flick up to the ceiling as he thinks about the structure of my family.

"Yeah, you got it," I say encouragingly.

"None?" Priya repeats. At my confused look, she continues, "You have more than one sibling?"

There's a bewildered silence as the rest of us exchange looks.

"Are you joking?" Lucy asks tentatively.

"What? No." Her brow furrows, uncertainty coloring her features. "I only know Laurent. Do you have another brother?"

I straighten and look Priya dead in the eye. I still can't tell if she's kidding.

"You have . . . two siblings?" she tries.

Am I being pranked? Does she really not know this? I shake my head. "I have five others. There's seven of us."

"No you don't," Priya shoots back.

My mouth falls open. "Uh, I think I do."

"Haven't you guys known each other for, like, ever?" Gia asks, pointing his fork back and forth between us.

"Yeah, but . . ." Priya trails off.

I finish for her, "We don't talk."

"So?" Gia points to a random camper at another table. "I don't talk to James Manor, but I know he's an only child and he grew up on an avocado farm. People know things about people they don't talk to."

"Oh. Yeah. James has zebrafish," I concede, biting my lower lip.

"I know things about Juliette," Priya insists indignantly. Facing me, she offers, "I know you don't have zebrafish."

"That's true," I say, pointing at her.

Lucy spreads her arms wide. "Yeah, but how can you not know *that*? It's one of Juliette's go-to icebreakers. Everybody knows she has six siblings."

"And she had rabies," Gia points out helpfully.

"And she won that singing thingy," Lucy finishes with a nod.

Priya is shaking her head at me. "How did you get rabies?"

I shrug. "Got bit by a raccoon."

"Wait. What?" Priya is flabbergasted. Raccoons, mythical creatures she just found out exist for real.

"Yeah, I was taking out the trash. I surprised a raccoon, and it bit me."

"Oh, gross." Priya scrunches up her face, eyes twinkling "Was it gross? Where's the bite? Did you, like, foam at the mouth?"

"No," I say. "To be fair, it wasn't really rabies, I was *treated* for rabies, preventively. But rabies actually has a hundred percent mortality rate once you show symptoms, so I d—"

"I don't think this is appropriate dining hall conversation," interrupts Galahad, appearing from nowhere to tower over us.

"Rabies?" I ask in disbelief.

She raises her eyebrows, but instead of answering me, she says, "And we could try not screaming."

"We weren't screaming." I know we weren't. I've heard Lucy get loud, and this is not it.

One of Galahad's eyebrows arches. "That's interesting. Then

how come I could hear you from all the way on the other side of the building?"

Before I can produce a brilliant comeback, Priya cuts me off. "Sorry. We were just excited about . . . Juliette's rabies."

"But we weren't yelling," I protest again. Even now, we're quieter than some of the surrounding tables.

I find myself wishing someone else would jump in, just so I stop looking like I'm being stubborn. Where's Lucy's rebellious streak when you need it?

Priya, the least-backboned of all possible choices, says, "But we'll be quieter."

My jaw slackens. This is why she and I don't get along. She's a people pleaser and I am a deeply displeased person.

I purse my lips, giving a small shake of my head, but I don't say anything.

Galahad watches us a moment longer than necessary, then says, "Juliette, Priya, I need your choices for the week."

Gia temples his fingers in front of his mouth, concealing a smirk.

"Theater, Archery, and Wilderness Adventure," says the Goody Two-Shoes.

Galahad turns to me expectantly.

"Circus," I say without hesitation. Only seniors get to do Circus and I've always had a sneaking suspicion I'd be good at the trapeze.

Galahad marks it down.

"Lakefront, Gymnastics—" I pause. I don't want to say

Wilderness Adventure because Gia is right. We will both get it. Then again, I can't change my whole life just for Priya. And, if I do, I can't let her know about it. "Wilderness Adventure."

Galahad gives a curt nod and reminds us about head count before walking off.

"We were not being loud. Why did you apologize to her?" I ask Priya. Then I whirl on Lucy. "And where were you, Miss Confrontation?"

Lucy and Gia, who both did an excellent job of fading into near-nonexistence just moments ago, speak over each other now:

"I handle my own shit, I don't meddle. How old is she? Like nineteen?"

"Damn, when I ran into Lynn at the assembly, she said Galahad was strict, but she didn't say it was like that," Gia comments, staring after Galahad's retreating figure.

"I think it's partially a me problem," I say, remembering the way she initially greeted me like I was any other camper. "She likes Priya." *Of course.*

Priya shrugs. "I don't start fights with her."

"I am not trying to start fights with her!" I object, forcefully readjusting the brim of my hat. "Some of us just aren't okay with being walked all over all the time."

"Ah." Lucy nods knowingly. "It's a D-Mo situation. You're lucky you have Polaris."

"What's a D-Mo?" Priya asks.

"He was Lucy's counselor from hell," Gia says.

Lucy tends to have more problems with authority than most people. According to her, she's had to be an adult for so long that she refuses to bow down to them now. And while most adults come to terms with her independence pretty quick, D-Mo, her seventh-grade counselor, didn't.

You can tell when a counselor hates their job. Some staff spend the whole summer wishing they were somewhere else—I have no clue why they don't just leave. The campers don't matter to them, fun doesn't matter to them; they mope around like it's a prison sentence. Even though they're usually only a year or two older than the seniors, they treat us like children.

D-Mo was one of those counselors, and when Lucy pushed back on everything, he punished her. No ice cream, "grounding" her, forbidding her from going to Quad 3, taking her name off hiking rosters. She could've gone to Pat, but I think she deeply enjoyed her journey of driving D-Mo to the point of quitting midsummer.

I, on the other hand, would rather not get into daily screaming matches with my counselor at the Gaga Ball pit.

"I can't be tamed," Lucy says, mouth full. "Makes people insecure. Especially the young ones."

Priya clinks her ice, considering me. "I could see that with Juliette. You are kind of—"

"I know," I cut in sharply.

Should I leave camp right now and get the word *intense* tattooed on my forehead, or should I wait until my birthday and do it as a present to all of humanity?

"Anyway," Gia says, leaning his elbows on the table, "not to lay it on too thick, but did we or did we not predict the schedule situation perfectly?"

Priya locks her fingers and places them at the nape of her neck. "You're right," she sighs at the ceiling. "You're all right. I don't know anything. Camp lost my forms. Juliette has enough siblings for a reality show. We weren't screaming. Rabies comes from raccoons."

"And bats. And skunks," I say, mock seriously. "Most people get it from raccoons or bats, but some people get it from skunks."

Priya's head is still tilted back on her hands, but she turns it to the side and locks eyes with me, heaving a long sigh. "And bats and skunks."

Later, as we leave the mess hall, Lucy and Gia flank me, squishing me between them. Once Priya gets a few feet ahead of us, they turn on me.

"Juliette," Gia starts. He's already flashing me his puppy dog eyes, so I know whatever's coming isn't good. "We're sorry."

"We're so, so sorry," agrees Lucy, her bottom lip pushed out in a pout.

"But we like her," Gia stage-whispers. He draws out the last word like he's afraid to let the sentence end.

"She's fun." Lucy squishes in close, sandwiching me tightly between them.

The news doesn't upset me like they thought it would. Priya is likable. It's a fact of life as reliable as gravity. Playfully shaking free, I point between them with mock contempt. "You two are traitors to your country."

I raise my index finger to my ear before tackling them both into the dirt in front of the mess hall.

# 8

# FUEL FOR THE FIRE

I get all of my choices for the first week.

Unfortunately, Priya does, too.

So, although it means I'll have to spend half my afternoon in her presence, it also means that I get a blessedly Pendley-free morning in Gymnastics and at the lakefront.

I've found that some of my high jump and long jump skills translate to the vault, and for someone who only gets five weeks of practice a year, I have a pretty decent tumbling repertoire.

The specialist, a Scottish college student with a thick brogue, shouts, "Walking feet!" at least a million times over the course of the session. She puts one senior in time-out for bouncing on things without supervision. A small group of his friends stands nearby and roasts him for the duration of his punishment.

In Windsurfing, I commit the ultimate camp sin, forgetting my sunscreen. So, I'm a little burnt and a lot sore when I arrive at lunch. Gia and Lucy wave me over to a table they've claimed to regale me with the stories of their mornings.

Lucy has a long-running crush on one of the hiking instructors, Euphrates. To be fair, he does look like a lost member of a K-pop group, with his boyish grin and swoosh-y silver hair. Everything I know about Euphrates was taught to me entirely against my will. I've never done a program with him, but I know all about his nature conservation efforts, his annual family vacation to Costa Rica, and which ice cream flavor he thinks best represents him. It's Moose Tracks.

*It's the sexiest flavor*, Lucy said when she told me last summer.

All of this to explain, when I say Lucy's distraught as she tells us Euphrates is sporting a shiny new engagement ring, I mean she is *distraught*.

"I bet his fiancée is amazing," she says, cupping her face in her palms. "They probably spend their weekends rescuing baby seals and cleaning up national parks."

Gia says something about how there are probably tons of men cleaning up baby seals.

Lucy's voice gets more muffled as she squeezes her face tighter. "Not ones who look like that."

I'm trying to decide whether it would help or hurt to remind her Euphrates is ten years older than us and never had any interest in dating a high schooler when I see Priya walk through the mess hall doors.

She's laughing, surrounded by known drama kids. I watch her grab a plate of fish sticks and look for a table with her new friends. When she disappears behind a pillar, I lose sight of her. Probably for the best. I can stay calm for Wilderness Adventure.

Except for Lucy's crisis. But she seems to have temporarily accepted the reality of Euphrates's marriage. Her hands still rest on her face, but they aren't squeezing anymore. She listens to Gia with a faraway stare in her eyes.

"We're working on self-portraits this week. I decided to do a self-portrait of Pat," Gia says.

The chair beside me scrapes back against the floor, and Priya drops into the seat. "Don't self-portraits have to be of yourself?"

"That's such a pedestrian opinion," Gia answers loftily, rolling his eyes. "Think outside the box, Priya."

I scrutinize her. "Why are you here?"

Her expression doesn't change, despite the question coming off much more aggressive than intended. She merely circles a finger in my direction and asks, "Haven't we been over this?"

"I mean, why aren't you eating with the theater people?" I clarify.

She hums and takes a bite of a fish stick. "They all have Art in the afternoon, so they're going back to Quad 2 to eat. Plus, I'm maximizing my Gia and Lucy time."

Gia preens. "As you should."

"Do you like Theater?" Lucy asks, valiantly resisting her heartbreak.

"Yeah, so far. We just voted on the play for the first three weeks. I wanted *Little Shop of Horrors*, but I think it's going to end up being *Into the Woods*."

"What part are you auditioning for?" Lucy asks.

Having indulged in a musical-theater phase myself, I wonder how I would cast Priya. Not the Baker's Wife or Jack's Mother. Maybe Cinderella. Little Red Riding Hood? She's annoying. It would depend on her—

Wait. "Can you sing?"

Priya scoffs. "No, absolutely not. I'm not auditioning."

"Then why are you doing Theater all five weeks?" I ask.

"Design," she answers. "I love costumes and set design. I think that's what I wanna do. You know, eventually." She gestures vaguely to the future.

"That's so cool!" Gia says, shooting me an apologetic wince.

"Thanks. I've been doing it for a while. I make all my clothes." She runs her hands down her body.

What? I examine today's outfit, a pair of well-tailored linen pants and a button-up crop top. Both white, of course. They don't look homemade.

"But I've been told I look like I'm a cult leader, so." Priya cocks an eyebrow at me.

Gia shrugs. "Well, if you're gonna be in a cult, at least you're the leader."

I rake my gaze over her, taking in the sleek low bun and pair of aviators perched atop her head. "You don't look like you're in a cult today. You look like . . ." I pause to think. "The world's cleanest archaeologist."

"Oh, yeah," Lucy says, tilting her head. "I see it."

Priya frowns appreciatively. "Hmm. I could be down to excavate fossils."

"Fossils are a step up from a cult," Gia says. Then he bites his lower lip to suppress a grin and continues, "That is not a sentence I ever thought I'd say."

Lucy shrugs. "I've heard you say weirder."

Gia manages to look affronted and pleased all at once.

Priya shoves the last of her fish sticks into her mouth and says, "Please. Say weirder."

I like wilderness survival as much as the next guy, but there is one reason and one reason only that I signed up to take it this week: Senior Twilight.

Every summer, the senior campers spend their last Friday night in the woods outside of Quad 3. The hiking instructors take them to different starting points, leaving them alone with a backpack of equipment and a walkie-talkie for emergencies. At dawn, they make their way back to the big fire pit at the edge of the woods. Every single person at Fogridge wakes up early to watch the seniors come home. All of camp sits in the field, bundled up in their comforters and sipping hot cocoa, to hear Pat announce each senior's name on a bullhorn as they break the tree line.

Obviously, it's not mandatory. Campers can opt out for any reason and many do. Gia, for example, has always adamantly denounced the Twilight. He maintains that one of these days a camper is going to slip and die and Fogridge will get shut down.

*And that won't be me*, he always says. *It will not be me.*

On the other end of the spectrum, Lucy has been begging Pat to let her participate in the Twilight since way before we were seniors. With the amount of hikes and backpacks she's done, she could probably survive alone in the nearby wilderness indefinitely.

Even though I'm not nearly as outdoorsy as Lucy, I can't fathom skipping it. To me, Senior Twilight is an essential rite of passage, like a quinceañera or walking at graduation. I want to stroll back into camp a triumphant badass, the way I've always imagined. I'll be damned if I'm the unprepared one who dies and gets Fogridge shut down. Or worse, has to walkie for help. So, as much as I'd rather be doing something fun for this activity block, taking Wilderness Adventure is a necessary evil.

But it's not worth anything if I can't learn to start a fire. I offer my tinder a telepathic bargain. *If you catch fire, I'll give you a million dollars.* Bark doesn't have a brain. There's no way it could possibly know that I don't have a million dollars.

I lower my flint and strike it with the steel. Not even a spark.

"Julia, use the magnesium," says the wilderness adventure specialist, Phantom. He's a short, ripped white guy with a blocky face. His haircut is precise, but his beard is wild.

"Juliette," Priya and I correct at the same time.

She's somewhere behind me. Our entire program group crouches in the dirt, trying to start fires. Unsuccessfully, needless to say.

"Sorry, Juliette." Phantom walks over and plants his Chacos right in front of me. "Go ahead."

He watches me scrape a mound of magnesium onto the kindling. I strike the flint again. Nothing happens.

"Use the flat edge," Phantom says, pointing at the steel. "Not the serrated edge."

I flip the steel over and strike the flint again. This time, there are sparks, but the bark still doesn't catch. I groan. Maybe it does know I don't have a million dollars.

"That's better, keep going!" Phantom's Chacos continue down the line of campers.

I rock back on my heels and massage my knees, taking the opportunity to survey the fire makers to either side of me. Phoebe, on my right, can't seem to build her structure before the flame goes out. To my left, James Manor, avocado farmer and zebrafish owner, has nicked his finger with the steel blade and keeps having to stop to wipe his blood onto his shorts.

"You okay?"

"It's not that bad. It'll stop," James says, though the frequency with which he wipes his hand only seems to increase.

Staring at the small stain on his thigh, I tell myself that I could probably get through one measly night without fire. But what if there's an emergency? What if I spill all my water and I need to boil some from a creek? What if climate change suddenly worsens and the temperature drops below freezing on a California summer night? What if I develop a debilitating fear of the dark?

I start in on the tinder again, trying to guess what it might find more useful than money. What does fire like? Houses? *I can get you a house.* Steel clangs against flint.

Suddenly, the bark catches. I scramble for my twigs, blowing gently on the flames as I build a little triangle. The twigs catch, but all at once, they go out again. I sigh and wipe my brow, frustrated. It knows. It knows I can't get it a whole house.

I grab a new handful of bark and shred it into thin pieces,

scrape the magnesium, and draw back the flat edge of the steel. *Okay, not a real house. But I could do, like, a little dollhouse or something. That'd be fine for you. You're only a little fire.*

The bark lights.

*I'll take Woodshop,* I promise the fire. *I'll build you a dollhouse. Two stories, if you want.* I prod the tinder. Licks of flame start to climb the sticks. They crackle as they burn.

"Yes! Good job!" Phantom shouts behind me, but halfway through my turn, he continues, "Priya, this is a beautiful log cabin. Everyone, come take a look."

I scowl at my fire. The last twig burns out, and the structure collapses into a black, charred heap. I kick a leg out, sending ashes flying.

*Whatever. Now I'm never going to take Woodshop.*

# 9

# THE COCKROACH
# OF BANKSTOWN

The second Priya steps through the door of Polaris, I jump on her. Figuratively, of course. "How do you know how to make a fire?"

Priya settles onto her bed and pulls off her shoes. The knees of her white pants are tinted brown with dirt. She scratches at the stains absently. "I like *Survivor*."

I shake my head. "Okay, you did not learn that from watching a reality TV show."

She whips her head up, an uncannily predatorial look in her eyes—a tiger about to pounce. "*Survivor* isn't *a* reality TV show. It's *the* reality TV show." Is she excited to yell at me about this? "And I didn't learn it just from watching. I learned it for my audition video."

I can't stop shaking my head like a malfunctioning robot. "You auditioned for *Survivor*?"

"No." She chuckles patronizingly. "I audition for *Survivor*. I have for ten years."

I'm still shaking my head in disbelief. "We were six ten years ago."

"I was seven." There's the Priya I know, splitting hairs over the four-month difference in our birthdays. She continues, "They never would've accepted me that young, but my parents let me apply anyway. It'll be a funny story when I win. I'll be like the next Adam Klein."

I don't ask who Adam Klein is; he's clearly a *Survivor* guy. I'm more focused on the way she casually threw his name out, like I should also be deeply familiar with this show's lore.

A myriad of questions swirl in my brain, but I go with "Do you think you could win?"

"Of course. When they finally let me on. It's all about winning people over and getting them to work with you. That's my area of expertise." Pausing, she squints at me, biting her lip.

"What are you doing?"

"Trying to decide . . . Are you familiar with the Cockroach of Bankstown?" She fights a smirk. "King George? Blessed by Macedonian Jesus? As strong as a Lebanese housewife?"

I feel like I've fallen into an alternate dimension. "What the hell are you talking about?"

She's so *alive* when she answers, her body practically radiating with a near-religious fervor. "There's an Australian version of *Survivor*. Not to be confused with season two of *Survivor*, which was filmed in Australia," she adds quickly.

"Oh, of course not," I say, amused.

"And there's a contestant, George Mladenov?" She waits for a reaction. I shrug, so she plows on. "I think you're him."

I roll my eyes, refusing to take the bait. "Don't fancast me."

The smile doesn't drop from her face, but there's a change

behind her eyes that I don't like. Gone is that blazing passion, extinguished in a moment. I want to grab it, bring it back.

I groan, loud and aggrieved. "Fine. Tell me why I'm George."

She lights up. "George's first season was Brains vs. Brawn. He was a brain—"

"You think I'm a brain?" I interrupt.

She waves a hand dismissively. "That's not important. Anyway, he was a mastermind. Absolutely ran the game. He gets to the final two, where you have to convince the eliminated players to vote for you to win, and just . . . gives the worst speech possible. He's like"—she affects a bad Australian accent—"'I was the king, and you were all my pawns.' He lost, clearly."

I stare, confused. "And that's me?"

"Just listen," she scoffs. "A few seasons later, they do Heroes vs. Villains, and George is cast as a villain." At my pointed look, she says, "Not important. He goes in with a huge target on his back 'cause he's a domineering a-hole, and they all want him out. But then he connects with people. He makes allies who respect the way he plays. He improves his past game's flaws. He wins them over, not by changing who he is completely, but by finding a middle ground."

This feels entirely too personal. "Are you . . . calling me a domineering a-hole?"

She pinches the bridge of her nose.

"Wait, am I the old George or the new George?" I frown. "Or is this like a 'two Georges live inside you, the one that survives is the one you feed' thing?"

"Well, when you phrase it like that, it sounds ridiculous." She laughs, rolling her eyes.

I can tell she's trying. So, I try to sound as nonjudgmental as possible when I ask, "And you think you know me well enough to psychoanalyze me like this?"

"That's the thing." Priya sighs, picking up her phone and popping it in and out of its case. "I'm not sure. I think you and I are still between seasons."

My cheeks suddenly feel like they're on fire. I step back, out of her sight, and press my hands to my face. "Did George win? That second time?"

I hear the smile in her voice. "You'll see."

My lips part silently, my thoughts scattered to the wind. "Oh," I sputter. "Are we gonna watch it?"

"If you want," she says lightly.

I laugh, but—it's the weirdest thing—I think I do want.

# SPACE GARBAGE

Fogridge is quietest in the morning, when the fields are wet with dew and exhausted counselors are asleep. I always enjoy being out here when it's like this, even if I've never loved the act of running itself. If I don't do it, though, I'll feel like a coiled-up spring all day.

Barto, a kayaking specialist, is hauling colorful boats into the water when I reach the lake. He waves without pausing. Only specialists, who live separate from the campers and have nights off, are out this early.

I bank east, toward Arts, to avoid Quad 3's busy morning setup.

My footfalls drum an unrelenting rhythm into the sand walkways of Quad 2. A slight mist hangs in the air, lending the area a magical feeling, though some of that is just Arts itself.

Each building has its own design, which specialists change whenever they get bored. Currently, Ceramics is *Alice in Wonderland*–themed. Its concrete platform, painted like a chessboard, sits under a big open-air tent. Gauzy mosquito nets hang down on all sides. Chairs are decorated like shiny technicolor mushrooms. A cartoonish bust of Pat wears a miniature crown adorned with heart-shaped plastic rubies.

Wind chimes, spiraling helixes, and pinwheels dance outside Painting. The converted barn that houses Textiles sports faux stained-glass windows from a project a few summers ago; they feature a saintly looking Pat fighting devil-Pat. The grassy lawn in front of Photography is littered with wooden standees, the kind you put your head in at carnivals. One is a kneeling knight, sword in hand. His word bubble reads I SOLEMNLY SWEAR TO ALWAYS SHOOT IN LANDSCAPE.

I pass paper lanterns and fairy circles, a freestanding doorway, books configured to look like a flowing river, and a slide shaped like a big shoe.

Arts is beautiful, but nothing here stays.

I used to love Ceramics. There was a ghost orchestra outside of the building. (It was a building back then, not just a tent.) The instruments, arranged to appear midperformance, were covered in pastel flowers. Daisies grew between piano keys. Poppies twined in the cello strings. Just looking at it was like making music. Growth and vibrance and feeling something.

Then one day I showed up, and they were gone. I was inconsolable.

Drell, the specialist at the time, just said, "Things change."

That was it. As if it were that simple. Things change.

I stopped going to Ceramics.

What I discover over the course of Wilderness Adventure is that fire making isn't Priya's only secret skill. She kicks my ass at everything from shelter building to basic first aid.

On one particularly strenuous hike, Priya tries to evangelize me into the cult of *Survivor*. My lungs crumple under the elevation gain while she prattles on about the difference between Redemption Island and Edge of Extinction.

When other seniors start climbing trees, I expect Priya and her flowing maxi skirt to sit out. Instead, she scoops up the excess fabric and, in a move that I do not understand the physics of, ties it into a pair of pants. In seconds, she lounges on the thick limb above me, grinning like the Cheshire cat.

During the foraging section on Thursday, she whips up a five-star meal out of leaves and berries. Meanwhile, I almost eat poison ivy. Twice.

On Friday, I step onto a fallen tree trunk. My foot crashes straight through the rotted bark, nearly sending me tumbling into a ravine. Phantom decides to turn that into a learning moment for everyone. I tune him out most of the time because there's a high chance that he's either praising Priya or critiquing me. I don't want to hear either.

For the entire week, I can't focus on the fun I'm having in my other three activities, let alone learn anything in Wilderness Adventure. No matter what I do, Priya does it faster and better, in a more stylish outfit.

I am good at camp. I usually thrive out here, but you wouldn't guess that from the number of cracked heel blisters I'm nursing by Saturday. I chalk it up to coincidence. I'm off my game because Priya's here. It's karma for getting all my choices on week one.

I choose Wilderness Adventure again for week two, hoping for a different instructor.

I want a fresh start.

Without Priya in Wilderness Adventure, and with a new instructor who is embarrassingly named Blaze, I do much better. I borrow Blaze's wilderness survival guide and read it multiple times, taking notes by flashlight long after lights-out. I learn to build five different types of fires—even Priya's damn log cabin—by spending all my free time practicing.

I feel nearly normal as Lucy and I relax in the center of the soccer field at the end of week two, drinking Gatorade and eating ice cream sandwiches. Some music campers rehearse covers of upbeat pop songs in the fire pit, loud enough for us to hear. For most of us, weekends mean free time. But for the campers who come for Fogridge's well-regarded music department, weekends mean practice.

I don't sing much anymore, but at one point in my life, it defined me. In fact, my mom originally placed me at Fogridge because of their music program.

Once I was old enough to audition, I already knew musical stardom wasn't in the cards for me. I could've still done it, but when the time came for me to choose my activities, I skipped music every time. Some habits just die, I guess.

Lucy is slaughtering a high note when a shadow falls over both of us.

Priya drops to a crouch in the space between our torsos and says, "Lucy, what time is this thing tonight? Also, is it like"—

she shimmies her shoulders—"regular clothes or bathing suits? Because I'm not trying to show up in a leather jacket with fringe and everyone else is in bikinis."

Lucy gives an answer that I only distantly hear through the rush of blood in my ears. I try to sound casual when I ask, "What thing tonight?"

Priya waves a hand at me. "The party thing."

I pause, blinking hard. "The party thing," I repeat. "A party thing tonight?"

They freeze, Lucy answering slowly, "Yeah, Tessa's birthday?"

"Hmm," I say, coaching calm into every muscle fiber of my body. "Cool."

"I told you about it," Lucy says, her voice a little too high.

She didn't. I try not to get caught up in whether she thinks that's true or if she's lying. It doesn't matter if my best friends—because if Lucy knew, Gia knew—purposefully excluded me or forgot about me. But invited Priya. All the options are bad.

"Probably did." I close my eyes like I plan to nap here, in the middle of the soccer field.

"Anyway," Priya says smoothly, "it's a big thing. So you're definitely invited."

Does she think she's helping? Inviting me to Tessa Rodriguez's secret party? The party I've attended every year since we all snuck out to the lakefront the night she turned thirteen?

My thoughts bounce wildly, a tennis ball at Wimbledon. A few times, I almost answer before I stop myself. I want to say, *Yeah, obviously I'm invited.* I also want to point out that if I were invited, I would have been invited. I want them both to feel as bad as I do and, at the same time, I want to make them feel better. I know it's not a big deal. It probably did slip Tessa's mind. And Lucy's. And Gia's. And Priya's.

But it's hard to find a place for these thoughts to coexist, especially when I try to think of a time when Lucy or Gia would have had the opportunity to tell Priya when I wasn't around.

I get a feeling in the pit of my stomach that reminds me of last week during trapeze. When I'm flying, there's a second my hands leave my bar and I'm reaching out into thin air. I don't believe, until their hands grasp my wrists, that my catcher will get to me in time. Logically, I'm aware there's a net if they don't, but my body doesn't understand it.

Lying here with Priya and Lucy, I feel as if I've just hit the height of my swing and am about to fall outside of the catcher's range.

"I'm gonna go," I decide. In one swift motion, I'm on my feet, striding off the soccer field. I tuck my hands into the pockets of my shorts to keep them from shaking.

I don't turn around when Priya and Lucy call my name. Neither of them follows me.

When I finally get back to the bunk, I collapse into my bed fully clothed. I don't fall asleep. I just stare into the middle distance and feel sorry for myself, embarrassed about how I acted on the soccer field, mad at everyone, and utterly empty.

I've said before that Priya and I are two planets orbiting the same sun, but in this moment, I don't feel like a planet.

I feel like space garbage. Straight-up low-orbit debris, incinerating in Planet Pendley's stratosphere.

# CALIFORNIA PENAL CODE 187 PC

Dear Alison,

My pen hovers over the shiny beige cardstock. Then I write the four words I never thought I'd say to any friend I share with Priya.

I'm breaking the pact.

I hesitate, contemplating tossing the letter in the trash and pretending this never happened. But my emotions are a herd of wild horses, suddenly realizing that the corral gate has been left open. They stampede over my reason and my pride, and I keep writing.

Does that make me a bad friend? I think it does. So, you don't even have to read this, or to respond. I'm not trying to put you in the middle, I just really need to speak. Or write, I guess.

Picture this:

You are a chameleon person. Not like a superpower. Not even on purpose. You've tried not to be a chameleon, but you can't help it. You just keep changing colors. This is your state of being and you've made your peace with it. But once in a while, in certain environments, you get to be chameleon colored! People notice and they say, "Hey, there you are! I can see you again!"

And that's cool because, after a long time of being invisible, you had almost forgotten that you looked like anything at all. So, you keep going back to that place where people can see you to remind yourself that you aren't a leaf or a tree trunk, you just look like one sometimes!

Still with me? I'm almost done, I swear.

Okay, so you're this chameleon. And you get to the zoo or whatever where people can see you, and the zookeeper says, "I'm glad you're enjoying the zoo and that you keep coming back! But don't forget that you're only allowed to visit the zoo ten times in your life." So each year you go to the zoo, you try to enjoy it because you're one visit closer to being invisible forever.

And then, on your tenth visit to the zoo, the last year you will EVER be allowed to visit, an eagle shows up (or whatever eats chameleons, idk). And no matter how hard you try not to be invisible, your animal instincts keep dipping you in and out of the chameleon invisibility juice.

Isn't that tragic? Everything just taken away from you without a goodbye?

Yeah, you know what's worse? Priya Pendley showing up at your summer camp. That's right. The chameleon? That pathetic invisible man? He should feel bad for ME.

Nobody is ever going to see me again. Unless . . . ?

*Is homicide illegal in the state of California? Just double-check and get back to me.*

*Juliette*

An indeterminate amount of time after dropping the letter in the outgoing mail, I wake to my flimsy mattress warping under someone's weight. I pull the blanket over my face and groan.

"Juliette Barrera-Wright," Gia says authoritatively. "Don't make me give you a pep talk. You know I'll take it too far. I love pep talks."

I don't respond, still half in the circus-themed nightmare Gia interrupted.

He pats my knee. "This is nothing. It's less than nothing. I love you. Lucy loves you. Tessa loves you. Everyone loves you!"

The blanket muffles my voice. "Not Priya."

Gia pauses for a second, then tilts his head in concession. "Well, maybe not Priya. But even she wouldn't exclude you on purpose."

I groan again, unwilling to acknowledge this.

"Think about it," he insists. "For years, you two have been . . . whatever you are. Has she ever not invited you to something?" When I don't answer, he shakes my leg intently. "Hmm?"

"No," I say sullenly.

"It was a mistake." He peels the blanket off my head.

Even under dim camp light bulbs, Gia is devastatingly attractive. It's not just his dark eyes, strong jaw, or deep dimples. It's not even his contagious confidence. There's a way he moves that's impossible to look away from.

Some people, Lucy for one, never finish a motion. She starts writing before she even picks up a pen. Others, like Priya, flow from one thing to the next, an eternal dance with their surroundings.

Gia stops.

When he smiles at me, he stays smiling a beat longer than most people would, saying without words that he took the effort to create that smile and, by God, he's going to get his money's worth. He doesn't tap his fingers on the table, he rests them still.

It's like he's a statue brought to life. At any moment, he could turn back to marble.

I force myself into a sitting position, my blanket pulled tight around me. "Maybe it was a mistake, but you guys don't understand. This is what it's like with her." I know I sound like a child. I can't help it. "When Priya's around, I don't exist. It *always* happens this way."

People like Priya better. That's fine! It's fine anywhere and everywhere else, but this is Fogridge. That can't happen here. It's unfair. It makes me want to stomp my foot and cross my arms until an adult forces Priya to give my friends back.

Expression softening, Gia holds my hand through the blanket. "Priya's great. But you—" He jabs a sharp finger into my sternum. "Are Juliette." Jab, jabjabjab. "Barrera." Jabjabjab. "Wright." Jab. "North Star. Superstar. Star . . . dew. And I won't hear another word about it."

I rub my knuckles over the spot he poked. "You lost steam there at the end."

"Or was I gaining steam in a different direction?" he demands, eyebrows dancing independently of the rest of his face. More seriously, he urges, "Come tonight."

"It's in like an hour," I reply.

He grimaces. "Actually, you've been here a while. It started like twenty minutes ago."

I flop back with a pathetic moan. "I'm not going."

Gia heaves a world-weary sigh. "No. You are. You're going, and you're going to have fun if it kills you." With that, he forcefully rolls me off the bed.

"Fine," I say, grabbing my blanket and draping it over my head like an ancient druid. "But I'm bringing the blanket."

I don't know if it's psychological—we're so far from the mess hall, after all—but no matter where I am in camp, it always smells like barbecue at night. I inhale deeply as we approach an area of the waterfront, hidden by a thick copse of trees.

A parade of fireflies sparkles across Lake Valerie. I once read that some places call them "lightning bugs." I tried it for a summer, but it felt disingenuous, like I was lying every time I said it. The next summer, I went back to firefly. Thankfully, that was my only weird phase. Lucy, however, spent two summers speaking in a British accent. (Don't tell her I told you.)

Tessa greets me and Gia, seeming pleased to see us. She doesn't comment on anything besides how cozy my blanket looks. The fact that she's acting normal does little to calm me.

My problem isn't with Tessa.

It isn't even with Lucy, Gia, or Priya.

I take up residence on a tree stump by the rocky beach and drag my foot in the sand, tracing and retracing a *J* with my toe. I can't be mad at Priya for being likable. I can't be mad at other people for liking her. There's nobody to blame except . . . me.

Me and my intensity. Me and my name that's too much for such a little girl.

I swipe the flat of my foot over the *J* and use the edge of my sole to carve a *B* and a *W*.

No matter what I do, no matter how many little pieces of myself I cut off to try to fit into a Priya-shaped mold, at the end of the day, I am still Juliette. I don't want to be sad about that; I like who I am, I think. I just wish other people did, too.

I want one person to look at me and not see a lesser version of somebody else. But Priya and I are attached by a cosmic rubber band. She goes where I go. I go where she goes. And we are both miserable about it.

I was cursed at birth, I decide. This is some misguided fairygodmother shit.

In the shallows, Priya is playing a game of freeze tag. She lies on her left side, letting the water lap at her white shorts and leather jacket. She catches me looking and waves tentatively.

I consider leaving. Leaving the beach, leaving Fogridge. Possibly fleeing the country.

"I'm not cheating! I'm taking a break!" Priya shouts, standing.

I watch with indifference as she plods over and sits down on the tree stump next to me. "You're sulking," she points out.

"Yup."

"Why are you sulking?" she asks, as softly as the crickets chirping in the grass.

Circling the initials of my last name, I say, "Oh, the usual."

"Is this about getting invited to the party?"

I squint up at the trees, envious of the fireflies blinking in and out of existence.

Priya blows out an annoyed breath. "Don't read so much into it, okay? Everyone didn't suddenly forget about you because I'm here. They just assumed you knew."

Again, I don't answer.

It causes Priya to crouch in front of me, centering herself in my field of vision. "Do you know how many parties I don't get invited to? People *always* assume I know. You are the only person who invites me every time."

"You should get better friends," I huff.

"Don't need 'em. I have great enemies."

This makes me look up.

She holds my gaze and gently, but firmly, bops my forehead with the heel of her still-wet palm. "They love you, you dweeb."

I smile and roll my eyes. With absolutely no malice I say, "Don't touch me, Pendley."

"How could they not?" she continues, ignoring me. "Look at this face!" She pinches my cheeks and I yelp, shoving her onto her butt. She laughs like it's the funniest thing I've ever done.

"Get up," she says. "I'll have no more sulking on my watch."

"You're a good nemesis," I confess, offering a hand to help her up.

She takes it with a smirk. "I know, I'm good at everything. That's why you hate me."

I shake my head, scoffing. "Oh, that's just one of the many, many—"

"—many—" she adds.

"—many reasons that I hate you," I finish.

We're sitting around the unlit campfire, watching Priya's brain combust as she tries to figure out classic camp riddles. She's begging for the answer to Green Glass Door when Gia returns from his bathroom trip, inexplicably holding a steaming bag of microwave popcorn.

He sends a piece arcing in my direction. I track it in the dark and twist my body slightly to the left, catching the popcorn neatly on my tongue. It gives a satisfying crunch when I bite down, releasing a burst of salty, buttery goodness.

"Me next!" Priya calls, raising her hand like Gia wouldn't know who said it otherwise.

He throws one. It bounces off her eye and into her lap.

"Bad throw!" She picks the popcorn up delicately and places it in her mouth.

"That was a great throw," Lucy and I protest in unison.

"Again," Priya demands. This time, the popcorn hits her forehead, then the ground. "Wind," she declares with kingly authority.

"What wind?" Tessa laughs.

Gia goes around the circle, lobbing popcorn into open mouths. Each person tries to one-up the person before. Lucy catches hers in a leapfrog jump over Dom's back. Charina covers her eyes and lets Tessa direct her.

At least half of the bag is wasted on Priya's insistence that "this is gonna be the time I catch it. I feel it in my bones." She misses every single one.

When Gia says, "Last piece! Who wants it?" the entire group is cracking up.

"Gia, let's go!" I call through my laughter, running backward.

He points skyward like a boastful sportsball coach, fighting giggles. "C'mon, Juliette!"

I'm wondering if I have time to complete a standing back tuck when it happens.

My heel catches on something unyielding, and in the space of a minute, I ruin my summer. My right foot lands on uneven ground, then all my weight crashes down on it.

I don't know if the shock, the pain, or the fear is worse. It all weaves together into the same heavy quilt of devastation, pinning me to the ground. I can't do anything but gasp and clutch at my ankle, trying to compress everything back to where it's supposed to be.

There's yelling, I think, but it sounds like I'm listening through a seashell. It makes me so dizzy. I roll onto my back, trying to find strength and solidity somewhere inside me, something that isn't broken or crying or nauseous.

But—in silent confirmation that I was indeed cursed at birth—the piece of popcorn Gia threw lands in my sobbing mouth, and I choke.

# NOT DEAD

Lucy reaches me first. I'm coughing from forcing down the popcorn, and she slides a hand under my head to help prop me up. Priya drops to her knees like she's about to do CPR. Gia yells something, but I don't know what.

I flinch as flashlight beams move over me, then quickly disappear toward the cabins. Oh. He was telling them to leave. I want to apologize to Tessa for ending her birthday party this way, but I can only whimper.

Priya curses quietly, grabs my hand, and squeezes it. Meanwhile, Lucy calls my name like she's trying to stop me from going into the light.

"I'm not dead!" I wail through tears.

Lucy swears, straightening my leg to judge the state of my ankle.

Gia appears above us, trying to catch Lucy's eye. He runs a hand through his hair. "I think we need to get you to the nurse."

I squeeze my eyes shut so hard they hurt. He's right, but I don't want him to be.

Lucy rests a hand on my calf. To the other two, she says, "You can go if you want."

Gia's voice is firm. "I'm staying."

Lucy tsks. "Priya, you go, then."

"Screw that," Priya says, her hand tightening around mine.

"At least one of you should go. We don't all need to get in trouble," Lucy says.

Nobody speaks. I almost volunteer as a joke. It would be so funny, but I can't bring myself to speak over the pain.

Gia huffs. "Okay, whatever. We can't stand here debating this while Juliette is dying."

I squint one eye open. "I'm not dying."

"Well, your face is killing me!" Gia quips, wincing. "Sorry, sorry. Not the time."

Priya whispers, "Terrible timing. Excellent delivery."

Lucy, the only one trying to fix the situation, suggests, "I guess we carry her?"

"Will we cause brain damage if we move her?" Gia asks.

"That's a spinal injury," I say, lolling my head to the side and narrowing one open eye at Gia. I follow it up with a quiet but forceful "doofus."

He makes an indignant noise, but Lucy interrupts, staying on task. "Let's pick her up."

"Don't pick me up," I command, but nobody seems to hear me. I repeat myself, "Don't pick me up. Do not pick me up."

"I'll grab her shoulders," Priya says. "Lucy, you take her torso, and Gia can get the legs."

I'm still protesting when they lift me off the ground. The movement sends a shooting pain up to my hip. They try not to look at my tear-streaked face as they clamber up the path to Medical, where Nurse Mari instantly ushers us to a padded exam table. The disposable paper liner crinkles when Gia, Lucy, and Priya set me down on top of it.

"What happened?" she asks, pulling up a stool and gingerly removing my shoe.

I grit my teeth, bracing myself. "I tripped."

"Over a tree root. Backward," Gia adds unhelpfully.

My sock comes off next. Nurse Mari is all business, poking and prodding. "Can you feel this?"

My sharp inhale answers for me.

She lifts my left shoe, causing Lucy to say, "She didn't hurt the other foot."

Nurse Mari continues fiddling with my shoelaces. "Anyone who doesn't have their nursing license can head to bed now." At their protests, she brandishes her walkie-talkie threateningly. "Before I call for Pat to come take her to the hospital."

"The hospital?" I squeak. I've spent my fair share of Take Your Daughter to Work Days there, and, I have to say, I'm not a huge fan.

"You need X-rays." To my friends she says, "You can't do anything else to help, so go. Before I start remembering names." She fixes Lucy with a look. "Miss Swen—"

"We're going!" Lucy blurts, grabbing Priya and Gia by the shoulders. "We'll remember you, Juliette."

"And plan a really nice funeral," Gia calls.

"Nicer than Priyatopia! You like Hozier? He'll come if my mom asks; he loves her."

"Funeraltopia," Lucy proclaims, steering them out of the building.

"I'm not dead!" I bellow after them, just as the door slams shut.

"I'll be honest," Pat says, striding into the medical center. Despite the late hour, he wears a long-sleeved white sun shirt and khaki shorts. Does he sleep in that? "I didn't think it would be Juliette causing problems after hours."

He holds the door open for the person behind him. I hear her before I see her.

"Well, who else would it have been?" asks Galahad pointedly.

That tree root should have killed me. It would be more painless than watching my plaid-pajama-clad counselor judge me so thoroughly.

Pat pulls a pair of blue gloves out of the box on the wall and slides them on. "I would've put money on Lucy Swentek." He takes Nurse Mari's vacant stool, examining my ankle.

"Swentek brought her in," Nurse Mari comments, typing away on her computer.

"Of course she did." Pushing off, Pat wheels the stool backward and drops his gloves into a trash can next to Nurse Mari. "EMS is en route. Did we call her parents already?"

"What?" I snap my head up from the exam table. "Why?"

He quirks an eyebrow. "What do the words 'legal liability' mean to you, Juliette?"

"I'll call," Nurse Mari says, grabbing a Post-it and scribbling down a note.

"I can call," Galahad offers.

I draw in a sharp breath to protest, but Pat replies first, "No, let's have Mari do it. They're doctors, so they'll want a nurse's assessment. We can also have Mari fill out the incident form, since you weren't there when it happened, Galahad."

He says it casually. Factually. While looking at his phone, even. She wasn't there when it happened, so it doesn't make sense for her to fill out the form. But Galahad reacts . . . weirdly. She blinks so intentionally that I almost wonder if it's Morse code. Her cheeks go berry-colored as she just stares at the back of Pat's head.

Exaggeratedly beleaguered, Nurse Mari says, "Oh, let's make Mari do *everything*."

"It's what I pay you for," Pat chirps. "Here's the number."

Watching Nurse Mari take Pat's phone, something occurs to me. "You aren't going to send me home, are you?" I look frantically between them.

Pat and Galahad begin speaking at the same time.

"Rules ar—"

"We'll see what the doctors say."

Galahad freezes, tension incarnate. Pat doesn't notice, too busy taking his phone back.

"Juliette, you're not the first camper to sneak out after curfew, and more importantly, your parents aren't the kind to sue." He nods benevolently. "You're a good kid. We'd all love for you to stay." I purposefully don't look at Galahad so I can pretend he's right. "But let's be realistic. Fogridge isn't safe for mobility issues right now. Depending on the diagnosis, it might make more sense for you to go home."

I want to say something, anything cogent that might convince them that doctors are quacks who know nothing about camp, but what comes out of my mouth is more of a "wuh!" followed by a "buh!" and then a sort of weird gurgling sound.

Pat disregards my attempt at speech and soldiers on. "Someone has to go with you, though," he says, frowning at his phone as he scrolls.

I cringe. The humiliation of Galahad hearing my personal medical details is unbearable.

"I'd prefer not to go," Galahad asserts.

"I wasn't going to send you." Pat stabs at his phone screen like he wants revenge against it. "You need to watch your cabin. And yesterday's backpacking group has a crisis that rhymes with bexplosive piarrhea, so I can't go. If this darn phone starts working, I'll ask a specialist."

Before technology can get it together, two sharply dressed paramedics breeze through the door, escorting a stretcher between them. Very dramatic.

I let them guide me onto it. One asks me questions while the other one talks with Pat. They boost the stretcher, wheeling me out the door and into the back of a bright ambulance.

In the only pleasant twist of fate today, TK's messy red hair pops up between the open bay doors. She wears a faded Mickey Mouse T-shirt and a dazed expression that makes it clear she was in the middle of a REM cycle when she was woken

WISH YOU WEREN'T HERE

up. However, she doesn't seem annoyed as she takes a folder from Pat and hops into the ambulance.

"Rough summer, huh, champ?" she asks, falling onto the little folding bench beside me.

I let the full weight of my head fall back on the stretcher. "The roughest."

"It's all part of the camp experience," she reassures me through a yawn.

"I wish it wasn't." I turn my head to grimace at her, but TK is KO'd. Her head droops forward onto her chest, mouth hanging slightly open. The folder Pat handed her starts to slip out of her grasp. I take it before it can spill (assumedly) the insurance information all over the floor.

Over the next few hours, I grow increasingly jealous of her ability to sleep—especially after we reach the emergency room. Pain, constant beeping, and the fluctuating volume of the world's oldest TV keep me awake long past midnight.

Between repeating infomercials, a doctor pulls my curtain back and enters. He doesn't introduce himself, but I know he's CHARLES HARBOUR, ORTHOPEDIC SURGERY RESIDENT because it's embroidered right there, over the breast pocket of his white coat.

He looks between TK, slumped in the corner, and the white blanket over my leg, not once making eye contact. "Hi, Ms. Barrera. How are you feeling?"

I don't correct him. That's how tired I am. "Okay."

"Good," he says to the sheet ghost of my foot. "Well, the

results of your X-ray are back, and it appears to be a simple sprain. So, good news and bad news. The good news is that it's not broken." He smiles like he just made a joke. "The bad news is that we can't do much for you except wait for the ankle to heal itself. I recommend restricted activity for four to six weeks."

Four to six weeks? There are only three weeks left of camp. My head spins as I think of the upcoming activities. Water Day. Color War. I feel all the blood drain from my face when *Senior Twilight* flashes in my mind like a neon sign.

"Do you have any questions for me?" Dr. Harbour is asking my foot when I tune back in.

I stare, helpless. He has to stay. He can't just leave me like this. He's supposed to fix me.

He observes my foot impatiently, so I blurt out, "Can I get it wet?"

His head twitches in my direction and I think he's going to look at me, finally, but he doesn't. "Can you get . . . your ankle . . . wet? Well, we're not—Yes. Yes, you can get it wet, but I'd stay away from water activities. Swimming could make the injury worse." He demonstrates with his hand, flapping it up and down.

So, I can't run on it? Can I do a straddle whip on the trapeze? Can I jump on the lake trampoline if I only land on my left foot? "Can I walk on it?"

The doctor nods, smiling. "Yes, in fact, research shows that may help it heal faster. But I do advise that you take breaks if it feels unstable. I'll have the nurse show you how to wrap it."

I don't know what else to say, and Charles Harbour, Orthopedic Surgery Resident, takes this as his cue to leave. At the curtain, he glances back at my foot. "Good luck, Ms. Barrera."

"Wright," I finish automatically.

"Right," he replies, clearly misunderstanding.

The curtain swings shut behind him, metal rings squeaking on their track.

Despite the ever-present noise of the hospital, despite TK within arm's reach, and despite the call bell in my lap that would bring a nurse running in within seconds, I feel completely and utterly alone.

## NOT BROKEN

"Good morning, sunshine," a cloyingly sweet voice chirps. My eyes drift open to see TK standing over me in her Mickey Mouse T-shirt, a stack of papers in hand. "Time to go home."

I don't remember falling asleep, but the clock on the wall tells me it's almost noon. I sit up, body achy from lying on the stretcher. TK pulls me to my feet and all but carries me to an old brown car parked right outside the ER entrance.

At my questioning look, she says, "My mom and dad dropped it off last night. They knew they'd be too busy to come get us during the day."

With her help, I climb into the passenger side of the Zimmermans' ancient car. TK has to turn the key several times before it catches in the ignition and the car finally shudders to life. The air-conditioning doesn't work, so I roll the window down with a hand crank. The drive back to camp is long, made longer by twisting mountain roads with low speed limits.

"Will your dad make me leave camp?"

She drums on the steering wheel, tilting her head. "I don't think so. The doctor said it wasn't broken, so as long as you're not doing backflips off the zip line, you should be fine."

I know she's right, but her answer does little to quell the

feeling of my life collapsing around me. My mind spins. My ankle throbs. My thoughts race. And the soundtrack to the end of my world is a nonstop stream of samey-sounding country songs blaring from the car's speakers.

We pull up to camp's main office in the late afternoon.

*It could be worse,* I tell myself.

I could be dead. At least I'm not dead.

It could be broken. At least it's not broken.

The path down to Polaris stretches endlessly ahead of us. We make it about halfway when a little Black girl pops up out of nowhere, the beads in her Fulani braids clinking. She headbutts TK in the leg, then grabs her hand urgently.

"TK, TK! Guess what?" she asks in a tiny voice.

"Margo, Margo!" TK says back, swinging their clasped hands between them. "What?"

Margo glares at me like I'm intruding. "You had a 'mergency last night."

TK chuckles. "I know, kiddo. I was there."

"Your daddy telled us 'bout it." Margo places a bead in her mouth, chewing thoughtfully.

TK expertly hooks a finger around the braid and extricates it from between Margo's teeth. "Oh yeah? What did he say?"

"Um." The little girl halts in her tracks, causing both TK and me to stop, too. She screws her face up in concentration, then shrugs, a big smile lighting up her face. Margo hums an "I don't know." "I was—" She clamps two hands over her mouth.

"You were what?" TK asks cautiously.

"Mmm?" The little girl is all innocence.

"Were you putting bugs in the cabin?"

Margo pulls free of TK's grip and twists her arms behind her back, giggling. "No!"

TK scoops her up, cradling her tiny body like a baby. "Are you lying, silly goose?" she asks in a fake-gruff voice. "Is the cabin full of bugs?"

Margo squirms wildly, still laughing. "Not full!"

TK shoots me a worried look. "Margo, are there bugs in the cabin?"

The smile Margo gives right before she wiggles out of TK's arms is wicked. The little girl takes off running, her arms flailing behind her like two scarves caught in the wind.

TK jolts, taking a half step in Margo's direction and then looking at me. "Are you good?"

I nod, though I'm not. "Go, get your bugs."

TK takes off, shouting incomprehensibly, and I trudge the rest of the way alone.

Only once I get back to Polaris do I realize my blanket is still at the lake. Knowing I'll be freezing in the morning, I slump onto the bed and fall asleep almost at once.

I startle awake to find the lights I had left on, off. It's dark out, and I hear Priya snoring quietly in her bed.

My cheek brushes something incredibly soft, a plush fleece draped over me. I run my hands down it and find a piece of paper resting near my hip. In the dark, I can't make out the words, so I pull the blanket over my head and shine my flashlight at the note.

Priya's handwriting is scary in its precision. There's a reason she always gets assigned to poster-writing duty in group projects. Even on the unlined sheet, the words run in an exacting straight line, parallel to the fold down the middle of the page. I'm pretty sure I could take a ruler to the letters and the standard deviation of their heights would be less than a millimeter. It's sick.

*Yours is in the wash. Don't spill anything on it.*

I chuckle to myself and slide the note and my flashlight onto the nightstand before cocooning myself in velvety softness and the scent of lemongrass.

Gia drops his breakfast tray with a clunk. "So, is it broken or what?"

The bacon is undercooked, which I usually hate, but I'm starving from missing dinner, so I shovel it down. I shake my head, chasing my mouth with my fork. "Nope, just sprained."

"Bummer," Lucy says, taking the seat directly across from me. "At least if it were broken, you'd have a good story. A sprained ankle is so much less interesting."

"Yeah, but this way it might heal by week five."

Priya exchanges a glance with my two friends. From behind her glass of ice water she remarks, "Juliette, you can barely walk. That was a hard fall."

My face flushes. I feel like a child caught running into the street after a ball. "It already feels better than it did yesterday," I say in a lie that I hope is obvious only to me.

Priya, who watched me wince as I did the compression wrap this morning, stays silent.

"Well, I hope it heals by Color War," Lucy says, giving me a nod.

"I don't," says Gia. "Feel free to stay on the bench, Juliette. It's our year, anyway."

At the end of the summer, Fogridge does Color War. The whole camp is split into three groups: purple, green, and orange. Three counselors are named Color captains, there's a huge reveal, and then we all participate in two days of wacky competitions.

The Zimmerman siblings who founded Fogridge were named Lazlo, Mary, and Donald, so it doesn't take a huge leap of logic to figure out why the purple team is named the Lazlots, the orange team is the Marikets, and the green team is the Dondos.

Lucy and I practically came out of the womb wearing purple *Lots go!* foam fingers. And though he remains a fiercely loyal Mare, Gia's orange team has come in last place for the past four years. And they'll come in last place this year, too.

I open my mouth to say as much, but he cuts me off. "I won't abide any Mariket slander."

Lucy and I laugh. She turns to Priya, "Are they letting you pick your team?"

Priya's eyes sparkle. "They sure are."

"You should be a Mare."

She gives Gia an apologetic smile. "That's okay. I don't like to lose."

I choke on my bacon, pounding against my chest as I cough and cackle simultaneously.

Lucy's mouth drops open, awed. She gives Priya a somber salute. "Absolutely brutal."

"The Lazlots corrupt even the gentlest souls," Gia intones, taking a sip of orange juice.

"Oh, there's too much purple at this table," says Priya. "I'm gonna be green."

"A Dondo?" the rest of us exclaim in unison.

"Priya, please. We can't have a Dondo in our friend group. We—" Suddenly, Lucy notices something behind me. Her demeanor breaks, and she drops her gaze to the table.

I turn and see Galahad approaching, weekly assignments in hand. But I didn't get a chance to choose. "Oh, Galahad, can I—"

"We already have your schedule, Juliette," she says, cutting me off swiftly.

"But I . . ."

This time it's Galahad's look, not her words, that stop me. "You broke your ankle messing around after hours. You *shouldn't* have a say in your activities this week."

"It's not broken," I say.

She doesn't dignify that with a response. "Priya, Theater morning and afternoon. Juliette, you'll be at Sculpture and Cooking for the morning. And in the afternoon, Theater."

I sit up like a marionette whose strings have just been tugged. "What?"

"Sculpture, Cooking, and Theater," she repeats with little patience.

I glance at Priya, and she raises her hands in surrender. *Wasn't me,* she mouths.

Galahad scowls. "Quit being a brat, Juliette. Be happy you're still here."

A wave of heat courses through me, a mix of too many negative emotions to name. I can't even look at my friends as embarrassment engulfs me. Am I being a brat? I don't know. For once, I don't want to fight. I just want the conversation to be over.

But I also really, *really* don't want to do Theater.

Galahad starts walking away. I call out the first thing that comes to mind. "But people have to stand in Theater!"

She doesn't turn when she responds, "Good thing your ankle isn't broken."

# 4

# I'M SORRY THAT I

I haven't entered the theater in years, but the smell of freshly vacuumed carpet brings me right back to childhood productions. My eyes find the seat I sat in as I watched the last play I was forced to endure—a barely coherent rendition of *Seussical Jr.*

"Do you want help?" Priya asks, pausing at the top of the aisle.

Swallowing my pride and accepting her help would make this easier. But I shake my head and furniture-surf down to the front row, where I collapse into a seat and massage my ankle.

In one fluid motion, Priya jumps up and perches on the edge of the stage. Her chunky white go-go boots swing, heels thumping against the wooden panels. She doesn't acknowledge the care I'm giving my injury, but I have a feeling she notices.

A specialist takes the stage, her red-and-white Fogridge shirt embroidered with the words TO SIT IN SOLEMN SILENCE. She's a tall, willowy Asian girl with a dancer's posture and a slick ballerina bun.

After introducing herself as Twee, she turns to the camper beside her and says in a bizarre mid-Atlantic accent, "Jeremiah, I'm so sorry that I killed your cat."

I recoil, but nobody else reacts.

The boy says, "I forgive you." He turns, taking another camper's hands. "Junior, I'm sorry I said *Doctor Who* was dorky."

Junior shakes his head stoically and answers, "Perhaps I may find it in my heart to forgive you one day, but today is not that day." To a blue-haired girl sitting on the floor between the stage and the front row, Junior says, "Rowan, I'm sorry I told you the baby was yours." He places his hand on an imaginary pregnant belly.

*Oh God.* I cringe with secondhand embarrassment when I realize it's some weird theater exercise. Anxious goose bumps crawl up my back. Keeping my face impassive, I slink out of my chair and stumble up the aisle. Walking is painful and tiring, but it's a fair trade to avoid *that*.

I burst through the heavy metal doors and immediately lean back against them, the last survivor in a zombie apocalypse trying to fend off the horde.

I'd like to amend what I said before: nobody is too much at camp, *except* the theater kids. I'm intense, but this type of intensity is not for me. I can't imagine ever playing that game without wanting to crawl out of my skin.

Instantly, I miss White Water Rafting and Rappelling. I even miss week one of Wilderness Adventure. I miss familiar places and things I understand.

I don't know how to act here.

When I eventually hear the unmistakable shuffling that comes with a teacher's dismissal, I work up the strength to push back through the door. It's heroic of me, given the circumstances.

Twee is still talking but is being largely ignored as people break off into groups. "I'll be around to run lines if anyone needs. Like, for example, if Etan still didn't know his lines. Then I'd be willing to run lines with Etan. Just for example. Etan?"

When it becomes clear Etan is not going to run lines, Twee dismounts the stage and strides over to me. "Welcome. Name and pronouns, new one."

Even just answering a simple question makes me uncomfortable. Jesus. *Get ahold of yourself.* I try not to squirm as I take her hand and say, "Juliette. Barrera-Wright. She/her."

"Good name. I just let the group know our second session musical is going to be *Beauty and the Beast.* Auditions are Wednesday." She smiles warmly at me. "I hope you'll try out. If you don't already have something else to do, I'm sure sets and costumes need help. Oh, hey!"

I follow her gaze and find Priya approaching us. I'm actually grateful, for once, to be foisted off onto her.

"Do you have anything Juliette could help you with?"

"Of course," Priya says, linking her arm with mine. "I'll take care of her, Twee."

Pleased, Twee raises a hand and drifts toward a group practicing choreography.

"Let's go, roomie," Priya says jauntily, angling her arm to support my weight as she leads me down the aisle. She helps me hop ungracefully up a set of steps and across the stage to a break in the thick velvet curtain. Holding it aside, she reveals an open door to a long, dim hallway. One side of the gray corridor acts as storage, piled high with metal grates, extra lights, empty clothing racks, stacks of chairs, and piles of fabric.

I reach out to use a sturdy-looking tower of wooden crates for stability.

"Don't," Priya yelps, catching and relocating my hand to her opposite shoulder. With my forearm draped over her back, I'm surrounded by lemongrass. "If you knock that over, they'll make me reorganize it."

I raise my eyebrows at the chaos. "That's organized?"

"Watch it," Priya says, her eyes exaggeratedly narrow.

She leads me to the end of the hall. A green sign that says THE WIZARD IS OUT hangs on the door. Priya flips it to say THE WIZARD IS IN before leading me into what I have to assume is the inside of a cinder block.

Priya's workstation is the grayest, most concrete room I've ever seen. Luckily, scattered projects lend some humanity to the space. I immediately drop onto one of the paint-splattered tarps, relieved to be out of sight of judgmental eyeballs.

"What're those going to be?" I ask as she drags over three slabs of blue foam, about seven feet tall.

She doesn't answer, attention focused squarely on her phone. A portable speaker bursts to life with the sound of men talking over each other, the intro to a song I don't yet recognize. The instrumentals kick in, and Priya hums along, pantomiming the choreography. It takes a minute, but the song clicks. "Sit Down, You're Rockin' the Boat" from *Guys and Dolls*.

My eyes widen as realization dawns. "Oh my God," I say. "You really are a theater nerd. I didn't believe you, but it's true."

She crosses her arms. "Can you ever just let me live?"

I pretend to give this some genuine thought before saying, "Hmm. I don't think so, no."

From my spot on the tarp, I watch Priya gather a metal paint can full of pointy wooden sticks and carry it to the blue foam blocks. The song fades into an upbeat number from *Rent*. This one I know, so I sing along as Priya traces rough rectangular shapes in the foam.

I cock my head. "What are those?"

Blue debris flutters to the floor, sticking to her white skirt on the way down. "Brick wall backdrops. They'll be good because I can reuse them for *Beauty and the Beast*."

"Can I help?" I ask, scooting my way across the floor.

Priya looks down at me, huddled near her feet like a Victorian orphan beggar child. "Sure, you can do the bottom halves. It doesn't have to be precise; they'll end up looking more realistic after we melt them." She hands me a stick from the can.

I pause. The stick hovers an inch away from the blue foam. "Melt them?"

"You have so much to learn," she says with a pedantic head-shake.

Carving the foam feels different than I expected. I thought it would be tough and stiff, like Styrofoam, but it crunches to dust beneath the stick. We fall into a quiet rhythm, her moving around me to keep foam chunks from landing in my hair.

We almost complete two foam pieces before Priya asks,

"Does Theater suck as much as you thought it would?"

I suppress a yawn, trying to recall the last time I was still for this long. "It's not so bad."

She shrugs. "You didn't seem super comfortable out there. I mean, you practically broke your ankle again running out during I'm Sorry That I."

I wince. "Yeah, that part wasn't great. And it's not broken," I remind her.

After she gives me an apologetic nod, she steps back to observe the progress we've made. I've noticed that when she's thinking, Priya draws both of her lips in until only the barest sliver is visible. She does that now, examining the project like it holds state secrets.

"Do you have to do them? The acting exercises," I add in case it wasn't clear.

Her mouth slowly unfolds into a full smile. "I volunteer to do them. They're fun."

"You're joking."

She laughs, dropping to all fours and scraping at a section near the ground that I carved too shallowly. "Juliette, I'm sorry that I tried to prompose to you by releasing all those painted chickens at homecoming. I thought it would be romantic. Please forgive me." She shoots me a mocking pouty face.

"No, eugh!" I shake my wrists violently and stick my tongue out, attempting to ease the chill running down my spine. "So cringe."

"Does that mean you're not going to prom with me?"

"Make it stop," I whine.

"Only if you do one back." She blinks, all innocence. "That's how the game works."

I shudder again. "I don't know what to say."

She sways close to and away from the set piece, chiseling confidently. "But there are so many options. Priya, I'm sorry I haven't watched *Survivor*. Priya, I'm sorry I never put any thought into your birthday gift. Priya, I'm sorry that I'm staring at your butt."

My eyes snap up. Priya grins at me over her shoulder.

"Oh my God," I whisper into the hands I've cupped around my face. I feel her smugness, even from inside my force field of mortification.

"It's okay, Juliette. It's a nice butt."

"I wasn't staring at your butt," I protest unconvincingly.

She doesn't answer. I part my fingers to find her sitting, facing me, wearing the most knowing look I've ever seen.

"I wasn't!"

She runs a finger over her lower lip, raising her eyebrows. "Sure."

My face burns. To be fair, I was staring at her butt, but it was *right there*. "I wa—Okay, I was, like, staring . . . at . . . it. But I wasn't *looking* at it. I—It was, like, in my line of vision, but I wasn't looking *at* it."

"Right." It's clear that Priya is trying to hold back a laugh. "You were looking *with* it. Near it."

I bring my hands together in prayer, dropping my forehead

onto them. "God, grant me the serenity to accept the things I cannot change and the strength to kick Priya's really nice butt."

She throws her head back with howling laughter. "So you agree? You think it's nice."

I scream quietly, uncomfortable and comforted all at once.

"Okay, back to work. Time is money," Priya says, expression serious. "Now, Juliette, I'm going to stand up and get some tools. Try to control yourself."

I huff, picking up a small chunk of foam and hurling it at her back. It gets caught in the breeze and ineffectually drifts to the ground.

Priya returns with two silver hair dryers, gesturing for me to watch. She raises one to the foam and turns it on. Slowly, the area under the heat begins to contract and contort.

Over the whirring, Priya yells, "It's easier with heat guns, but they won't get me one!"

I glance around, sure that I noticed a table with a saw on it when I walked in. "They won't let you have a heat gun, but you can have a saw?"

Priya grins. "The saw was already here! Twee isn't super vigilant! As long as I don't cut my arm off, she won't notice!"

"You better hope Pat doesn't find out," I caution. "Lawsuits give him hives."

"I'm not worried. I have good luck."

"Luck isn't real," I scoff.

"Sure it is." She tilts her head at the foam, then shuts off the hair dryer. "We'll see how that looks once it's cooled down."

I survey the block she was working on. The brick really does look more realistic now. If you ignore the fact that it's still blue. "How did you learn to do this?" I ask.

Priya sits, tucking her legs underneath herself. "My ex-girlfriend was into set design. That's kind of how I got started. She taught me a lot."

I practically concuss myself, whipping my head up so fast. "Wait, your—I thought . . . ? Aren't—What about Barry?"

Priya furrows her brow. "Christine was before Barry. She was the first person I ever dated. But she moved back to the East Coast when her mom got some banking job in New York." A wistful smile comes over her face that makes my stomach clench.

"Oh. I—Oh, I thought—" I've never acted like this about any of my other queer friends. I'm reacting more like a libertarian mom than a twenty-first-century teenager, but I can't stop. My mouth moves a few more times. Maybe it even makes noise. I don't know.

It was that whole thing about her butt. It threw me so hard that my soul astral projected. I hope my spirit is violently kicking my head in an attempt to reboot my brain.

Priya's lips quirk up. "I'm bi, Juliette."

I groan internally. Obviously, I had inferred that. Am I acting so clueless that she thinks I don't know what being bi is? In California? You can't throw a rock without hitting a bisexual or a tourist in a Joshua Tree T-shirt. Usually, it's the same person.

"Do your parents know?" Oh my God. What is wrong with

me? My astral-projected self is searching for another body to inhabit right about now, and I'm a little jealous of her.

"Yeah," Priya answers with a wave of her hand. "I would never date anyone without their approval. They have good-person radar."

"And they're cool with it?" My stomach recoils.

Priya's eyes sparkle with amusement, but I'm grateful for that. I'd rather she be laughing at me than be angry, or worse, ashamed because I can't get a grip. "Yeah. Dad doesn't care, and you know Mom. She just loves people. She's always telling me which of my friends she wants me to date." She watches her reflection play with its hair in a fish-eye mirror mounted on the wall. "She's tried to convince me to ask you out more than once. She doesn't know that we're—" She gestures between us. "Eh."

God, I love Deepika. "Honestly, if it meant Deepika would be my mom, we could skip dating. I would marry you."

*What.*

Am I dead?

This is hell, isn't it? I'm being psychologically tortured. Possessed by a demon of embarrassment. Cursed by a vengeful wood nymph. Punished by the camp gods.

What is going on?

Priya angles her head, studying me thoughtfully. She starts, "I wo—"

I grab her hair dryer and slide the switch up. It screams back to life.

She jumps, looking down to the dryer and then up at my

face. I shrug and motion toward the foam block. Beyond the whine of the motor, I make out a ballad from *Waitress*. I throw my whole chest voice into it.

I work as if the last few misguided moments never happened. Priya never finishes her sentence, and I drown my thoughts deep underneath the noise I create.

# 5

# EXPERIMENT IN PROGRESS

My brain betrays me in the morning by forgetting that I'm injured. It's only after I slam my feet into the ground that I remember. The scream and bone-deep pain occur simultaneously.

Priya jolts awake like Frankenstein ('s monster. I know, I know. Relax). "What?"

"Nothing," I grunt, clutching at my throbbing ankle.

Priya rises to her feet and stretches, yawning deeply.

I glare, fumbling for a small roll of compression tape. "Don't gloat."

"You know. You're not doing a great job at convincing me that you're 'fine.'"

"I don't have to convince you." I smooth the end of the tape. "I just have to convince Pat."

"Oh, that won't be hard." She materializes at the foot of my bed and extends a hand to help me up. "As long as he doesn't see you, hear you, or otherwise perceive you in any way for the rest of the summer."

"Ha, ha." I take my first step, stiff and sore. "Let's go to breakfast."

She escorts me down the stairs of Polaris. I try not to

appear injured as we descend. I don't do a great job.

Once we're on flat ground, Priya drops into a starting crouch—the kind we use in track—and lifts her eyebrows. "I'll race you."

"Okay," I say. "It'll be the only time you ever beat me at anything."

Twee hands out modified scripts at breakfast, but I don't even look at mine.

In Cooking, we make personal pizzas, which I'm excited about at first. Then it takes the cooking specialist thirty minutes to finish lecturing us on kitchen etiquette and hand out our supplies. My usually overactive bones hurt from sitting still for so long, but standing hurts even more.

When we finally start cooking, I'm so zoned out that I accidentally put the sauce on top of the cheese. I think I can just remake it, but I return to the ingredients bar to find that all the cheese has been used up.

"Don't worry," the cooking specialist says to me when he notices my despair. "It'll melt down. Pizzas all taste the same in the end."

It does not taste the same. Even though they share the same components, the thing I made tastes distinctly more like a grilled cheese sandwich dipped in tomato soup than a pizza.

The sculpture specialist teaches us to make themed bas-reliefs on metal. Mine is a bear fishing in a stream. As the week goes on, the specialist tells us, we'll fill in more details with these tools that look like the blunt end of a paintbrush. Eventually, we'll get to paint the metal.

It's fun, and I'm not bad at it. I share a workstation with a girl from Fullerton who's attempting a portrait of her cat. We have a nice conversation; she makes me laugh a lot.

It's fine. It's all fine. But I don't love it.

For the first time ever, I'm not excited to be at camp. It's not just that I don't get to do what I want, but that I *won't*. I want to be stand-up paddleboarding. I want to be flying down the zip line. I want to go on my morning run. And the reality is that camp will end before I'm well enough to do any of those things again.

On top of that utterly depressing thought, every inch of my skin feels tight. The most exercise I've gotten in days has been walking between buildings. I'm bouncing off the walls.

Moodily, I trudge to Polaris, passing a group of campers seated just off the path. A hush falls over them as I approach, their little eyes tracking me with wild excitement.

In the middle of their semicircle, closest to the path, sits Flagstaff, blindfolded with a white tube sock. He cradles a handwritten sign that sloppily proclaims *Experiment in Progress*. It's upside down.

I come to a stop and the boys snap to attention like a group of excited meerkats.

"What's the experiment?" I ask, shifting my weight onto my good foot.

Flagstaff tilts his head from side to side, like he's trying to clear water from his ears. "Say something else. Not your name," he clarifies quickly.

"She sells seashells by the seashore." It's the first thing that comes to mind.

He snaps, grinning. "Miss Juliette Barrera-Wright."

His group swings to face me, so I shrug. "Yes?"

The boys grumble, throwing their hands up. Accusations of cheating ring out.

"I am not cheating," Flagstaff announces haughtily. "Jordan, add it to the list."

A scrawny redhead holding a clipboard adds a check mark to a long list of checks and x's.

"We're conducting an experiment," Flagstaff says.

"I see that." My gaze sweeps over the boys. "Is this . . . for an activity?"

"Oh, yes," Flagstaff croons. "I'm running a program this week. Flagstaff Hour. I bet the boys that I could guess the Fogridge Fam by voice alone. If I get more than seventy-five percent right by the end of the week, I get to paint little Flagstaffs on their faces."

I bite down on a smile. "You should paint yourself doing a victory dance."

"No!" the boys wail. One fixes me with a glare and demands, "Why would you say that?"

Flagstaff gasps. "That is an excellent idea, Juliette! Jordan, write that down."

"Okay. How do you spell 'victory'?" Jordan asks, his face the picture of concentration.

"V, as in Vlagstaff. *I*, as in Ilagstaff. *C*, as in Clagstaff. *T*, as in Tagstaff—"

They all groan and one of them throws himself onto Flagstaff, placing a tiny hand over his mouth. Flagstaff keeps spelling out the word, but it's muffled behind the boy's hand.

He pries his camper's hand off his mouth and calls out, "Juliette, before you go: Are any of my troublemakers eating worms?"

I let my gaze slide over them. Some of them pat the dirt suspiciously, but I don't see any chewing. "I'm not sure," I say truthfully.

Flagstaff sighs. "Isn't that always the way? How many miscreants we got back there?"

I count the boys. "Fourteen."

"Okay, who's missing?" Flagstaff shouts. His blindfold threatens to fall off at the reckless speed with which he waggles his eyebrows.

The boys all cry out, some of them in hysterical laughter and some in mock annoyance. "Nobody!" they say.

Flagstaff puts his hands on his hips. "This is a fifteen-person group."

The boy who had previously launched himself onto Flagstaff's lap now grabs Flagstaff's face on both sides and looks deep into his blindfold, saying, "*You* are the fifteenth person."

"Are you sure?" Flagstaff asks dubiously.

The little boy nods Flagstaff's head with his hands. "Yes!"

The boys rise to their feet, some climbing on Flagstaff, some jumping up and down in a mix of frustration and excitement. Only Jordan remains seated, watching his peers with a weary authority.

Flagstaff's knowing smile causes another laugh to bubble out of me. "But what about . . . Schmibley Greebles?" he asks.

Shrieks. Bloodcurdling shrieks ring out from the mob.

"No!"

"Schmibley Greebles isn't real! You made him up!"

"I did not," Flagstaff insists. "What a mean thing to say about your friend. Juliette, you've met Schmibley. Tell them he's real."

I nod gravely and address the boys. "You know, I have met Schmibley. He's my cousin. On my mom's side."

"Now, see!" Flagstaff exclaims as the boys slander my good name. "Schmibley! Schmibley, come back! You always do this! You can't just leave the group whenever you want."

I shake my head, limping away, grinning ear to ear. Flagstaff's voice calling for Schmibley follows me the entire way back to my bunk.

Flagstaff's fake camper in my group was Redmock Frampto. I smile, remembering how worked up we'd get when he would say things like, "Of course you've never seen Redmock. He likes to swing in the trees like a monkey. Don't look now—you'll embarrass him!"

None of us believed him, but I secretly spent that entire summer watching the trees. Just in case.

# BITTERSWEET AND STRANGE

"Audition for Belle," Priya says, leaning her face in between the slats of the banister. In her right hand, she holds the *Beauty and the Beast* script, rolled up like she might swat me with it if I disobey.

"Why?" I ask, narrowing my eyes.

"Because I want you to! It'll be fun," she singsongs.

I shake my head. "Nah."

"C'mon," she groans. "I know you don't have stage fright and I know you can sing, so why not?"

"You've never heard me sing," I say, waving her off and returning my gaze to the book in my lap, a fantasy called *Lying for Prophets*. I'd bet money the main character, a witty pirate queen, dies at the end.

"Come on." Priya falls dramatically forward into the railing. "You've been singing in the workroom since Twee announced the play. If I had a fraction of your talent, I'd sing constantly."

Truthfully, I'm staring at the book more than reading it. I skim the sentence "The moon was more than just a door" over and over, the words a treadmill for my eyes. "That's in the workroom. How do you know I don't have stage fright?"

"My mom dragged me to every single one of your Little Star Search performances."

I turn a page of my book, for flavor. The sentence at the top of the new page reads, "The rain was polite enough to wait until just after Isadora got inside to start coming down in sheets." I make a mental note to actually read this book. "That was like nine years ago," I say to Priya.

She thwacks the rolled-up script against one of the wooden rods. "You are so annoying."

I turn away instead of answering. Within seconds, she's stomping up my steps, but I pretend the book has my full attention. How interesting: "The rain was polite enough to wait until just after Isadora got inside to start coming down in sheets."

Priya plants herself on my mattress and pushes the book away.

"Hey! I was reading that," I protest.

"Didn't you spend Tessa's birthday party talking about how much you hate me being the center of everything all the time? Now you get a chance to be the lead and you're just not going to do it? For what?"

"I did not 'get a chance to be the lead.'"

"Juliette!" Priya snaps. "You know you'd get that role the second you sang."

Despite my success on Little Star Search (a talent competition for *children*, by the way), I have no illusions about getting onstage again. I haven't done it in years. When the time came for my mom to choose between singing lessons for me and computer coding classes for my teenage sister, she chose Eloise. Because, she'd said, coding is a real skill that Eloise can make a real career out of someday. Singing is fine for fun, but we need to live in reality.

And do you know what? She was right. Now that I'm faced with college and the real world, I see that I never could have made a career out of my voice. People rarely do. Famous artists get famous because they have connections or they're extremely lucky, or both. Priya Pendleys get famous. Juliette Barrera-Wrights get steady white-collar jobs at The Business Factory and try to suppress the knowledge that once upon a time they were good at the trapeze.

Not all of us can follow our dreams.

She holds the book back with minimal effort when I try to grab it. I can't have this conversation. She doesn't understand. I'm not going to sit here and pretend I've had a hard, impoverished life, but there's still a gap between Priya's opportunities and mine.

I give her a version of the truth. "I can't major in singing at Yale."

"Uh, I think you can," she says, wielding her words like a whip.

I roll my eyes. "I know *people* can. I mean *I* can't. Anyway, I don't want to act. I want to be doing Water Polo and Climbing."

Priya shoves my shoulder like she's trying to wake me up. "First of all, I know what you meant. I meant *you*, Juliette Barrera-Wright, could major in singing. Second, this is a camp production of a knockoff of *Beauty and the Beast*. Nobody wins an Oscar here. Your voice will be more than enough to wow them. And third of all, Water Polo and Climbing are off the table, so stop being a baby and audition."

I push back on her hands. "Priya. Voices change over nine years. I'm not doing it."

The weight disappears from the mattress, and I hear her retreat down the steps. Just when I think I've won, she says, "Your voice hasn't. You are auditioning for Belle if I have to drag you onstage and move your mouth for you."

A deeply unsettling mental image of Priya moving my jaw up and down to the tune of the musical's opening song pops into my brain.

She's right. My voice hasn't changed. I mean, it has, but it's only gotten better, richer. The breath control I've gained from track has helped.

My singing isn't the reason I don't want to audition. When I sang in the workroom, I knew Priya was listening, and it felt . . . good. If I'm being honest, I miss it.

You know I can't watch *The Voice*? I spend the entire time thinking, *That could be me. That could be my four-chair turn. It could be my talent the judges are arguing over.*

But what if I got up onstage and nobody turned? What if I'm not as talented as I think I am? What if I am as talented as I think I am, but that's still not good enough?

If I don't even try, I can go on thinking, *That could be me,* for as long as I want. I'd never have to sing the last note of a song while staring at the backs of four unturned chairs. If I know that music will never be my career, I won't be sad when my career isn't music.

But . . . I wonder if Twee would turn.

---

I walk—by which I mean limp—into the theater the next day, determined to paint sets. It's dark and quiet, which is odd. Programs started five minutes ago, so *Into the Woods* prep should be in full swing. I flip all the switches on the panel beside the door. High above, eight industrial bay lamps thrum to life in quick succession.

I proceed down the aisle, startling when I get close enough to register the bizarre scene illuminated at center stage. Priya, who disappeared immediately after breakfast, sits in the center of a circle of campers. They look up at me as one, an enormous hive mind.

"This is eerie." I set my water bottle down on an armrest in the front row.

"We're staging a sit-in," Priya explains serenely. She spreads her arms wide, the picture of innocence. "Until you audition. I showed them videos of you on Little Star Search, so there's no way out of it now."

I furrow my forehead. "How did you get those?"

"The internet never forgets," Priya says ominously.

"That's why nobody should send nudes with identifying features," a senior named Maris says, waggling his eyebrows. The girls seated near him giggle at his suggestiveness, but they'd react the same way to anything he said. He seems to have that effect on people.

"Maris!" Twee snaps.

"What? It's good advice!"

Now that I'm close enough, I see that much of the circle is composed of campers I just met this week. I'm sure a few of them would like to be Belle themselves, but they all watch me with enthusiasm. Of course, if anyone could convince them to do this, it would be my roommate.

Twee smiles encouragingly, gripping her calves with both hands. Her shirt today simply says ACT. "It's up to you. But we'd love to see it."

Priya leaps to her feet and pushes me to the mic stand. The pressure of her hand disappears just before we reach it. She jogs past me and plants herself right at the edge of the stage. I make a big show of being annoyed; she just watches expectantly, hands framing her face like a child waiting for story time.

It's been a long time since I've felt comfortable singing, but the girl I was when I used to perform is still in me somewhere. I would never have chosen to get on that stage by myself, but now it feels out of my control.

It's kind of a relief.

One last step places me behind the microphone. I take my time adjusting it to my height, worrying about whether I can do this the way I used to, especially without warming up. Because my primary audiences over the last nine years have been my steering wheel and the showerhead, it's a genuine concern.

Then the microphone is adjusted. I'm there on the stage. And there's nothing left to do but sing. In the moments before I open my mouth, I try to recall years of training. Feet shoulder-width apart. Stand tall. Loose knees. Breath support from my diaphragm. Lift my soft palate. Relax my jaw. Remember which vowels work best for me. Don't screw this up. Don't rest in my head voice. Stay on key. Stay in the pocket. Emote.

I yawn, inhaling deeply one last time.

All my fears subside as the opening note escapes me. My brain forgets, but my body remembers. Everything comes back as easily as breathing.

I step back into myself, for the first time in a very long time.

Twee offers me the part before I even leave the stage.

# THE FIRST PRIYATOPIA

Lucy and Gia are drumrolling on the table when I pull my chair out and sit.

"Bum-buh-dah-bum! Congratulations!" says Gia. He stops drumming and starts clapping.

"How did you hear?" I set my plate of salad on the table. A smattering of leftover grilled cheese bits masquerade as croutons. One tumbles off the plate and onto the table.

"Etan's in my bunk. He knew I would care, so he told me right after you got it."

Lucy leans forward. "Are you going to lose your shit spending so much time with Priya, though?"

"It's fine," I say, carefully inspecting a fork laden with grilled cheese croutons. These have to be a health violation. "It hasn't been as bad as I thought. Living with her, I mean."

Gia wrinkles his forehead. He points at me, consulting with Lucy. "Mind control or replaced with a clone?"

"Not sure," she answers slowly. "Let's see the back."

They both crane their necks at me.

I rush to slap a hand over the back of my head. "I can admit when I'm wrong."

"Clone," Lucy concludes, settling back into her chair, arms crossed.

At the same time, Gia laughs. "No, you can't! You very much can't."

I roll my eyes and take a bite of the croutons. They taste just as bad as expected.

"Where is the queen, anyway?" Lucy asks, nodding toward Priya's empty chair.

"Dunno," I say with a shake of my head. "She's been missing all day. It's probably *Into the Woods* stuff."

"Oh, yeah. Are we going to that?" Gia looks at me expectantly.

My brow furrows. "Why would we?"

"Because Priya's been busting her ass on set design stuff for weeks?" Lucy posits. "Gia and I even helped her paint the cow as white as milk last week."

Gia nods, his eyes flashing with excitement. "Hell yeah. I wanna see that guy. He's a star. I *did* initially paint spots on, but we fixed it. In my defense, I've never seen the play. She said it was a cow! What was I supposed to think?"

Lucy nods sympathetically.

My fork clinks against my plate as I put it down a little too hard. "She didn't ask me to help." I conveniently ignore the fact that I spent all of yesterday painting with her.

"She probably didn't think you'd want to," Lucy says with a shrug. "I mean, you are pretty open about your feelings toward her. I know you two are friends-ish now, but I was surprised you even let her sit with us for meals at first."

I run my hands lightly over my hair, careful not to flatten the curls. "Of course I let her sit with us; I'm not mean!" Then I breathe out a sigh as the possibility hits me. "Am I mean?"

WISH YOU WEREN'T HERE

Lucy and Gia don't hesitate to assure me that I am, in fact, not mean.

"You're just protective of camp." Lucy shrugs sympathetically. "Listen, in this world it's gatekeep or get gatekept. I'm with you. Gia doesn't get it, though."

"Yeah," Gia says with a shake of his head. "I'd much rather girlboss than gatekeep."

"What is this?" I look back and forth between them. "A meme?"

Gia and Lucy exchange amused looks.

Mouth full, Lucy asks, "How old are you, again?"

Gia slams a hand against his forehead, as if he's just had a eureka moment. "This entire time we've been focused on the Priya and Juliette dynamic, when the bigger issue is how to exorcise the ninety-year-old ghost living in Juliette's body."

Lucy's eyebrows shoot up. "Gia, chill," she stage-whispers. "Think about it: that ghost has probably been there this whole time. We can't banish her now. She's our buddy!"

His eyes flick up at the ceiling, thoughtfully. "Yeah, I guess you're right. And what if the actual Juliette is, like, a racist? Things would really suck for me." He gestures at Lucy. "You'd be fine, though. You're as white as the back of my eyeball."

"Oh, nice!" Lucy shadowboxes the air. "Once again, being white in America works out in my favor."

"I would love to get off this topic," I say, speaking over the start of Gia's next sentence. He glares at me. "I guess we're going to *Into the Woods*."

"Are you kidding?" Gia says, stabbing a fork in my direction.

"I'm not going to watch *Into the Woods* with a racist ghost."

"No," Lucy corrects. "The ghost isn't racist. The ghost is our friend. *Juliette* is racist."

"Oh my God! A little quieter!" I stage-whisper, ducking my head. My eyes dart, acutely aware of Galahad's supernatural ability to hear everything we say at this table. "Can we not spread rumors that I'm racist, please?"

Lucy pats Gia's shoulder. "That was a good bit. We're funny."

He nods at her, smiling, and scoops up more croutons and pops them into his mouth.

"Those are disgusting," I say, frowning. "I don't know how you eat them."

Gia's eyes widen in surprise, and I can physically feel him getting ready to set up another comedy routine that's going to go on forever.

I cut him off, "What? Was that racist, too?"

"Juliette!" Lucy gasps.

With a hand pressed to his heart like a southern grandma, Gia says, "Wow. Joking about racism. That's low, even for you."

The two of them shake their heads, ever in sync, and high-five without looking.

Foolishly, I assumed that, because I know the movie so well, *Beauty and the Beast* wouldn't be hard to memorize. But once every little detail was changed so Fogridge wouldn't get sued by a certain infamously litigious company, the script became unrecognizable. Twee says there's zero chance of legal action, but Pat is insistent. He stops by the theater at least once a rehearsal to remind us that he cannot afford a lawsuit.

Everything in the play is off brand. My favorite is the dinner song, with the lazy new title "She's a Guest." The good news is that Twee and the music specialist, Legato, didn't set the musical in space or turn it into a hip-hopera. That's how embarrassingly low my bar was for the rewrite. The bad news is that, because everything's different, I spend an infinite number of hours learning the Uncanny Valley versions of beloved childhood songs.

Priya promises to help me rehearse, but only after *Into the Woods* wraps. At first, Gia and Lucy were super into running lines. Around the fourth rerun of the opening scene, they lost all enthusiasm. When we hit seven, they officially resigned as "good friends" and told me they would not be helping anymore.

"It's not you, it's us," said Gia.

"But it's also a little bit you," Lucy added, with a mock sad face.

Those are the reasons I'm by myself on Thursday night, deep in the trenches of the Week Three Slump.

It's always the worst week, without the novelty of the first two weeks or the anticipatory nostalgia of the last two. Camp delirium, the inevitable few days where everyone at Fogridge seems to temporarily lose their minds, doesn't even hit until the beginning of week four.

I'm resting on my back with the script on top of my face, hoping to absorb the lines through osmosis, when Polaris's door swings open. I sit up quickly, surprised to see Galahad, not Priya. Her eyes cut straight to me, and she marks her clipboard and turns to go.

"Priya'll be back soon! She's not missing!" I call, trying to prevent a camp-wide search.

"I know, Juliette," Galahad says flatly, and lets the door click into place.

Priya waltzes through the door nearly an hour later, and I don't know why I'm so upset with her. I pretend to be asleep. When she doesn't notice that I'm pretending, I sit up loudly.

"Oh, hey," she says, looking up from her mirror. "I thought you were asleep."

"I *was*," I lie.

Priya continues taking out her braids as she apologizes. "Sorry, I didn't realize I was being loud. It's been a long day, and I just want to get in bed as fast as possible."

I soften, unsure why I even wanted to pick a fight in the first place. Ugh, what is wrong with me? "Are you guys ready to open tomorrow?"

"Maybe. I think *I'll* be ready, at least. I'm not sure about the cast." She grimaces. "They were struggling today. Twee chewed them out. *Into the Woods* is just really complicated. I'm glad we're doing something simpler for the second session."

It doesn't feel simple to me, but I don't say that. "At least you won't be onstage."

She laughs and goes back to the mirror. "Thank God. I'm a terrible actor." Her short hair falls in loose waves around her head once she has her braids out.

"Funny how acting didn't matter when you were trying to get me to audition," I remark.

"I was lying. Obviously. Can I hit the lights?" She gestures at the switch by the door.

"Go ahead."

The lights click off, plunging us into darkness. The night at Fogridge is so much darker than back home. If the moon is full, it's not so bad. The moon isn't full tonight. When I first started camp, I missed the way headlights rolled across my bedroom ceiling. I missed the constant glow of streetlights. In the silence—without the sirens, the talking, doors opening and closing at all hours—my ears rang constantly. I wonder if Priya is experiencing the same thing.

Probably not, actually. I don't imagine there's a lot of sound in the Pendley house.

The sheets rustle as she climbs into bed. "I can't believe you'd take my word on anything acting-related. Don't you remember when I performed *Stop, Drop, and Dance*?"

"Oh my God. Wait," I say, barely choking back a laugh. "I do."

*Stop, Drop, and Dance* was a one-woman play (in the loosest sense of the word) that Priya spent every recess of third grade rehearsing. I don't think it had a plot, but there was definitely a bright tracksuit and sideways baseball cap.

I smile. "That was at the first Priyatopia, wasn't it?"

"Actually, no. It wasn't the first." She hesitates, her voice soft and a little sad. "I'd tell you about the first one, but you'd be weird about it."

I adjust my pillow and turn, facing her even though it's too dark to see anything past the shadowy banister. "I will not. Tell me."

"Fine. Don't be weird." She inhales. Exhales. "My nani—my grandma—and I had the same birthday. We always celebrated together, which most kids probably would've hated, but she was so great. I've never met anyone half as fun as she was."

"This is Deepika's mom?" I ask.

"Mm-hmm."

"Okay, I love her already. Go on."

"As you should." The smile is so clear in her voice. "Anyway, she got pancreatic cancer when we were in sixth grade. It has a horrible prognosis." Here, her voice changes and becomes a little huskier. "Like, less than a year to live, constant pain, nausea. And she was so vibrant, always dancing and laughing. She didn't want to live like that, so she arranged to have medically assisted suicide done at her house."

There's a long pause during which the only thing I can hear is Priya's breathing.

I'm about to reassure her that she doesn't have to tell me any more when she continues shakily. "She threw this huge goodbye birthday party called Anitatopia. She invited everybody she'd ever met, and they all got up and told stories about her. We played her favorite songs and served her favorite food. Oh my God, the butter chicken, Juliette?"

I laugh, sniffling.

"It was so good. I don't even eat meat, and ugh. That chicken. And she wore this beautiful sari and a tiara." She snorts a laugh. "A freaking tiara. It was wild. A total celebration of life. You could feel the love everyone had for her, and even though we were saying goodbye, it was on her terms. She was super stubborn, so that was kind of fitting that she got to die when she said it was okay. I'd never seen anyone truly celebrated like that. So, the next year, when our birthday came around, I asked my mom if I could have an Anitatopia and she said yes. So, you were right-ish. That was my first Priyatopia, but . . . not *the* first."

My heart feels so heavy, mixed emotions fill it to bursting. "That is . . ." I pause, searching for the right word. "Weird?"

Priya gasps in surprise, choking back a laugh. "Thanks a lot. I open up to you and that's all you have to say?"

I laugh breathily, my throat tightened by bittersweetness. "No, no. It's nice. It's a nice story. But the fact that your 'next Coachella' birthday ragers started as your grandma's euthanasia party? Don't tell me that's not objectively weird."

The sound of Priya's pillow flying into the wooden slats that separate us startles a "Sorry!" out of me.

Priya's snicker choruses with the groan of the bed as she rises to retrieve her pillow. When she reaches the railing, I hear her lean into it, the slide of her hand around a post, the creak of the handrail under her weight.

By way of apology, I say, "Sometimes my mouth speaks before my brain can stop it."

In a low voice, Priya says, "She would have really liked that about you."

It feels unusually intimate, speaking to someone I can't see. Like the night itself is listening in on our conversation.

"You think so?" I ask, matching her volume.

"How could anyone not?"

# LINE

Priya moans into her pillow, her first sign of life since *Into the Woods* closed yesterday and she collapsed into bed. She sits up, needlessly shielding her eyes with a hand. The sunlight is long gone. Apart from the glow of the lamp on my bedside table, Polaris is dark.

The show was *very* good. I've been humming their knockoff version of "Agony" all day. Seeing Etan and Maris play the princes gave me goose bumps, making me even more excited that they're costarring in *Beauty and the Beast*. Etan's sick, rumbling baritone shakes the air. Maris's technique isn't perfect, but his stage presence is magnetic. Based on the casts' performances, I'm shocked Twee gave me Belle. My voice is a gift I'm lucky to have, but if you compare my acting to what was on the stage last night, I'm Priya in *Stop, Drop, and Dance*.

Groggily, my roommate asks, "What time is it?"

"Six," I reply, glancing out the window into the darkness.

She groans. "Oh man. I missed food."

Her voice is so full of despair that I decide to tell her immediately instead of messing with her first. I grab the plate of tacos off my dresser. "Here. They're vegetarian."

When she spots the food, she snaps to attention. "No. Really?"

"Unless you'd prefer gorp." I crouch awkwardly beside her bed, holding the plate. "Twee said you might have a post-show hangover." I nudge her exposed elbow with the plate until she takes it from me.

"A post-show hangover. Is that what this is?" She lifts a taco and inspects it. Sauce drips from the hard shell, causing Priya to flinch. Gingerly, she lowers the taco onto the paper plate and looks up. "I ask this in the most respectful way possible: Can I eat this on your bed?"

I laugh and swing my body around, motioning for her to follow me up the steps. Settling myself cross-legged against my headboard, I say, "You're a freak."

"White is hard to clean, dude." Priya sinks onto the foot of my mattress. She looks around, searching for something as she holds the tacos aloft.

"Wear another color, then." Realizing what she wants, I pass her a handful of napkins.

Though her white sheets are safely halfway across the room, she still performs a very delicate balancing act with her plate, the tacos, and the napkins. She covers her half-full mouth and says, "I can't do that."

"You actually can. Get new clothes. It's that easy."

She finishes one taco with a crunch and starts on the other. "You don't get it."

For once, I agree with her. "Yeah, I don't."

Priya looks like she's about to explain, but shifts topics. "Want me to help you run lines?"

I sigh, pulling the booklet off my bedside table. It's deceptively thin. "Don't you want a break from theater stuff?"

Priya nods, dabbing at a line of taco sauce running down her chin. "This is a break from my theater stuff. If I'm not sewing or painting, it's a break. I am really excited for these costumes and sets, though. *Into the Woods* was pretty monochrome."

"Monochrome?" I look her up and down. "I guess you are the authority on that."

She scowls, taking the final bite of her taco before looking around again. I motion for the plate and place it on the nightstand.

I hold up the script. "Do you want to be Gaston or the Beast?"

"Gaston," Priya says without hesitation. "I've always liked him. Is that weird?"

I raise my brows. "The hot popular girl liking the hot popular guy? No. That's expected."

Priya tsks and swats my calf. "That's not why I like him."

"Oh, come on," I sigh. "You're dating Barry. You have a type."

Amusement crosses Priya's face. "I'm not."

"Not what?"

"Not dating Barry."

I can't tell if she's joking. "Yes you are?" I try, tentatively.

She laughs again, her whole face lighting up. "I'm really not. We broke up in, like . . ." She stops to think, her eyes flicking to the ceiling. "May, I think."

"But he was at Priyatopia," I insist, like it's proof of anything. Like I could convince her that they are, in fact, dating. "You guys were hanging out."

Priya shrugs and looks off in a "Can you believe this?" gesture at some invisible ally. "Yeah, because he was invited. We're cool, just not dating. You know Barry. He's good people."

I put that information in the back of my brain to process later. "Okay, well if you don't like Gaston because he's hot and popular, then why?"

"He's easy," Priya says, drumming her fingers on the corner of the bed. "He doesn't play games. If you're wondering what he's thinking, it's whatever he's saying. The whole-ass village knows he's into Belle and he's not messing with anyone else. He's fun and athletic. He can sing. When he realizes that a bear-creature kidnapped her, he genuinely tries to help. Nobody in the village likes her, and he still gets them to go on a rescue mission. What makes Gaston a villain? He's just a community organizer who needs to take some gender studies classes. And he uses antlers in all of his decorating. I mean, c'mon. Heart. Throb." She sticks her tongue out.

I shake my head. "First *Survivor*, now this? Someone needs to take your TV away."

"My screen time is embarrassingly high," she admits with a laugh.

"Okay, you got the part. Be Gaston."

"Gladly." She bounces on the mattress, jostling me.

"We get it," I grouse. "You're in love with him. Let's start with act one, scene three."

As Priya thumbs through the book, her brows knit together in concentration. "Got it." Deepening her voice, she says, "Belle, what a lovely surprise."

I slip into character, affecting a soft lilt and batting my eyelashes mischievously. "A surprise? You've been following me since I left the butcher's shop."

Priya rolls her shoulders. For all her talk about being a terrible actor, she's not half-bad. "The surprise is how you manage to get more beautiful every time I see you," she says, her eyes locked on mine. She grabs my hand and mimes kissing the back of it.

Like the script tells her to. Just following the script.

I feel a blush creep across my cheeks and bow my head shyly. Because I am Belle. This is Belle and nothing else. "Sire, you flatter me."

Priya reaches out and hooks a finger under my chin, lifting it up until I'm once again looking into her eyes. Her stare—Gaston's stare—is dark and heavy. She lied. She's a good actor. "No need to be so formal. Call me Gaston."

My breath hitches. I duck out of her reach. "I'd rather not."

Priya pretends to snatch something from my hands. "Is this venison?" she asks, pawing through the imaginary grocery bag. "Belle, when we're married, you won't have to buy venison from the butcher, you know."

An uncomfortable ache settles into the pit of my stomach. "I quite like the butcher."

"Yes," Priya huffs impatiently. "But wouldn't you rather have a nice, strong hunter to rely on?" She fights a grin as she follows the line direction: kissing her biceps.

"I quite like the butcher," I repeat. "I care not for the amount of meat my husband can bring home. I just want him to be smart and brave, like my father."

"Am I not brave?" Priya asks, scooting closer to me. "Have you seen how big deer are?"

I turn my face away. "I cannot say I have."

"And as for smart," Priya leans in and whispers, "I'm smart enough to know I want you as my wife."

The line is supposed to be funny, but it feels really unfunny in the moment. I'm suddenly aware of the rise and fall of my chest. My palms tingle, a sensation that's both uncomfortable and pleasant. I'm struggling just to breathe evenly when Priya scrunches her nose, confused.

I shake my head. "Sorry. Line."

"'My father says only a fool claims a wife based on looks,'" she reads.

I echo her words, my head swimming.

"Your father? Your father *is* a fool."

"Don't say such things! He is a wonderful man."

Priya's leg presses into mine as she moves closer. She lifts her hand. It hovers beside my cheek. I feel the heat coming off of it. "Sweetheart, you'll know nothing of the meaning of 'wonderful' until you have known me."

Gaston is supposed to read as creepy in this scene, but Priya is playing him so straight that I automatically lean my face into her palm. Every inch of contact sets my nerves on fire. A shiver runs through me, causing an involuntary neck flinch that presses my cheek harder into her palm. My eyes flutter closed for a brief second, and then I freeze.

What the hell is wrong with me?

Half-developed excuses swirl weakly in my mind, but I can't

bring myself to open my eyes or mouth. Priya's hand hasn't moved either, probably waiting for my line. Her fingertips press deeper into the hollow near my ear, the slope of my jaw, and the corner of my lips.

"You're unreal," she whispers. Her words, like a rock thrown into a pond, ripple across my skin, leaving goose bumps in their wake.

The words have all left my brain. Not just my lines, but my ability to speak and think and, and . . . and think. I open my eyes.

Priya's full lips quirk up at the edges. "Juliette?"

I choke out a questioning noise.

"That's your line. 'You're unreal.'"

"Oh, the—?" I still. Because she's just . . . staring. Her intense gaze is fixed on my mouth.

Speak. Goddamn it, Juliette. Say anything. My lips part. No words come out.

Her eyes slowly travel my face and when they finally lock onto mine, she smiles. It's not a big toothy Priya grin. This feels more personal. Her smile is usually the sun, but right now it's a candle, just bright enough to see by.

Our faces are so close, and I am hypnotized by the leisurely blink of her long lashes. The dark way she lowers her eyes back to my mouth. A shiver runs down my spine as her hand drifts, gentle but sure, from my face to the nape of my neck.

A millisecond and a millennium pass.

I feel like I'm dreaming. Spinning. Floating. Drowning. Flying.

Then Polaris's door opens.

We spring apart. Priya nearly falls off the bed trying to put space between us. My head thumps into the wall. I barely feel it with the amount of adrenaline coursing through my veins.

"Head count," Galahad announces, looking up from her clipboard.

"Yup," I answer, steadying my voice.

"I'm up here," Priya says, gathering her empty plate and the script before realizing that the script is mine. She starts to hand it to me, then thinks better of it and places it on the blanket.

"Okay. Night." The door closing is the loudest sound I've ever heard.

Priya and I each pretend to get ready for bed like whatever just happened didn't happen.

I can't fall asleep, though. I lie in bed, staring at the ceiling until Priya flips the lights off without asking. Polaris is plunged into darkness, except for the dim moonlight that stripes my bed through the blinds. Her socks pad softly across the carpet. The bed frame creaks under her weight. I expect the blue-tinted glow of her phone screen to light up her face, but it doesn't.

My fingers sear a path across my jawline and down my neck. When I notice, I rip my hand away, but it has a mind of its own. It finds its way back.

"Priya," I call into the darkness.

Her mattress creaks as she shifts in bed. For a breath, I'm convinced she's going to answer, but she doesn't.

I rub my palms over my face, not sure what I would have said had she answered. As I fall into a fitful sleep, my mind turns itself over and over, looking for some sort of hidden mechanism that might stop the sensation of falling I feel.

# IN THE MOMENT

"Sweetheart, you'll know nothing of the meaning of 'wonderful' until you've known me."

I dodge the extended hand as if we're dancing. Shaking my head, I say, "You're unreal."

Etan grins, big and unbothered. "Why, thank you."

"Okay, cut! Let's run that scene one more time and then we can move on to Maurice's first encounter with the Beast?" Twee, from her spot in the front row, points a finger at me. "Juliette, I need you to be in the moment. Are you here in the moment?"

No. "Yes."

Twee frowns. "Okay. I need to really feel it, though. Connect with him. Do you remember the last time you really connected with someone?"

My eyes dart offstage. Yes. "No."

She rubs her forehead. "Mama, you gotta give me something. We have two weeks. Let's go again from"—Twee looks down at her script—"'Belle, what a lovely surprise.'"

I feel the distance between me and the lines as I speak them. I know I'm not a great actor; that's why I try to put as much as I can into my songs. When I sing I can make each melody feel like a victorious clap or a sputtering gasp above water. This scene doesn't have a song, though. I sigh internally and deliver the lines again, not surprised that I somehow do even worse.

Twee's face betrays her true feelings, but she says, "Good work. You both . . . know your lines. That's great. Juliette, your homework is to find someone you have strong feelings about—positive or negative—and really focus on how you feel when you have a conversation with them. Go see if sets or costumes need help. Can I get Phoebe and Junior downstage?"

Etan and I exit. He's been frustrated with me all day, so I agree easily when he suggests we split up. I agree again, but much less easily, when he insists on taking on costumes, sending me down the hallway toward Priya.

I haven't seen my roommate all day. Her bed was empty when I woke up this morning.

A loud, rhythmic whirring buzzes from the set room. The sign on the door says THE WIZARD IS IN. I enter with a knock she probably won't hear.

Priya slices planks of wood with the table saw. She's angled away from me, a dusty orange apron over her white sundress. The upper half of her face is obscured by thick goggles, and she scrunches up the lower half in concentration as she pushes the wood forward. I'm unsure what to do, not wanting to startle her.

She surprises me by stopping the blade and turning to face me. "What's up?"

"How did you know I was here?" I ask, stepping closer to inspect the machinery. She holds a hand up, a clear safety barrier that I happily stand behind. I'm trying to leave this room with the same number of limbs I came in with.

Priya indicates a fish-eye mirror mounted in the corner opposite the door. "Not everyone is so considerate about their entrances. I put that up week one so I didn't accidentally chop off a hand." She pushes her safety goggles up like a pair of sunglasses. Again, she asks, "What's up?"

My hackles rise. "Just checking to see if you need help."

Priya reaches back, slides a gloved hand along the rim of the table. I don't think I've ever seen her so disheveled—her hair sticks out in all directions from under her goggles. I definitely haven't seen her in Home Depot–commercial orange. Unsurprisingly, she pulls the color off.

"Twee asked you to," she says. It's not a question.

There's a challenge in those words that I think I understand, but I put on my best oblivious face. If she's not going to talk about last night, neither will I. "Right."

Her hand stills on the table, an inscrutable emotion behind her stare. She draws in a deep breath, and I can't keep my eyes from dropping to her parted lips.

I feel hot. Exposed under the fluorescents. But I force myself not to turn away.

Priya's words seem to escape before she can stop them. "Juliette, are you i—" She exhales and turns her head, laughing with an invisible audience.

"Am I what?" I raise my eyebrows, daring her to finish. I'm genuinely curious. I don't know how that question ends.

She presses her lips together in a thin line, fighting back a smile. "Nothing." Priya spins, pulling down her goggles and realigning the wood in front of the saw blade in one swift motion. Without looking, she points to the right-hand side of the room and says, "Make yourself useful and paint those bushes green. Forest green, not lime green."

I'm not sure if she's watching in the fish-eye mirror. In case she is, I mouth *coward* at her reflection.

I head for the messy tarp, where three bush standees lie beside sealed paint cans. I pry the forest-green one open with a nearby screwdriver and quickly find a rhythm, swirling the brush in patterns to simulate leaves. I'm not an artist, but I destroyed my fair share of coloring books as a toddler. This is the level of creativity that I'm comfortable with. I'm considering adding some lime green—against Priya's orders—when I'm startled by her voice right behind me.

"Excellent job, Michelangelo," she teases.

I turn to look up at her. The goggles and apron have been abandoned, and she's back to her normal self. Even her previously wild hair looks professionally styled.

I gesture to the chaos of the room. "How come you can do all this stuff wearing white, but you had to eat your dinner on my bed?"

Priya crosses her arms, running her tongue along her top teeth. "That's a good question." She can't fight the smile that pulls at the edges of her lips. "Let me know if you figure it out."

I swallow against the sudden dryness in my mouth. Is she . . . toying with me? Trying not to burst into laughter, I mimic her stance, sinking back and crossing my arms. "Priya."

"Juliette," she says, humor in her voice.

We hold each other's stares, eyes narrowed playfully, chests rising and falling beneath our folded arms.

She dips closer, bending until her body is within a hair's breadth of mine.

Every atom of my being goes motionless. Her hair brushes my cheek. Her shoulder presses into mine, but she keeps leaning, reaching for something behind me.

When she straightens and the warmth of her body leaves mine, she's holding the lime-green paint can. A knowing smirk lights up her face.

"I don't trust you with this," she whispers, slinging it over her shoulder and walking away.

# 2 0

# END, BUTT, HEEL, BEST PART

Priya stands completely still on the wood chips of the playground, wearing a blank stare like she's looking into the future and it doesn't impress her. Both her hands white-knuckle a paper plate with a sandwich on it. Her long wrap dress billows in the breeze. She's a painting of a lone angel—breathtaking and crestfallen.

This has been happening more and more, weeks of late nights at the theater catching up to her. Lucy and Gia don't seem to notice, which is unusual because they notice everything.

"You okay?" I ask quietly as I drop onto an Adirondack chair near the slide, every muscle in my body slackening as the backs of my legs meet the sun-warmed plastic.

Priya shakes her head quickly to clear it before flashing me a bright smile. "Always," she says cheerily, taking a seat on the swing beside Lucy's.

According to every piece of media ever, there should be a moment where her expression drops. There should be a second, even a millisecond, where someone who's been living with her for over three weeks could read the truth on her face and know she's lying.

There isn't.

Priya's smile reaches her eyes every time, like she believes it herself.

But I don't. Because, though nothing in her appearance betrays her feelings, she's definitely taking up less space in the universe.

Priya chuckles with Gia, waggling her eyebrows, and I can't help wondering how many times I've bought this act. There's a time and place to interrogate her, but it isn't here and now. I dog-ear the thought and bite into my sandwich, letting my concerns fade beneath the taste of sweet strawberry jam, bright on my tongue.

"Can you believe we're halfway through week four?" Lucy asks, her voice fading in and out as she swings.

"Don't remind me," Gia groans. He sits up from his spot in the grass and shields his eyes, watching Lucy pump her legs back and forth. "I don't want to think about going back to school."

Priya drags her feet, barely leaving the ground at all. "I can't believe it's moving so fast."

I take another bite and I try to just be where I am, listening to my friends' chatter and the squeak of the swings. Fallen leaves pepper the lush green lawn. A soft breeze tumbles them across the mown grass and something about the sight makes me feel . . . sad.

The end of camp always brings out my worst habit, one that's only gotten worse this senior year: the urge to think about the Lasts.

The Last Time we sit on the playground. The Last Time we

all do Color War together. The Last Time Pat calls an All-Camp. It doesn't help that I had so many without proper goodbyes because of my ankle. I didn't make those Lasts special. And now I'll never do them again.

I wish things were different.

After taking the last edible bite of my sandwich, I stand to throw the crust out. A dollop of jelly drips onto my thigh, just missing the hem of my shorts. I scoop it up with a finger and put it in my mouth.

My eyes flick up to find Priya staring at the crust in my hand like it's the holy grail. "You aren't going to eat the crust? That's the best part."

Her voice lacks the teasing tone she normally uses on me. I don't know how to fix this.

I start by offering her the worst part of my sandwich. She snatches it from my hand.

While Priya eats, making noises that definitely aren't camp appropriate, Gia and Lucy launch into a bread debate. Gia insists the end of a loaf is the heel. Lucy calls it the butt. I start to say they're both wrong—it's called the end—when a flash of color catches my eye.

I imagine strawberry preserves dripping from Priya's lip and landing on her sweeping white skirt, staining it irreparably. I move so fast I make sound waves, reaching out to brush my thumb across her mouth. Priya freezes, her mouth opens into an O.

In that instant of surprise, the galaxy shifts as the Priya I know returns to herself, filling the vacuum of space she'd left behind. Her bewilderment—which turns to understanding as she notices what I've done—buoys me.

I still wish things were different, but I do not wish *this* were different. I'll always mourn goodbyes I never got to say, but at least I learned how to put that confused smile on Priya Pendley's face.

I consider my new revelation, the flush on her cheeks, and the glistening strawberry jam, before bringing my thumb to my lips and licking it clean.

The remaining crust tumbles from Priya's hand and into the dirt.


She slips in the door just before curfew on Monday, doing a double take when she finds me sitting on her bed with my arms crossed.

"Bruh," I say with a reproachful head tilt.

Priya holds up a hand. "I'm too tired. Yell at me after *Beauty and the Beast* closes." She circles me, shedding clothes—shoes, cardigan, socks, and earrings—with each step.

"I'm not going to yell," I say, twisting to follow her movements. "I'm worried about you."

She wilts into bed, narrowly avoiding a collision with me. "I need sleep. I think that I'm starting to hallucinate. I imagined you said you were worried about me."

I'm temporarily stunned by the sight of her lying there, curled up on her side with her hair fanned around her head like a halo.

Eyes half-closed, she hugs a pillow to her chest. The corners of her mouth turn up in a sleepy smile.

I clear my throat and say, "Good night."

Priya's hand wraps around my wrist, pinning me in place. Images flood my mind. More than half of them involve Priya pulling me down beside her. I won't be examining that desire.

"Tuck me in," she demands weakly.

I scoff, but when her hand loosens, I do tuck her in. She lifts her body in increments to allow me to tug the white comforter out from underneath her. When one-third of the blanket is free, Priya falls asleep. Her face relaxes, the line between her worried brows disappearing for the first time in days.

I stand beside the bed for a moment, thinking. Then I retrieve my own blanket—the one Priya rescued from the lakefront the night I went to the hospital—and drape it over her.

# BREAKDOWN

By some miracle, we don't fall to our deaths on the way down to the costume department. Like everything else backstage, the walls of the stairwell are coated in thick black paint. Luckily, the cavernous room below is brightly lit, or I'd probably get lost in the jungle of clothing racks.

While Priya agreed to mostly do the set work for this show, she told me she insisted on making my ball gown. After weeks of refusal, I've finally finagled a sneak preview. She parts the sliding metal rows like the Red Sea to reveal the most gorgeous thing I've ever seen.

"So?" Priya asks.

The dress is a swirl of yellow-gold tulle, draped and gathered and sculpted into a masterpiece, with a heart-shaped neckline and full skirt. I'm entranced by this apparent cloud plucked directly from the Pacific Ocean sunset.

"You hate it," she suggests tentatively.

My eyes stay locked on the dress. "You are out of your damn mind."

"You . . . like it," she says in the same slow, nervous tone.

I turn back to the gown, tilting my head to the side. "I want to eat it. I wanna sleep on it."

She laughs. "Let's check the fit. It's built for a quick change," she explains, sliding it off the mannequin. "It has a magnet closure down the side. Put your arms out and I'll show you."

I look down at my track jersey and shorts. "Do you want me to take this off?"

Priya's amused gaze cuts me from head to toe. Her mouth closes around a W—but she interrupts herself with a lick of her lips. She gives me a crooked smile and overenunciates, "I . . . don't need you to. You'll have your other costume underneath during the show, anyway."

*What was that?* my brain screams.

*Aaahhhhhhhh?* I scream right back.

Priya nudges my arms up, sliding the airy balloon sleeves on. She wraps it around me, and the magnets snap the bodice together with a series of dull clacks.

While she assesses her work, I shift from side to side, watching the skirt swish and float with my movements.

"You should wear yellow to your wedding," she says suddenly.

Though I'm at a standstill, I nearly stumble. "Priya." I shake my head. "That is a bizarre thing to say to someone."

She shrugs, casual as ever. "It's your color. You always look good in it."

It's suddenly very warm down here.

"I'm not thrilled with the fit, to be honest," she continues, running a hand over her exhausted face. "I'm gonna redo those stitches. Let me just pin it real quick."

I stand still as she reaches for a stuffed tomato stuck full of straight pins. She begins gathering excess fabric and piercing the metal through it to shape the dress to my body.

"We'll have to do another fitting, but I don't know how long it'll take. And I think the skirt's a little short. I might need more trim at the—"

"No." My gaze settles on the dark circles beneath her eyes.

"No?" she repeats. "No, what?"

I shrug, waving my hand. "No, don't fix the dress."

"Hmm." There's a beat of silence as she kneads her lower lip between her thumb and forefinger. Finally, with a click of her tongue, she announces, "I don't get it. What's the joke?"

"Oh, it's actually really funny." I hold my right sleeve still with my left hand, attempting to extract myself from this death trap without puncturing a vital organ. "What do you get when you cross a perfectionist with an indentured servant?"

Priya narrows her eyes at me, stepping forward to steady the pins and save her carefully placed measurements. "Are you gonna make fun of me right after I said you looked beautiful?"

I'm not sure that I manage to keep my voice level when I respond, "I don't recall you using that exact word."

She raises her chin defiantly and loftily huffs, "It was implied."

Her hands join mine, helping free me from the dress. If ever I've had a Cinderella moment, this is it. Princess to pumpkin in two seconds flat.

"Hey."

She doesn't look up, carefully spreading the gown over a worktable, arranging it so the pins are visible. "What?"

"Leave the dress. It fits fine." There's no indication she heard me, so I add, "Please."

Her hands still, flattening on the table. With her back to me, she takes several slow breaths. "I—I don't make things that are 'fine,' Juliette."

"Well, maybe you should," I say gently.

She combs a hand through her hair and turns sluggishly, fixing me with vacant eyes. Fatigue rolls off her as she drops her head back, exposing the long column of her throat.

"I'm tired," Priya sighs, voice gravelly.

"I know," I say, closing my arms around her in a hug.

When exactly I got close enough to do that, I'm not sure. One second, I'm out of arm's reach, the next Priya's collapsing into me. With a low groan, she goes limp, dropping her forehead onto my shoulder, knocking me off balance.

"I might be dying." Her voice, barely above a whisper, sends tingles down my spine.

I squeeze tighter, tucking her into me. "We'll get it done, Pendley. It's gonna be fine."

Priya pulls back and gives me a skeptical squint. "I don't think you understand. I'm not doing this half-assed. It's like if you got onstage without knowing the songs. It *will not* happen."

"You." I lean in, hands braced against the table on either side of her. "Need." When we're nose to nose, I say, "Therapy."

Her sharp inhale melts into a barking laugh. "Shut up," she

says, flattening her palm against my clavicle like she's going to push me away.

I lift my hand off the table and press it over hers, curling my fingers and trapping her in the space just north of my heart. "I swear to you, we are going to figure this out. When this show goes on, you'll be proud of everything you put on that stage. I promise."

She responds in a wordless breath, flared nostrils, pupils blown wide.

The tension shrink-wraps my skin, tightening until I can think of nothing but how to escape my own body. I've never missed being able to run more than I do in this very moment.

"But this is all you get. This one, single enabling, and then I'm back to heckling you," I joke, relaxing my posture and starting to turn away.

Priya catches my arm. "Juliette, wa—"

Then a blaring alarm rings through the building, and the moment dissipates like smoke from a post-wish birthday candle.

# BREAKOUT

F ace stricken, Priya shouts, "What the hell is that?"

"Fire alarm!" I reply, but she can't hear me over the relentless blasts of the siren.

"What?" she yells.

I shake my head and grab her arm, tugging her back through the costume department, up the stairs, and out of the theater. A crush of bodies herds us toward the lakefront, the designated meeting spot for all camp emergencies. Around us, counselors exchange uneasy looks. If this were a drill, they would've known beforehand. Something is up.

When we reach the lakefront, different leadership staff members shuffle us into order based on grade and group. I push Priya ahead of me, making sure we stay together.

A hand lands on my head. "Fifteen." The hand moves from my head to Priya's, and I see who it belongs to: Galahad. "Sixteen."

"Galahad, you got everyone?" the senior division leader, Zoo, shouts over the din.

Galahad gives Zoo two thumbs up before turning back to me. "Juliette, let's go. Get with the group," she commands, voice hard.

I notice she doesn't say anything to Priya, but we silently join Galahad's single-file line, facing away from the water.

The Minis are the last group to arrive. TK comes chugging down the path in her little green train. The air fills with happy screams when the Minis see their older siblings in the crowd. I try to remember ever feeling that way about one of my older siblings, but nothing comes to me.

Once the counselors finish their group counts and the division leaders signal them to Pat, he takes his place in front of us, microphone in hand. He taps it twice to get our attention, his face grim. "Thank you all for remaining patient. We have almost everyone accounted for, but we're missing three staff members."

My body is one step ahead of my brain. My palms start sweating, and my heart speeds up.

Pat frowns down at a list in his hand. "Has anyone seen . . . Eleazar, the soccer specialist?" He pauses, looking up toward all the specialists, grouped together without any campers. Nobody says anything. The sports director shakes his head, eyes trained on the ground. Pat continues, "What about Lovelace from fifth-grade girls?"

The fifth graders break out into a low buzz, their voices melding into an anxious symphony. "No? Quiet, please. Quiet. The last missing staffer is"—he squints at the paper again—"from third-grade boys: Flagstaff."

That's the moment I know. I try to school my features into disinterest.

An office worker runs up to Pat and whispers in his ear. His frown deepens. Into the mic he says, "All three of them were last seen at the lake. Does anybody know where they are?"

At that moment, the rumble of motors drowns him out. Every single person turns to see three colorful jet skis slide into place, facing the camp. One green. One purple. And one orange. The riders' outfits match their boats' paint, including shiny helmets with dark visors.

"What . . . is going on?" Priya whispers.

"I don't know," I lie, but I can't hide my grin any longer. A shudder of electric excitement courses through me, and I bounce on the balls of my feet. "Just watch."

Other campers who have caught on start screeching, their voices nearly louder than the engines. Counselors cover their mouths, their eyes, the top of their heads, like they need to be protected from their own anticipation.

Pat's voice booms over the speaker system as all three motors cut out simultaneously. "May I introduce to you"—each of the three riders stands up, balancing on the outer edges of their jet skis—"this year's Color War captains!"

The crowd drowns him out before he can even finish. Even Priya is caught up in the giddiness, coming dangerously close to blowing out my eardrums with her screams.

"For the Dondos, Flagstaff!" Flagstaff, grinning from ear to ear, frees his head from his helmet and cups his hand around his ear, signaling for us all to get louder. We obey, of course.

*Traitor!* I think, even as I roar his name. If I had to pick one captain for Priya, though, I couldn't have chosen anyone better than him.

I crane my neck to see Flagstaff's boys going absolutely bonkers. Their entire grade has turned into a little mosh pit, little bodies frantically bouncing off each other, little voices joining in a little roar.

"For the Lazlots, Lovelace!" The girl in purple whips her helmet off, shaking free a mane of golden waves. She's white, with a deep tan and plum-colored lipstick. She pumps a fist in the air and executes a skillful backflip into the water.

I don't know her, but I already love my captain. My voice joins the chorus of voices.

"And for the Marikets, Eleazar!"

Priya cheers, but I know she's having a distinct experience from me right now. Years of camp drama are layered into everything at Fogridge, but especially Color War. Even as a camper, I've caught snippets of the Eleazar saga. He's a polarizing figure, because while he's one of the most passionate and beloved staff members, he isn't gentle the way a lot of the staff is. He spends most of his time standing on the sidelines of some field or court, red-faced, screaming at the top of his lungs like an NFL coach. He's not my favorite employee, but the kids who love him *love* him. They cling to his side like he's their mama bear, and when they win sports tournaments, Eleazar hand-makes them matching jerseys and crowns.

I shouldn't know this, but he was chosen as the Mare captain two years ago. A few days before the reveal, Pat pulled him from the position for fear of "potential bad sportsmanship." Eleazar's boyfriend was a lifeguard at the time, which is how I overheard. He was so upset that he accidentally called "buddy check" six times during Swim. It's usually only called once.

Competitive athletes howl their approval as Eleazar violently rocks his jet ski from side to side, chanting, "Mare-uh-kets! Mare-uh-kets!" Nearby, a sporty camper-turned-counselor and die-hard Eleazar stan chokes back tears.

In an impressive show of physicality, while pitching ferociously from side to side, he tears his orange T-shirt in half, revealing an identical one underneath. Only, this new shirt has JUSTICE 4 ELEAZAR written in block letters across the chest. It's hard to tell from so far away, but it also seems to be covered in campers' signatures. I wonder if they knew he was a captain when they signed it. Based on the bird-like squawks of astonishment, I'm guessing not.

I search for Pat, expecting disapproval upon his face, but when I find him, he seems to be covering a smile. He's far away, so I could be wrong, but I swear his eyes shine with pride.

Eleazar has worked here a long time, and I can tell he's been waiting for this a *long* time. Love for camp radiates from him in palpable shock waves. I don't know him, not really. But I feel proud of him, too.

Pat's voice booms over the mic. "Color War starts now! Campers and counselors, you have twenty minutes to get in your colors and meet me on the soccer field."

## WHEN, JULIETTE?

I don't go right away, instead staying to watch Flagstaff and Eleazar dismount their jet skis, helmets in hand. They meet Lovelace in the lake and somehow manage a group hug. Their giddy laughter echoes off the water. A pang of wistfulness rolls through me, and I realize I'm sad for future Juliette. I miss something that hasn't even happened.

When I finally tear my eyes away from them, camp is a different world. Orange, purple, and green ribbons wrap tree trunks like maypoles. Fairy lights twinkle from branch to branch. Every staff member—apart from the captains—stands along the path. Their chants form an indistinguishable cacophony. Noisemakers clack, cowbells clang, party horns wail.

A purple maraca appears in my right hand and, instead of questioning it, I start shaking it as vigorously as possible. I glance around, worried about how Priya is handling the sudden change in atmosphere, but, of course, there she is, blowing shamelessly into a green vuvuzela.

I grab her shoulders and steer her like a plow, breaking through the crowd.

When we reach the fork in the road beside the pavilion, she laughingly sidesteps my grip, and I stagger, grimacing at the twinge in my ankle.

"Sorry," she yelps, grabbing my elbow and guiding me off the dirt path, safe from the stampede of eight-year-olds screaming a Lazlot chant. "Did I hurt you?"

"Physically, emotionally, or spiritually?" I ask, gingerly rolling my foot in a circle.

"Ankle-ly." Priya just barely brushes the toe of her sneaker against the toe of mine, but I still feel the contact deep in my bones.

I clear my throat. "No, I'm good. I think it was more surprise than anything else."

With an exaggerated sigh, she pretends to wipe off her brow. "Phew. I wouldn't be able to live with myself knowing I'd maimed Juliette Barrera-Wright right before Color War."

"I wouldn't be able to live with you either," I say. "You'd have to move into the forest."

She clucks her tongue at me, watching two counselors karate-kick their way back to their bunk as their campers mimic clumsily. "Not the forest. The theater is much closer. And it has indoor plumbing."

"Juliette!" Lucy singsongs as she passes. "Stop schmoozing and start face-painting."

"There's still time," Gia adds, dancing to the sound of campers chanting Eleazar's name, "to switch to the winning team."

I scoff a laugh, exchanging a knowing look with Priya.

"Anyway, speaking of living in the theater." Priya jerks her head at the path to Quad 3.

"Wait." I cross my arms and hope she isn't saying what I think she's saying. "What?"

Priya frowns. "I need to be in the theater today. I told you already, I have so much to do."

My mind is a spinning roulette wheel. The dice tumble past *Are you out of your mind?* and *This is camp, not a job* before landing on "I don't think you can just skip Color War."

She matches my stance, leaning into one hip and folding her arms. "Are *you* gonna tell Galahad?"

"Of course not," I sputter.

I don't want to force her to do anything.

But Color War is special—how strangers become best friends just by screaming the same team chant, how blood-thirsty crowds are drawn to even the most innocent game in Mini Camp.

I frown. Priya only has one opportunity to experience all the drama and silliness and fun of this. And she doesn't want to. How can she say she went to Fogridge if she doesn't sing "Take Me Home, Country Roads" at the closing ceremonies? If she doesn't choke on breathless laughter and lemon sorbet as she watches counselors dance badly? How can she understand me if she doesn't have to scrub off so much body paint that it clogs the shower drain?

When the world comes back into focus, Priya is examining my face wearily. "I'm sorry, I want to. But . . ." She thumbs in the direction of the theater.

"Wait," I say. "Come to Color War. Please. I swear I'll help you get everything done."

"When, Juliette?"

Nothing changes in her face. Soft smile, warm eyes, everything as it always is, but again I sense the emptiness beneath it. I want to drag her back to the surface, just like at the playground. The moment isn't the same, though.

My eyes keep catching on the stragglers making their way up the path—middle-aged specialists who have little stake in Color War chatting amicably, counselors herding the short-legged and easily distracted, and TK's train.

This moment is much less private, but I channel the protective Priya I glimpsed earlier. "What do you need to get done? Woodworking? Painting?"

She bobs her head from side to side. "Yeah, among other stuff."

"If I switch my activities to Woodshop and Painting this week, would that help enough for you to come do Color War?"

Priya purses her glossy lips and exhales, slow and controlled. "Yes, but Galahad would never let you do that."

I hold my hands up, glancing down at my watch. "Stop talking and start walking." I encircle her wrist and pull her toward Polaris, away from the theater.

"Juliette," she whines, straining against my hold. "You can't just sw—"

I cut her off, eyes locked on hers. "I can and I will. Trust me?"

She swallows. Then, with a nod, she intertwines her fingers with mine and suddenly she's the one tugging me up the path.

When I emerge from face-painting in the bathroom, Priya gives me a wide grin. "Ready to go?"

"You can't wear that." I shake my head, scanning her typical all-white.

She looks down at herself, wrinkling her nose. "Why not?"

"It's *Color* War. You have to wear your color." I scan a hand down my body, from the neon-purple spray dye in my hair to my plum sneakers.

Priya's hands come down on my shoulders, forcing me to look at her.

It's cloudy outside and the muted light that streams in through the window makes her eyes shimmer. Long grass blowing in the wind.

"Try to remember who you're talking to. Do I have green clothes?"

Goose bumps trail up my arms. I take a deep breath, ducking out of her grip. "Right. You can borrow my clothes. Just for Color War," I say firmly, already making my way up the steps to grab an old green camp shirt and bright green bike shorts. I reach into my bottom drawer, jammed with a rainbow of tutus, and grab the green one before turning toward the stairs. Midpivot, my brain short-circuits, and I stop dead in my tracks.

Priya is facing away from me, pulling her shirt over her head. She shakes her hair free of the neckhole as she just stands there in a nude bra. When she starts to unbutton her shorts, I make a strangled noise.

"Hhnh?" I choke out.

"Hmm?" She twists to look back at me, fingers threaded through her belt loops. When she catches sight of my face, she pauses and crosses her arms in front of herself. "Sorry, are you . . . ? Are you not okay with this? I know . . . I just figured since you're in sports, you'd . . . ? I can . . ." She trails off, pointing to the bathroom.

She's right. I have been doing sports for years. In track, I undress in the locker room without a second thought, and being in the room while people change hasn't bothered me for a long time. So why do I feel like I'm actively fighting the urge to cover my eyes?

"No, I'm fine. Uh, you just caught me off guard for a second."

Before she can shimmy out of her shorts, I toss her the clothes and busy myself with something important—and invisible—on my bed. I fumble around with my sheets until I hear Priya stop moving. When I finally chance a peek at her, I find her yanking at the hem of the green T-shirt uncomfortably.

"I look wrong," she says, craning to catch a glimpse of herself in the mirror.

"You look normal. It's camp," I tell her.

To be honest, she does look kind of wrong, but it's more about the way she stands—unsure of herself, shoulders hunched forward, arms hugging at her waist. She's a supernova, a star collapsing in on herself with the intention of winking out of the universe.

Priya moans in dissatisfaction, tucking and untucking the green shirt, wiggling like she's going to jump out of her skin.

I feel a sudden fondness for her, the way you do when you're afraid of something, but your little brother is even more afraid and you have to comfort him.

"Don't make me get Gia to give you a speech on inner

beauty," I say, pulling her attention from the clothes. "You know people don't just like you because you wear white all the time, right?"

Her mouth falls open in feigned shock. Pressing a hand against her heart, she gasps and says, "Juliette Barrera-Wright! Say more nice things about me."

I give her a playful side-eye and shove her out of Polaris, trying to slam the door loud enough behind us to drown out the echo of her gasping my name.

---

# LIFE, DEATH, MUSICAL CHAIRS

Nothing fills a child with bloodlust faster than a game of musical chairs.

Pat tells us as much in his opening speech, where he very carefully outlines the numerous actions that would get a camper disqualified from Color War altogether. Personally, I don't think any of us are as close to hunting humans for sport as Pat seems to think we are, but then I catch sight of Lucy on the other side of the purple crowd. She crosses her arms, frown deepening with each new stipulation.

No shoving. The corners of her lips turn down.

No tripping. Her brows furrow.

No forcibly removing campers who are smaller than you from their chairs. Flames erupt from the side of her face. Rolling her eyes, she whispers to the person beside her. I have to imagine it's something like "How does he expect the youth to learn if he keeps coddling them?"

Perhaps some of us do need the warning.

"The first game," Pat says, "will be played by your captains. Can I please have Flagstaff, Eleazar, and Lovelace?"

Eleazar and Lovelace step into the center of the large circle we've formed around the folding chairs. Seconds later, I hear raucous laughter from the Dondos. Heads turn in waves and bodies shuffle as Flagstaff shouts, "Excuse me, excuse me, please. Make way for your king."

All eyes are trained on the line of green when the final camper steps aside to reveal Flagstaff, moving clumsily through the crowd, an airplane seat inexplicably affixed to his butt.

He struts (more or less) up to Pat and crows, "Let's get this party started!"

After a theatrical slapstick performance, Flagstaff is forcibly removed from his airplane seat. He and Lovelace lose a quick game of musical chairs to Eleazar, and then it's our turn.

No sooner has my foot crossed the sideline than I'm stopped by a grim-faced Galahad.

"I don't think you should participate in this, Juliette." She tilts her head in the direction of my foot. "It's not safe."

*Not safe?* I huff a laugh. "It's . . . musical chairs?"

Annoyance practically vibrates the air. Once again, I've accidentally given her attitude, but I can't help myself. It *is* musical chairs. Trying to stop me from playing feels like more of a power trip than an actual attempt to help.

"I saw you hurt yourself while *walking* earlier." Her tone is clipped, accusatory.

The crowd around us thins as campers choose seats and division leaders remove excess chairs. I swivel my head around and catch Lucy darting glances to the chair beside her, a silent *Get over here already.*

"Juliette," Galahad says authoritatively.

It's a command. And it sends a weird reactionary chill down my spine. How is any of this fair? It's not. It's literally freaking *musical chairs.* I'm not gonna die playing this.

I know it's the wrong thing to do as soon as I raise my hand. I wave to catch Pat's eye and Galahad stiffens. It doesn't matter. The childish part of me wants this to happen. I'm not irrational, I'm right. The other part? She's gone now—living out the rest of her life under an assumed name in Paraguay just to avoid the interaction I'm about to have.

"Pat," I call, voice shaky.

"What ya need, Juliette?"

Everyone who's playing is already seated. Division leaders finish clearing the empty spaces, and then all eyes are on us. There's time to stop, but I won't. What is Galahad even punishing me for?

I ask, "Am I good to play this? With my ankle?"

Oblivious to the tension between me and Galahad, Pat shrugs. "Sure. It's just musical chairs."

I hear Galahad's head pop off her body and launch into space, like a bottle rocket fueled by anger. Good.

I sprint over to the chairs, stand beside Lucy, and wait for Pat to count down the start.

We start with hundreds of seats, but Pat is ruthless with the music, an upbeat Olivia Rodrigo song that isn't yet overplayed. Division leaders pull empty seats and disgruntled campers from the fray until just about half of us are left.

"Hey, Juliette," a sultry voice calls from behind me.

I don't turn. "You can't trick me. I'm not paying attention to you."

Gia laughs, low and grumbly. "We already won once."

"*Eleazar* won once," I correct. "He's a sports specialist; he's going to win every time. It doesn't count."

The music cuts, and I lunge for a seat that's empty one second but Gia'd the next.

He watches me fall into his lap and pats the top of my head. His deep brown eyes sparkle irritatingly. "Sorry, buddy. All's fair in love and Color War."

I glare at him and join my eliminated teammates.

"Did you let the gorgeous man distract you?" Lucy asks, dropping into the grass beside me with a sympathetic back pat.

"He's too charming for his own good," I grumble. When I scan the remaining players for Gia, however, my eyes land on someone else who's too charming for their own good. Someone who is somehow even more distracting. And more gorgeous.

Priya, lips pursed in concentration, side-shuffles, hovering above the chairs. I have to cover my mouth with a hand to suppress my proud cackles as she deftly secures her spot in round after round. Of course Priya is good at musical chairs. She's good at everything.

Finally, with about ten people left, another camper slides a chair out from under her just as she begins to sit. The crowd gasps, groans, giggles when Priya falls backward and collides hard with the ground, her whole body collapsing.

I'm on my feet before I register what's happening, hand

pressed into my chest, heart racing with—I don't know. Fear? But a second later, Priya sits up, howling with laughter. I'm so relieved it makes me light-headed. Teary-eyed.

Overwhelmed by the seismic shifts in emotion, I want to close my eyes. Let my body sag back to the ground and rest my head in Lucy's lap as she calmly eats her gorp.

But I can't stop watching Priya and her unruly hair, speckled with grass and dry bark. Her dirt-smeared fingers hiding an expression that's half smile and half grimace. She allows Flagstaff to pull her to her feet, and they jog back to the Dondos together. The back of her—my—shirt is soaked with something. Sweat? Dew?

She's the Priya I've always known, but . . . somehow completely different. This Priya is a mess, far too human in her embarrassment. But she glows, radiant with joy.

As if she feels my gaze, she squints in my direction. I look away before she notices me watching. Retraining my view on Flagstaff, I realize something that feels simultaneously like a surprise and the most obvious truth in the world.

Fuck.

I like Priya Pendley.

# THE SQUEAKY WHEEL
# OF THE ROUND TABLE

I wipe my hands on my shorts and push open the door to the Round Table. The scene inside catches me temporarily off guard. Girls hang upside down from the top bunks, chatting with their friends below. Laughter explodes in firecracker bursts from a game of Uno. The smell—sunscreen and the woodsy fragrance Polaris would have if my roommate were different—hits me hardest.

This is what every summer at camp is supposed to be, but I don't want it like I used to.

At the center of everything, like Jesus in *The Last Supper*, Galahad sits cross-legged on her bed, filling out camper forms.

"I need you to switch me into Woodshop and Painting for this week," I say, approaching her bed. Nobody pays me any mind as I walk past, each of them engrossed in their own activity.

"Can't do it," she says, flipping a page over and starting the next one.

The sudden answer stuns me; I expected at least a chance to explain myself. "Why not?"

Her pen moves in sharp, definitive strokes. "Because the

schedule's already set. I'm not going to inconvenience the staff just because Juliette Barrera-Wright wants to take Woodshop."

The way she says my name grates at me. She chants it, like a schoolyard rhyme.

"It's not that I *want* to take Woodshop," I begin, exasperated.

"Great." She flips another page. "Problem solved. Good night."

I sit myself down on the very end of her bed, making it clear I have no plans to leave. "Priya is on the verge of a nervous breakdown."

"Which you no doubt aided and abetted," Galahad mutters under her breath. Her pen stabs at the paper.

I drive a hand down into the mattress. "I'm trying to help. Haven't you noticed how late she's been staying at the theater? Don't you care?"

That gets her attention finally. She sucks in her cheeks, eyebrows arching in icy irritation.

It takes all my self-control (of which there is very little in the first place) not to drop my head into my hands and groan. Apparently, I don't possess the gene that tells me something is the wrong thing to say *before* I say it. "I just mean . . . I want to help her. If I switch to Woodshop and Painting, I can work on sets and props. It's my play, too."

She briefly looks right through me, sighing. "I don't believe you."

I gape at the top of her head, bowed toward the papers on the bedspread. "I'm not lying."

"And I'm not changing my mind. Good night." Her dismissal is downright cheerful.

Under any other circumstances, I'd walk out without a word. I could go straight to the specialists—Gia's brother, Dyson, at Fishing and Poplar at Nature Crafts—and explain the situation. They'd happily let me drop their programs. Pat, too.

Even if that didn't work, I like my activities. Gia's brother was born to teach fishing, somehow making it interesting enough that he has a waiting list for sign-ups. And Poplar was my fourth-grade division leader before she switched to work in Quad 2. She's great.

Except, I can picture the hundred-watt smile Priya'd give me as she says it's no big deal. *I got it, Juliette. Don't worry about me.*

I've never been so senselessly angry at something I, myself, imagined, but I'm practically feral at this. It hasn't happened, but I know it would—it will—if I walk out of here without fighting for her, or if I go behind Galahad's back and put Priya in the middle of it.

I want to spend more time with the Priya who got knocked on her ass at musical chairs. I won't let her act like I'm just another follower who believes her social media sleight of hand.

For once, I want to be intense. I want to be pugnacious—the word my older brother used when I tackled some high schooler after he called Laurent a slur. I was in middle school. I walked away with a bruise the size of Texas and a bleeding lip, but Laurent rubbed my shoulders like a boxing coach all weekend, proclaiming that his little sister was his new bodyguard.

I was never proud of that moment, but now that same surge of protectiveness gives me a respect for my younger self. I cared then. I care now. I'm just fighting in a different way.

I can't believe I'm catching feelings for Priya Pendley.

It's sick.

Adrenaline forces one last desperate question from me. "What if I skip Senior Twilight?"

The slack-jawed look on Galahad's face is priceless. That alone is nearly worth what I've just agreed to. Nearly, but not quite.

In her silence, I repeat, "I'll trade. Senior Twilight for Wood-shop and Painting. I know you think I don't deserve to go."

Though I can't help but tack on the ending like a petulant child, I still expect Galahad to protest my claim. It's what any other counselor would do.

But Galahad isn't any other counselor.

She inclines her head, gaze cast heavenward. "You're right, I *don't* think you deserve to go. You broke the rules and there should be consequences for that."

A huff escapes me. "You put me in Theater, wasn't that a con-sequence?"

"Oh, because being given the lead role was such a cruel pun-ishment?"

I rear back, her implication stinging like a physical blow. "I auditioned?" I mean it as a statement, but disbelief turns it into a question. More forcefully, I say, "I earned that role."

Her lip curls. "And how many plays have you been in before this?"

"None, but I've—"

A wide, wolfish smile spans her face. "Yeah, you really earned it, then."

My lips part, but I'm at a loss for words. Am I not supposed to make the best of my circumstances? I didn't even want to audition. I would have been fine painting sets for a week and then leaving the theater altogether!

I—

I did earn it. Didn't I? I thought I did.

I know that, despite my efforts, I'm not the best actor. My vocal talent is undeniable, but I guess that doesn't mean much. Just look at Maris, who carries his performance with his presence, not his singing ability. Twee didn't need my voice to make the production good.

My heartbeat speeds. The more I think about it, the more I see Galahad's point. What if Twee just gave me the part because I'm the North Star? How many of the theater kids hate me for taking a spot I didn't deserve?

*It doesn't matter right now.* I subtly smooth down my goose bumps. *Focus.*

I told Priya I cared. I told her I would help. She deserves to have someone help.

I straighten, channeling all the too-muchness I possess, and demand, "Well?"

Galahad's jaw tightens. "No Senior Twilight?" she asks.

I nod sharply, afraid to speak and shatter the fragile armor I've pulled together.

"Fine."

# TRAGEDY PLUS TIME

Priya's voice drifts into the bathroom as I brush my teeth. "So, she just agreed to let you switch activities? Just like that?"

"No," I say, toothbrush still in my mouth so it sounds more like "Nugh." I hold my hair out of my face and duck my head under the faucet, catching water and spitting it out. "Not just like that. It took like thirty minutes of pretty intense groveling."

Priya's fingers drum on the doorframe. "Noooo," she says, drawing out the word. "It wasn't that easy. What did you have to do?"

"Well, I did have to give up something." I wipe my face on my towel and swivel past her into the main room of Polaris.

She follows in lockstep. "What?" she asks urgently.

"My first-born child. And something called a soul? I don't know what that is, but she made me sign a contract."

She blows a raspberry, trailing me up to my loft. "Did you really trade something?"

"Yes," I say, exasperated.

"What?"

"I *just* told you. A. Soul." I barely manage to keep my voice serious.

Priya groans.

I lower my weight onto the creaky bed, pulling my script into my lap. Since leaving the Round Table bunk, I can't seem to let the pages go. I want to prove Galahad—and anyone who agrees with her—wrong. And I think I can, as long as I spend this week eating, sleeping, and breathing *Beauty and the Beast*. Maybe I can get Priya to run lines while we paint.

She stands on the top step, leaning her face into the banister. It squishes up her left eye as she analyzes me. "I don't get it."

My abs flex defensively. The idea of telling Priya I gave up Senior Twilight feels like an incoming karate chop to the stomach.

First, because I want to be as *good* as she is. She wouldn't complain. She would just do it—with relentless positivity, at that. The second reason is, if I tell her, she'll make me go back to Galahad and say I changed my mind. That is not a conversation I want to have. And lastly, it was a crappy deal. And I don't want to have that conversation either.

"I'm not gonna tell you—" I start.

She cuts me off, shaking her head. "No, not that."

"Then what?"

"How do you . . . ?" Priya looks up, searching. "How do you ask for things?"

The script crunches, surprise tightening my fist around it. I scramble to flatten it out, glad to have something to concentrate on as I say, "I don't know if I can answer that in a way you'll understand. It's like if I asked, 'Priya, how are you likable?'"

"Hmm." There's a thick silence as she contemplates this. "I see. You're just so—"

"Intense?" I prompt.

She shakes her head. "Independent. Assertive."

"Oh." I roll and unroll my script, giving her the canned response I stole from my older brother years ago, "When you're competing with six mouths, you speak up or you don't get fed."

I expect this to be the end of the conversation, but Priya leans harder into the banister, like a child who's about to throw a leg over and slide down. "Was it tough?"

"No," I say, restless fingers pinching at my blanket. Again, I remind myself that Priya doesn't need to know about how my bargain with Galahad truly went. "She likes you, so I just explained that you're seconds away from an emotional break-down. Next time you see her, try to look frazzled or something."

Priya bats my response away. "No, I meant was it tough growing up with six siblings?"

The question shouldn't surprise me—lots of people ask— but it does. Her shining earnestness pulls the truth out of me. "Sometimes. It was hard to be a *person* in our house. I just always felt like . . ." I pause, tilting my head. Priya nods encouragingly. "Part of a set, I guess? Another name on the chore wheel. Until I came to camp."

She gives me a thoughtful hum. "Do you know all your siblings' names?"

"You're such an only child," I say, snorting. "Yes. Of course I know all my siblings' names."

A slight blush rises in her cheeks. I worry her embarrassment will keep her from continuing the conversation, but she says, "Tell me about them?"

"Why?"

She barks a laugh, nose crinkling. Leaning her entire torso onto the railing, she says, "You're always so suspicious. I just want to know. Please?"

If she looks at me like that and says *please* again, I'll tell her anything.

Ugh. There is something seriously wrong with me.

I gesture to the bed. When she takes a seat on the edge, I start, "Arthur is the oldest. He's a photographer." I think of the black-and-white portrait of his son, Teddy, that hangs in their living room. "He was already in high school when I was born, and off to college in Maine before I learned his name. He always came back for Thanksgiving, though. I like him. He's . . ." I trail off, pressing my lips together. I don't know what else to tell her. "Balding," I decide.

Priya nods, attentive. I don't know how this could possibly be interesting to her. It's not interesting to me, and they're *my* siblings.

"Laurent is five years younger than Arthur." An image pops into my head of Laurent dangling me out of a second-story window by my ankles, but I decide not to mention it. With Priya's gentle, lonely childhood, she might misread it as a bad memory. It's not; I wanted to see the robin's nest tucked onto the branch above the kitchen window. "He's the tallest. He lives in San Francisco with his boyfriend, Benji. They're pretty serious."

"Do we like Benji?" Priya asks.

I give a nod. "We do. He works for some tech start-up and

donates like half their money to homeless youth organizations."
After a second, I add, "Benji's also very tall."

Her eyes sparkle softly. "Good. Next."

"Then Ariadne. She's twenty-three and goes to a community
college in San Diego. I think she feels bad about that, but she's
probably the smartest of us."

"What does she study?"

"Uh, something with forests? I don't know. Conservation?
She doesn't talk about herself a lot." I think of Ariadne and how,
even when we were children, she always had her nose buried in
a textbook. Last time I saw her, she was reading some statistical-
looking paperback in a tree. *Nobody bothers you when you're
reading in a tree, Juliette.*

"Then you."

I nod. "Mm-hmm. Then Eloise. She should be in school with
us, but she's a computer genius, so she goes to some fancy vo-
tech near Irvine." I hear the pop of her gum and the click of her
acrylics against a keyboard. "We used to share a room, but she
got her own after convincing our parents that she needed more
space for her mainframes, or whatever."

Priya smiles. I bet the idea of sharing a room is a quaint novelty to her.

"Henry is next. He's my favorite." I'd tell her not to tell anyone, but Henry is everyone's favorite. "He's ten and plays the
drums surprisingly well. He and Arthur—the oldest—talk a lot."
I'd never thought about how funny it is that Henry's best friend
is our thirty-two-year-old brother. "Arthur plays guitar, so they

have a little band. They make up songs about *Minecraft*.

"Lizette is the youngest. She's six and very angry about it. She takes steroids for asthma, so she gets roid rage." I think of Lizette, tearing apart the couch like Godzilla when she found out Baby Yoda wasn't real. "It's very funny."

Priya stares, as if she expects me to say something else.

"What? Was that mean to say about steroids?"

She rolls her eyes. "You missed one."

I frown, reviewing the names in my head. I do have a lot of siblings, so maybe I really did forget one. Arthur, Laurent, Ariadne, Eloise, Henry, Lizette. "No, I didn't."

She gives me a pointed look. Oh, right. Me.

"You already know me." I shake my head.

"I know school you and camp you. What about Barrera-Wright you?"

I click my canines together in thought. "I'm . . ."

"You can't say 'intense,'" Priya commands sternly.

"I am intense."

"Sure, but you're other stuff, too."

Every nerve in my body tingles with awareness. I feel it all acutely. The backs of my legs touch the bed. The blanket touches my legs. My hair touches my neck. Priya's gaze touches my face. Heavy silence presses me into the mattress.

"I guess," I exhale, watching Priya blink her long eyelashes hypnotically.

She tilts her head, rolling her full lips together and releasing them thoughtfully. "Tell me about it, the other stuff."

It's not a command and, arguably, that's worse. It's painful to sit here with Priya—and her tentative smiles, and her olive branches, and her interest in *me*—while my foolish brain talks me out of things that I know to be true, because I am helpless to stop myself.

Priya is just being nice.

Nothing has changed between us.

She looks at everyone with this same dizzying heat, this heady affection.

I don't want her so much it hurts. I wouldn't take anything she'd give me.

After a moment of vertigo, I'm not sure where exactly I am or what's happening or why I'm so overwhelmed. Priya, Polaris, it all falls away and I am just . . . afraid.

And then I'm nothing.

Whatever decision needs to be made, whatever truth I have twisted, I won't deal with it right now. I can't handle it. The same emptiness that grounds me also numbs me. It makes me say, "There isn't anything else."

Priya looses a breath. I've never seen someone hold so many emotions in a twitch of a smile and a glance downward. Compassion and disappointment. Sadness and amusement. Frustration and fondness.

On her next inhale, all emotions disappear behind the safety of cheery neutrality. Without looking at me, Priya stands and walks down the steps. She pauses at the front door, resting a hand on the light switch.

I want to be upset with her for putting the mask back on. But I put mine on first.

"Good night, Juliette," she says, her back still to me. The cut of her top scoops low, displaying the strong lines of her shoulder blades, the indentation of her spine. "We'll try again tomorrow."

The switch clicks, plunging us into darkness.

## 2 7

# IT'S NOT A THREAT,
# IT'S A WARNING

"Here," Priya says, shoving a plastic stage makeup palette into my hands.

The included sponge tip applicator is hardened by years of face paint caked on top of even older, even grosser years of face paint. Eons from now, I bet alien anthropologists cut this open and study the strata to understand human behavior.

When Priya notices the future artifact, she plucks it from my grip and tosses it into the wastebasket beside her bed. "Don't use that." She reverently unlatches a tall, heart-shaped leather case and removes a small makeup brush. "Use this."

The handle is made of smooth pink wood and embossed with a little white heart. It screams Priya, right down to the angled brush's half-pink and half-white dye job that resembles her own bleached tips so closely it's almost suspicious.

I laugh. "You want me to use a hundred-dollar brush for this?" I tap the palette.

A smile spreads slowly across her face, breaking into a wheezing laugh. "Juliette!" She tries to sober, but ends up hunched over giggling as she spits out, "A hundred-dollar brush?"

I fight my own laughter at the sight of her trying to regain control of her body. "Two hundred?" I suggest.

"TWO—" She chokes, then rushes to the mirror. "My eyeliner, my eyeliner. Stop." Using her forefingers like windshield wipers, she clears stray black smudges from under her eyes. When she returns, she's utterly smug as she says, "Seven dollars, Juliette. Seven. No eye shadow brush costs two hundred dollars. But it was free; I'm on the founder's PR list."

"Oh." I turn the brush over in my hand, examining the way it gleams under the fluorescents. "Looks more expensive."

Priya smirks. "I'll tell Trixie you said that."

Hearing her say another girl's name makes me nauseous. I hand the brush back. "Either way, anything more than a Q-tip is too expensive to use with Fogridge stage paint."

In one swift motion, I coat the pad of my thumb with thick green goop and step in to her. It feels a little like a triumph to watch her breath hitch and head tilt back.

With all the care of a Martian archaeologist, I smooth two stripes along her cheekbones. Green, a shade darker than her forest-floor eyes. Nobody should look hot dressed like a tailgater at a Sacramento State game, and yet.

"How do I look?" she asks, though she could easily turn and look in the mirror herself.

I consider, and for a moment, it's like I can see into a parallel dimension. And in this parallel dimension, the space between us closes. The warmth in my chest spreads, setting my entire body on fire as I wrap Priya's hair around my fis—

But I am a wimp. And I live in this dimension.

I take a step back. "Like someone whose team is about to lose Color War."

Outfitted in the most outrageous monochromatic tactical gear, Flagstaff, Eleazar, and Lovelace somersault around the soccer field, ducking around obstacles. Flagstaff, clad in eye-aching neon green, crouches behind a hay bale with his paintball gun cradled to his chest. Lovelace has one gun in each hand, crossing and uncrossing them in a parody of a Western. Eleazar box-jumps onto anything sturdy, his gun raised over his head like a barbell.

Instead of shooting, because Pat is nominally still explaining rules to the handful of campers who are paying attention, our captains make soft *pew-pew* noises at one another.

Finally, we're dismissed to get our supplies from the division leaders. I make it to the huddle of senior counselors before Pat catches up with me. I'd know that sound anywhere—his distinctive jog, long shuffles of grass against sneaker soles.

"Juliette? Can I speak with you for a moment?"

Galahad turns at the sound, and I watch her gaze lock on Pat with something close to alarm. I'm sure I look the same, because Pat doesn't use that tone for just any old chat. Nope. That inflection? The one with the false cheer and an upturned ending? That's bad news.

The look on his face says everything. He smiles, but it's agonizingly joyless. This isn't bad news; it's *bad* news.

I decide to go with a preemptive strike: "Pat, do not say whatever you're about to say."

He asks, "Can we talk by the picnic tables?" But he isn't look-ing at me as he nods his chin toward the row of wooden tables between the field and the path. His eyes stay fixed on Galahad.

I immediately *know* what's coming. I just know Pat is going to take me over to those benches and tell me not to participate in paintball. The reality of it settles over my body like a weighted blanket, comforting in how evenly it crushes my dreams.

Nodding, I gesture for Pat to lead the way, but once he's a few steps ahead of me, I whirl on Galahad. There are so many feelings fighting their way out of me that the only thing I can do is grind my molars together so hard it makes my ears ring.

Her brows are drawn. "J—"

I snap. Winding my hand back, I hurl the water bottle I forgot I was even holding into the ground beside me. It bounces once, metal clang dulled by the dirt, and then rolls away. I say the only thing I can think of, tears in my eyes. "Am I *that* bad of a camper?"

Before she answers, I fall into line behind Pat with a grim acceptance, almost hoping it's worse than I expect. Maybe Pat will tell me I've been kicked out of camp. The entire Theater company rallied together in protest because they hate me. Not only am I banned from paintball, I'm banned from the rest of Color War. For the rest of my life. Even when I work here as a counselor, I'll be chained to my bed on Color War days, like a werewolf during the full moon. And no matter how loudly I howl, I won't be released until a winner has been crowned.

Fogridge is beautiful. I try to focus on that.

Trees shade the area, protecting the tables from a sun that

gets brutal come midday. In the early morning though, the trees are just decoration. Light filters through the sparse umbrella of leaves, laying dappled shadows on the surface of the table we seat ourselves at.

Wisely, he's taken the bench facing the field, so I don't have to watch everyone getting ready for a game I'm not allowed to participate in. Unfortunately, I still have to hear them. The laughter reverberates off the surrounding mountains, sound waves bouncing from trees to bodies and eventually finding their way back to me. It's an echolocation of my rock bottom.

"You're in the play, right?" Pat asks, fidgeting with his phone. He juggles it nonchalantly, like it isn't contraband in anyone else's hands. "How's it going? Twee keeping you all in line?"

If the bench had a backrest, I'd let my head collapse onto it. Instead, I steeple my hands over my nose to support the unbearable weight of my own body. I'm just so tired of this.

Excitement, setback. Anticipation, defeat.

I barely keep my eyes open behind lids that are heavier than they've ever been.

Truly, I could fall asleep right here.

"Yeah. I am." I sigh. "Just tell me, so I can go back to Polaris and get in bed."

He doesn't look confused by my words, which I take as a bad sign. He taps his fingers on the back of his phone. Tucked inside his clear case is a Polaroid of the Zimmermans' youngest grandson. He's a cute kid with shiny blond hair and a peeling temporary tattoo of the Batman logo in the center of his forehead.

"Galahad told me you decided not to do Senior Twilight."

I whip around, cracking my back as I search for the life ruiner herself.

Most of the crowd that had been on the field is gone now, dispersed to change into messy clothing and receive final talking-tos about not aiming for the head, no matter how many points it is in *Fortnite*. But Galahad is still here, staring directly at us and chewing on her bottom lip.

"Yeah," I say flatly, turning back to face Pat. "I did."

His fingertips can't find a steady beat. They speed up and slow down in turns, finally stopping when he claps his hands together in thought. "I worry about you, kiddo."

"I'm okay," I insist miserably.

"I don't want to take this away from you, but if you pulled out of the Twilight because of your ankle . . ." He raps his knuckles on the table while a fist squeezes around my heart. "I want to be safe."

I resist the urge to scream, to tell him that I'm not a child and he should stop treating me like one. All this front-loading isn't making it any easier for me.

"I'd like to tell you a story, Juliette. And I'd really like for you to listen to it. Then, afterward, we can discuss the modifications I'd like to make to your participation in Senior Twilight. Does that sound okay?"

I frown. Modifications.

Modifications? What does that mean? "Wait. Are you gonna let me play?"

"Would you like to listen to my story?"

He doesn't ask it condescendingly, the way every other adult in my life would have—that *I don't know. Can you?* that teachers do when you ask if you can go to the bathroom.

Of course Pat can tell me a story. He's going to let me participate.

"Yes," I say, folding my hands in front of me. "I'm listening."

"Did I ever tell you that I did gymnastics in high school?" he asks.

I take in his bony frame, his uncalloused fingers. "No, I don't think so."

"I did. Pommel horse, mainly, and I was pretty good. In fact, when I was your age"—he gives me a meaningful nod—"I qualified for nationals.

"The weekend before the comp, I was doing a tumbling pass and I tweaked my wrist." He turns his right hand over and back gingerly, as if he can still remember the feeling. "I competed anyway. Actually, I kept competing that whole season. And the next one, despite the pain. I was much more senseless than you are, of course, but I'm trying to tell you that I know how you can love something so much that you convince yourself it's worth anything."

He tucks his arm up to his chest and uses his left hand to pull the long sleeve of his sun shirt back, past his elbow, then he presents it to me. A gnarled scar, at least three inches long, extends down his inner forearm. Small lines hash across the main scar, like rungs on a ladder. It's the kind of surgical incision you only see on old people, done back before they had lasers.

"I've had over ten surgeries on this wrist, but the pain always comes back." He pulls his sleeve down again. "It hurts whenever it rains. Or when I carry Thomas for too long." Pat taps the boy inside his phone case. "And do you know how much I care about gymnastics now?"

I shake my head.

"Not. At. All. I haven't cared about gymnastics for at least thirty years, but I still suffer because once upon a time it was the love of my life. Your body isn't something to mess around with. You only get one."

I roll my ankle under the table, considering his words. It's hard to focus, drained as I am by the emotional roller coaster of the last few minutes.

"I understand, I think," I say with a slow nod. "So . . . you want me to sit out?"

Pat's head tilts so far to the left that it's nearly parallel to the ground. "No," he says, but it doesn't sound like a no. It's flat, like I asked what he was drinking and he said water. "I want you to take what you need from that story and apply it today. And tomorrow."

My forehead creases. "But . . . still play?"

"Within reason." He flourishes a hand. "I'm proud of you for making one responsible decision, and I'm giving you information that may help you make another. This isn't a punishment, Juliette. It's a cautionary tale."

# THE GOD OF FINGER GUNS

I take the long way to the senior bunks, avoiding Galahad by rigidly following the path instead of cutting through the soccer field. Behind her bunk, Lucy shimmies into a purple jumpsuit. Her hair is pulled back into a low ponytail, covered by a paisley bandana.

"I look like a grape," she says in greeting, not seeming upset in the least.

"Kinda. Does your counselor have extra purple stuff? I don't want to talk to Galahad."

The corner of Lucy's mouth twitches—probably one of her most mischievous-looking expressions, though after years of friendship I've learned it's her version of a shrug. "Snorkles," she calls over her shoulder, in the direction of her bunk's open window.

A counselor appears behind the dirty window screen. With false grumpiness, she asks, "What do you want?"

"Do we have extra equipment that Juliette can use?"

"Oh, yeah. Lazlots, right? Give me a sec." She disappears from view and then reappears, rounding the corner with a handful of purple denim and a paintball gun. A full-face helmet dangles from her pinkie. She jingles them at me with playful impatience until I take them.

When she turns the corner again, I make a face at Lucy. "You're lucky you have a good counselor."

"Snorks? Yeah, I love her. But it's more like *Galahad* is lucky she doesn't have *me*." She grabs her helmet from the base of a tree. "I don't put up with an ego trip. She'd learn not to try it with me. Quickly," she adds.

I pile my hair on top of my head and slide my helmet on before I do anything else, wanting to be unrecognizable if my favoritest counselor walks up. Inside, it smells like a department store bicycle aisle in the best possible way—new rubber and faint disinfectant.

As I step into the jumpsuit, I protest, "I *don't* put up with it."

The built-in visors have a faded oil-slick sheen, so I don't see the side-eye she gives me, but I do feel it. "Juliette," Lucy admonishes. "Come on. We both know it's not the same."

She's right. At the intersection of Lucy's self-assurance and her freckles, there's a Bermuda Triangle that authority figures get lost in. With the exception of D-Mo, she's generally gotten away with murder. Meanwhile, they burn me at the stake anytime I step a toe out of line.

Gia explained it perfectly once:

*You are a piece of paper and Lucy is a knife. A knife cuts you because you were careless. It doesn't surprise you; that's what the knife was made to do. You should have been more careful. When a piece of paper cuts you, you're pissed because it was made for other things—to create and write and draw and document. It wasn't supposed to hurt you.*

WISH YOU WEREN'T HERE

"You're the knife," I say.

She lifts her helmet to flash me an impish smile, her round cheeks rising to squish her eyes. "Freshly sharpened, baby." She settles it back on her head and hooks an arm through mine. "Now let's go find our friends and make them cry."

Once I explain Pat's nonpunishment to Lucy, she summarily abandons me, saying, "Sorry, Juliette, but you'll only slow me down. Godspeed, you weak link."

The weird thing is, not only has Pat's story burrowed its way into my thoughts, I've started to believe it.

I play paintball without Lucy's dramatic lunges and leaps, without climbing on top of sheds. When someone targets me, I throw my arms wide and say, "Kill me, then." Usually, one shot to the torso is enough of a victory before they return to chasing more agile campers.

It turns out to be a fun game in and of itself, strutting around camp like I'm invincible. I wander from specialty area to specialty area, eventually finding myself in the no-combat zone of the art buildings. Because so many of the projects live out in the open, pylons and caution signs rope off the entirety of the quad.

Specs, the bushy-mustached woodshop specialist, is posted up in a folding chair at one of the Quad 2 entrances. He and the metal shop specialist, a gray-haired woman named Laith, play a game of cards on a TV tray table. All their paintball gear lies unused in the grass, though they do occasionally pick up their guns and shoot at a nearby tree, seemingly without reason.

"Who goes there?" Specs asks, inspecting his cards closely.

I pull off my helmet. "Just me."

"Oh, hello, Juliette," he says, giving me a nod as he lays down a pair of kings. "I hear you're with me this week. That's gr—Well, who do we have here?"

I turn to find the Minis' train cruising down the dirt path toward us. They aren't allowed to participate, but TK drives them around, commentating through a bullhorn like a safari guide. A clear vinyl tarp shields the little ones from stray projectiles, and they squeal delightedly whenever it does its job.

TK brings the train to a halt and raises the bullhorn to her lips. "If you look to your left—that's this side, Aiden—you can see Mr. Specs and Ms. Laith playing cards. Wave hi!"

The babies crowd up against the barrier, their tiny noses squashed beneath the plastic. They wave, as instructed.

"Oh no," says TK. "What color is Mr. Specs wearing?"

Specs is adorned in his usual yellow Color War outfit. For as long as I've known him, he's pretended to be clueless about the team colors. Anytime a camper reminds him that yellow isn't a team, he pretends he just forgot. But, of course, the next year, he comes in yellow again. Diehard Specs fans wear yellow bandanas as an inside joke. Gia's considered it but always chooses to fully commit to orange. The year they finally win (which, as a reminder, will be never), he wants to be fully dressed in his color.

"Yellow," the Minis giggle.

"And is yellow a team, friends?"

"No!"

Specs smacks a hand into his forehead. "Jeezle Pete, that's right! I'll get it next year."

The practiced choreography of his answer is so well known that Laith lip-syncs along with him as she lays down a set of cards. She even gets the "Jeezle Pete" correct.

"Isn't that so silly of Mr. Specs?" TK asks, preparing to return the way they came.

"TK!" a little voice calls. "Is that your grandpa?"

TK thinks for a moment before lying, "Yes. Yes, he is. Say 'Bye, Grandpa!'"

They follow her instructions and Specs waves back jovially. Quietly, he says to Laith, "I don't mind more grandchildren. As long as I don't gotta give 'em money."

Laith guffaws, swatting him with her hand of cards. "Ain't that right?"

"Oh, look! There's our friend Juliette! Everybody say, 'Hi, Juliette Barrera-Wright!'"

They don't say that. They say something more like "Hi, Chulatet Baowite!"

I've never been so delighted by someone getting my name wrong. I follow the train, waving until they're out of sight, but then a voice sounds behind me, low and serious at first but breaking character to laugh by the end.

"Say your prayers, Baowite." A pressure pushes into my back, and I can picture the spy movie pose Priya has taken to aim the barrel right between my shoulder blades. I pivot to face her, expecting a paintball gun to be pointed at the center of my chest.

It's not. The gun itself hangs by her hip, strap slung cross-body like a bandolier. What presses into my sternum, instead, are Priya's gloved fingers, clasped together.

Even with her arms extended, we're close.

Our eyes meet and everything falls silent, a force field suddenly separating us from the rest of the world. The laughter dies on my lips. I'm panting, my chest rising and falling with such intensity that it moves Priya's arms.

I glance down at her hands, then back up. She looks like an abstract painting, streaks of orange and purple covering her entire body.

"Who am I praying to? The god of finger guns?" I joke, taking her hands in both of mine and lowering them to her sides.

"Well, I wasn't going to point the gun directly into—Lucy!" she shouts abruptly, interrupting herself. Priya rips off her helmet and tucks it beneath her arm. Her thick hair cascades right into place, no evidence of the helmet-hair I'm sure I have. "That's Lucy!"

I swivel, but I don't see anyone. "What's Lucy?"

Priya grabs both my elbows, eyes intent. "Lucy is the god of finger guns!"

My jaw slackens at her fervid desperation. Then I laugh, so hard I nearly fall to my knees. Not because what she said was particularly funny but because the moment she wraps her hands around the angle of my arms, I am pulled out of my body.

I see us now, Priya in her messy green jumpsuit, earnestly screaming at me about one of my oldest friends. I see us in school with a near-tangible wall dividing us, even as we work together on an APUSH handout. I see every picture containing the smallest sliver of the other person, right at the edge. Every sigh of resignation and every outraged eye roll.

I laugh because that's funny—the idea that Priya and I are the same people we've always been. It's so funny.

"That was good, right?" Priya asks, pulling her helmet against her chest. With raised eyebrows and open-mouthed anticipation, she waits for my response. For *my* approval.

I collect myself, straighten to full height, and meet her eyes with sincerity. "Priya" is how much I manage to spit out before every muscle in my body gives out from hysterical laughter. I crumple to my knees, gasping for breath.

Priya sinks down beside me, clutching her stomach. Through gasping breaths, she chokes, "I should have killed you when I had the chance."

# THAT'S MY CAPTAIN

Color War always ends with a camp-wide relay for a massive number of points.

Normally, I would be running the relay. Strat would be sprinting next to me, cheering me on. My knees would scrape the ground, my hair catching on the rough net of the army crawl. I'd tag Lucy to start her section before tumbling down the other side of an adrenaline spike.

I'm not doing that. And, shockingly, I don't want to be.

I've been avoiding Galahad since my talk with Pat, so when I saw her walking up the Polaris steps this morning, I flung myself under Priya's bed.

"Juliette?" she called, opening the door. "There's a letter for you." A soft sigh, the sound of something being placed on the carpet, and the door clicking closed again.

I wormed out from under the bed to find an envelope addressed to me on the floor. Not from Galahad, though. From Alison. I'd completely forgotten I wrote to her. I took it up to my loft and hunkered behind my bed to read it, in case Galahad came back.

Dear Juliette,
I looked it up and homicide is illegal in California, I'm afraid.

WISH YOU WEREN'T HERE

That sucks. Forreal, though, I'm sorry you're having a crappy
summer. I know Priya can be intense sometimes,

My head snaps up. I reread the line, and then I read it again
to make sure I'm not misreading my own name. Priya? Intense?
Flipping the envelope around, I check the recipient one more
time. Juliette Barrera-Wright. That's weird.

but camp will be over before you know it. Just try not to
pay attention to her and keep reminding yourself that once this
is over, you only have to deal with her for one more year.
One more year.
One more year.

In solidarity,

Alison

PS one more year.
PPS one more year.

Before I compacted it between my hands and hooked it
into the garbage can, I thanked the Fogridge gods that she was
wrong. One more year? Not if I have anything to say about it.
So, when my division leader asked if I preferred to cheer or
to participate, I said I'd gladly be the cheering section for the last
camper leg, fire making.
Priya huddles over a pile of supplies, working diligently as
Flagstaff bounces on his toes at the start of the captain's leg—
which ends in the woods, to keep the final scores a secret until
the reveal.

I scream when Priya gets fire *eons* before the campers on the Lots and the Mares.

I follow her the short distance to where she high-fives her captain. Flagstaff leaps into action, high-stepping through tires, holding up his tutu while leadership members pelt him with water balloons. He laughs, open-mouthed, at each and every splash.

Priya anxiously tracks him across the last part of the relay that camp can see.

But, for my part, I'm transfixed by Priya, killing her first Color War. I smile, taking it all in, paying her all the attention I have to give.

It's silent as we gather into our teams.

I keep sneaking glances at the sea of green clear across the field, but Priya blends into the chaos despite her distinctive hair. Before she left my side, she wished me luck with a wink that sent my stomach plummeting to the center of the earth. Since my return from the planet's molten core, I've been wandering aimlessly, looking around like I'm trying to catch sight of a ghost.

Everyone else's eyes are trained on the rainbow parachute in the middle of the soccer field. It's the kind kindergarteners play with but bigger. About five minutes ago, Flagstaff, Eleazar, and Lovelace all ducked underneath. Now the mushroom of air they created is slowly deflating, the parachute sinking like a soufflé in a noisy cartoon.

"Good afternoon, Fogridge!" Pat's voice booms from the

speakers just seconds before I spot him emerging from beneath the parachute, microphone in hand.

"Good afternoon, Pat," we sing back.

The camp's owner struts down the field toward us in his sun shirt and khakis. He smiles toothily before continuing, "Today is a big day for the Fogridge community. For some of you, this was your first-ever Color War. For others, it is potentially your last."

I swallow a gulp of air, fighting the knife-in-the-gut feeling Pat just inflicted upon me.

Lucy clicks her tongue. "He's just trying to make us sad so we'll come back as staff," she whispers.

I guess she could be right, but part of me thinks Pat must live for camp the way we do. I imagine him as a child, standing on this very field at the end of Color War, knowing he was going to be running it one day. This ceremony has to mean something to him.

"Is it working?" I ask Lucy.

She scowls, regarding me with derision. "Of course."

"Before I reveal the Color War winner for this year," Pat says, surveying the crowd deliberately, "I want to congratulate all of you for the gusto you've shown these past two days."

There are too many campers at Fogridge for Pat to look each one of us in the eye as he speaks, but I swear he does. His gaze locks with mine, eyes creasing at the edges.

"I know our staff has done a good job when I see campers on one team cheering for their friends or counselors on another team. And that's why I'm awarding the Spirit Stick to the team I've seen be the most encouraging and positive over the past few days." He lifts a baton above his head. Red and white ribbons twine the pole, and each end has a shiny gold pom-pom attached.

The Spirit Stick is both an achievement and a failure. The winner of Color War never gets the Spirit Stick. It should be an honor, but it also guarantees a second- or third-place finish.

"That team is . . . drumroll please!" Hundreds of kids slam hands into thighs arrhythmically until Pat finally shouts, "The Lazlots!"

A half groan, half cheer arises from the crowd around me. A Lots counselor I don't know valiantly leads a chant that would make an outsider think she cared. My voice joins in, but my attention is fixed on the parachute in the middle of the field. By this point, it's deflated to half its original height. I can only imagine the weird postures the three captains are assuming to keep from creating outlines in the fabric.

"Congratulations to you all, and your fearless captain, for setting such an incredible example for our community."

I think about how I purposefully tripped Gia during a low-stakes sack race. Oops.

"Now, the moment you've all been waiting for: this year's Fogridge Color War Champions . . ." Pat pauses for dramatic effect as several leadership staff grab at the parachute and yank it away. "The Dondos!"

Flagstaff rockets out of a cloud of green smoke, jumping

higher than I've ever seen a human jump in my life. He hefts a golden paddle toward the sky, the Color War Oar. Lovelace and Eleazar are nowhere in sight, concealed by the green smoke bomb.

All at once, I don't care that it isn't the Lots. I don't feel conflicted at all as I cup my hands around my mouth and shout, "That's my captain!"

I've always imagined yelling that for him. He's still my captain, even if he is a Dondo.

In a thundering deluge, Flagstaff's entire team rushes the field. I watch him grab several campers and line them up in a triangle formation. He jogs back away, turns, squints at them, and finally mimes throwing a bowling ball down a lane. Up until this point, the campers looked as confused as I felt, but now they laugh and topple to the ground with synchronized accuracy. Flagstaff throws his hands up in victory, running laps around his bowling pins.

Through the chaos, I see it. Not a face, but a flash of half-white hair. My green camp shirt, with a blur of signatures on it, races toward . . . me.

Lucy catches my neck in an aggressively friendly choke hold, admonishing me for cheering for the enemy. Gia guffaws in my ear, cursing his perennial last-place finish. But it's Priya I'm focused on, as she finally breaks through the crowd to pull us all into a group hug.

"How does it feel to lose, losers?" she crows.

My frenzied brain doesn't know if I answer or not. I can't tell if the warmth flooding my senses is from the Southern California sun or from somewhere deep inside me.

Then there's a singular instant where all the noise fades except for Priya's laugh. A long smear of dirt stripes her nose. Two faint green bands crest her high cheekbones. And when she wraps her arms around my neck, she is beaming, in a full-body smile.

My heart feels so full it could burst.

# 3 0

## TINE AND TINE AGAIN

I barely have time to I-told-you-so Priya about Color War before she disappears. When I get back to Polaris after masterfully evading Galahad, the cabin is dark. I fall asleep before Priya gets home. When I wake the next morning, I can tell she's been here. The white sneakers she sprayed green—the ones she was wearing yesterday—sit in a tidy pair beside the door.

She doesn't come to breakfast, and I feel almost guilty when I tell Gia and Lucy I don't know where she is.

For the briefest of milliseconds, I convince myself that she saw the letter from Alison. What if she thinks I don't like her? What if she thinks "one more year" is what I want?

But before I can fall down that well, I remind myself that this is Priya Pendley. Priya, who tells me exactly what she thinks whether I want to hear it or not. Priya, who met with every single cast member of *Into the Woods* before setting needle to fabric because "everyone should have a say in what they put on their bodies." In an infinite number of multiverses, zero versions of Priya disrespect me enough to go through my trash and read my mail.

No, the reason Priya has suddenly fallen off the face of the earth becomes clear the second I step into the demolition zone that is the Fogridge theater.

She looks relieved to see me, allaying all my fears with a frazzled wave. I drop my things and immediately get to work.

For the next few days, most of the cast spends their waking hours building props, adjusting costumes, and rehearsing. We squeeze in what sleep we can on the stunt fighting crash pads. They line the floor of a cool, dark storage room that Twee supervises with a vigilant eye.

In Woodshop, Priya writes out a to-build list, and we slowly cross each item off. A window, a walking stick, wagon wheels. Specs patiently explains the basics to me. I notice that he gives Priya little direction, trusting her to use tools he won't let anyone else get close to. I feel a twinge of pride at that.

Priya stops working exactly once, just to pack her supplies for Senior Twilight. I fight my heartbreak by mercilessly making fun of the items she chooses.

"You're bringing your phone?" I tease once she returns to the theater.

We take spots on either side of a large dining table, to which we have hot-glued ten place settings. Because she's an overachiever, everything is accurately laid out for a Parisian-style twelve-course meal. Now, you may be thinking, *What makes it Parisian-style?* Well, in formal Parisian dining, the cutlery is placed tine down—something I only found out *after* I had already painstakingly glued thirty-three individual pieces of silverware with their tines pointing up.

To my horror, Priya insisted I fix it.

"They are in France, Juliette," she whined, running a hand

over her anguished face. "Everybody knows that. It's canon."

Looking over the table, I pleaded with her, "The audience won't even be able to see it. No one will know."

To which she replied, "I will know."

All 110 utensils are now tine-down.

Priya bends her knees and grabs her edge of the table, gesturing for me to do the same. "One, two, three," she says, and we lift together. "Yeah, I'm bringing my phone. It's a clock, a flashlight, an alarm. What am I supposed to do alone in a tent all night besides scroll?"

"Sleep, meditate, worry about bears," I list as we maneuver the table out of her workroom and down the narrow hallway.

Walking backward, Priya carefully tilts the table to avoid knocking over the props stacked against the walls. "This was a lot easier before it had legs."

"Your battery is going to die," I point out.

"What?"

"Your phone battery."

"Jesus, who closed this?" She lets out a frustrated huff. The table jostles as she backs into the push bar of the stage door, swinging it open. "I have two battery packs, I'll be fine."

"Will you even have signal out there?" I ask, but she doesn't answer. The stage booms with the sound of theater kids talking over one another.

Priya shouts over the noise, "Twee, where do you want this?"

The reply comes from above us. I look up, finding Twee untangling a mess of electrical cords in the scaffolding. "The table can go along the back wall, next to the bookcase!"

"Got it!" Priya yells back.

The groups part for us, joking about how strong Priya is, how she must not skip leg day, telling her to be careful not to Hulk out and upend the fake wine glasses. She chuckles at every comment, kissing her biceps when we set the table down.

It brings me back to the first line read we did together. A blush rises in my cheeks. And seeing her here in her element, with her easy authority, it's kind of . . . hot?

A hand claps my shoulder. "C'mon, Grandma. Let's grab the chairs."

"Are you calling me weak?"

"No," she sighs, grabbing my wrist and leading me back through the stage door. "I'm calling you old. This isn't the nineties. There's 4G everywhere."

I stop in my tracks and paste on a serious expression. "Rude. Carry your own chairs."

She sticks her lower lip out in a pout. Her hand slides up and down my forearm coyly. That's flirting, right? Isn't that flirting? I think it is. Either way, the caress sends goose bumps rippling across my body.

"Please? You look so cute when you carry things."

Okay. That is flirting. It has to be.

She flashes a winning smile. "Plus, if you help, we only have to make two trips."

I'm giving myself a headache. To put an end to my internal debate and save my brain from combustion, I say, "Fine. I'll help."

"Yay!" Priya exclaims, wrapping me up in a big hug. Her cheek presses into mine, her smile palpable against me. She makes a small, pleased noise in my ear that's going to be lodged into my thoughts for years to come.

*This.* If this isn't flirting, then I give up.

When she pulls back, I expect a mirror of my yearning on her face, but there's only mischief. She skips off down the hall, chanting, "Two trips, two trips, two trips!" She spins, pointing at me. "Hurry up, loser. These chairs aren't going to move themselves."

I don't know what anything is anymore.

The to-do list dwindles, albeit slower than Priya would like. But for me, rehearsals fly by with barely any errors. I'm dedicated to proving that I can do this, regardless of why I was chosen to be Belle. Every reflective surface becomes an opportunity to practice emoting. I free my phone from the prison of my bedside drawer and play my songs while I sleep. I drink so much chamomile tea that I'm sure I'll smell like the floral steam until the day I die.

Priya and I are half hovering out of our chairs at breakfast on Friday morning—show day—when Pat announces, "Campers who will be participating in the Senior Twilight tonight, please meet me at the pavilion directly after this for gear distribution instructions."

I look up at Lucy, excited for a second before remembering the promise I made Galahad. My eyes flit around the mess hall for my counselor, finding her looking right at me. She cocks an eyebrow. The time has come to pay the piper. I hate the piper.

Priya and Lucy both stand, then they pause, expectantly. I shrug and wave them on.

"You're not coming?" Lucy asks.

I shake my head and try to think of a plausible explanation.

Priya turns, sending her hair flying. Her eyes, pupils blown in confusion, say everything.

Frowning, Lucy prompts, "Is this because of what Pat said before paintball?"

*Yes!* I think, giving Lucy a mental fist bump. "He has a point."

Lucy crosses her arms. "He doesn't know what he's talking about. Your ankle's fine."

Looking between us, Gia asks, "What did he say?"

"Basically, that if Juliette goes on the Senior Twilight, she'll injure her ankle and be in pain forever," Lucy says with a dismissive eye roll.

I purse my lips to one side. "I mean, it wasn't *that* dramatic."

"It was that dramatic," she insists. "Otherwise, you'd be coming to the pavilion with us right now."

"I don't know. I've always said that would happen," Gia says.

Lucy shoves him. "You aren't helping."

He shrugs, biting a piece of French toast in half. "I wasn't trying to. I'll support whatever y'all do, but you know how I feel about Twilight."

"It was a cinematic triumph and the baseball scene will be forever iconic?" I suggest.

Gia snaps in agreement. "That. It's the only Twilight that matters."

Priya scratches her jaw, staying suspiciously silent. Her eyes are fixed on me so intensely that even when I look away, I can still feel her stare burning the side of my face.

"You guys should go," I say. "We'll talk about it later."

Neither of them moves. Finally, I stand to get more apple juice, and when I return to the table, Lucy and Priya are gone.

"So, you're gonna tell me, right?"

I look up from the wood I'm painting. Priya hovers over me, hands on her hips.

"Tell you . . . ?"

She fixes me with an annoyed look. "Oh, stop. Why aren't you doing Senior Twilight?"

I try to resume working, but Priya steps closer and drops to one knee. She levels her face with mine, and I am pulled into her green eyes.

"Juliette," she warns. The low hum of her voice sends a shiver down my spine.

"Priya," I reply calmly even though I'm melting under her stare. Even breathing near her feels like flirting, the slow rise and fall of my chest a loud mating call. "I've been on my feet a lot. I want to focus on the show. I just don't feel up to a twelve-hour forest adventure. Accept it."

She raises her eyebrows. "Okay, yeah. I would accept that. *If* it were true, which it's not."

I heave a dramatic sigh. "This production goes on in like"—I glance up at the clock on the wall—"six hours, in case you've forgotten. I don't have time to argue about this."

Her fingers tap on the wood paneling beside her foot. Finally, she stands and rolls her shoulders. "You're doing Senior Twilight."

"I don't want to," I say to the paintbrush. Brick-red goop falls from the bristles, landing on the set piece with a plop. I inartistically scrape at it until it forms a semi-even layer.

There's silence from Priya, but her shoes don't move in my peripheral vision. Tension builds as I continue to ignore her. Finally, a hand slips under my chin and tilts my head up so I'm face-to-face with Priya's crouching form.

We're upstage left, surrounded by people working on last-minute tasks. But the proximity, her whisper, and the firm press of her fingers on my jaw—I'm entranced. Nothing has ever existed besides me, Priya Pendley, and this moment.

"Tell me again," she whispers, "that you don't want to go, and I'll believe you."

I almost do. I don't know what holds me back. It's such an innocuous thing to lie about, but I'm frozen under her scrutiny.

Priya holds my gaze for a minute, and when I don't give her a response, she grabs my hand and tugs me to my feet. "Come on," she says. Then, to a passing stagehand, "Would you mind finishing up that set piece, Anton?"

Anton grins, his curly black hair bouncing with every step. "I got you." My mouth twists in distaste at his overly familiar tone.

"Where are we going?" I demand.

She drags me backstage, toward her workroom. "To play a game."

I pull back against her hand, bringing her to a halt. "I don't have time for a game."

"Then you better play quick." She continues down the hall. Her grip on my wrist is firm, and though I do want out of this situation, I can't pretend that I want her to let go. A shudder goes through me as my body recalls the physical memory of her guiding my chin up. How easily her hand could have wandered to my cheek or my neck or—

*Jesus, Juliette!* My cheeks heat. *This is not the time.*

She pushes the workroom door open, and I'm hit with the comforting scent of sawdust. The area is empty, most of the props having been moved into the hallway or backstage. A plastic guard covers the circular saw, since Priya finished all her big projects days ago. The concrete is graffitied with splotches of color around hard, clean squares where cardboard protected the floor from the worst of the spray paint. Priya tests one patch for dryness with her white sneaker before sitting down cross-legged.

She gestures at the space across from her. I don't bother checking for wet paint before I take a seat.

"Truth or dare." She presents the options as fact, as if to a finicky toddler: We *are* playing this game. You cannot choose not to play; you can only choose between truth and dare.

"Dare," I say.

"I dare you to tell me why you aren't going to Senior Twilight."

"Okay, it doesn't work like that." I start to stand, but she puts out an arm to stop me.

"Fine, fine," she says. "I'll go first. Truth."

I scoff, throwing my hands up in an exasperated shrug. "I don't know what you want me to ask you, Priya. I just want to—"

"The truth is," she starts, cutting me off, "that you've put a lot into helping me this past week and I'm afraid I know exactly why you aren't doing the Senior Twilight and I want you to tell me I'm wrong."

She doesn't know. How could she know?

"Truth or dare?" Priya asks with her mouth set in a somber line.

Faced with the reality that she won't let me out of this conversation until I give her what she wants, I say, "Truth."

Her words come out haltingly. "Did you really trade Galahad something to switch activities?"

My mouth falls open. "What?"

"Did you trade Senior Twilight?"

The connection between my mouth and brain has died of shock. Though I'm thinking, *No, nope, don't tell her,* I end up saying, "How did you know that?"

She flashes a humorless smile. "I wouldn't be a particularly good *Survivor* player if I didn't understand people. But mostly, it was a lucky guess."

I sigh, more out of habit than actual annoyance at our inside joke. "Well, Lucky, ya caught me. Can I go back to prepping now?"

Her hands encircle mine in a cocoon and I nearly flinch.

"I wish you hadn't," she says, eyes soft. "Why did you do that?"

A loud bang erupts in the hallway, followed by laughing and shouted apologies. Priya glances over my shoulder at the door.

The temporary reprieve from her attention clears my head. "You needed help."

She focuses on me again, the noise in the hallway forgotten. Cocking her head to one side, she opens her mouth, then closes it again with a huff. At once, she's on her feet and walking away from me. I'm not sure what happened or why she's leaving.

"Wait," I call, and in that single word I hear all the desperation I didn't know I was feeling.

Priya must hear it, too, because she falters with a hand on the doorknob.

"Are you . . . ?" I have no clue what to ask and she can sense it. Her arm flexes, grip tightening. Anxious for at least one clue to what is happening, I blurt, "What are you doing?"

She turns her head to the side, looking more at her shoulder than at me. I can't discern anything from her profile.

"You didn't say 'truth or dare.'" She opens the door and steps out, letting it swing shut behind her.

# THANK YOU, PLACES

For the rest of the afternoon, I am rattled by that conversation with Priya. Whenever I try to talk to her, she barely slows, pointing in the opposite direction and saying, "I gotta..." I catch sight of her a few times: carrying an armchair, helping Twee in the rigging above the stage, and repairing the loose hem on Etan's Gaston coat. The fourth time she makes it clear that she won't speak with me, I give up and focus on the things I need to get done.

"Circle up," Twee calls as Frankie rolls a rack of costumes through the stage door. We all pretend to pay attention to her while sneaking glimpses of our outfits. "Is everyone here?"

I scan the circle, but I already know who's missing.

Frankie says, "Priya."

Twee waves a hand in the air. "Oh, that's fine," she says, like she was expecting it. Her tone surprises me, but I force myself not to think about why our director doesn't seem bothered about the disappearance of a key crew member less than an hour before curtain. "It's been a pleasure working with you, team. I'm proud of the show we're going to put on today, but before we get in costume, I want to do one final game with you."

I've come to like the games. Well, certain games. I'm Sorry That I still makes me cringe.

"Just to help us loosen up," Twee continues. "Let's Zip, Zap, Zop. Who wants to start?"

"I'll start," I say, clapping my hands together. If I can make enough noise, I figure, I can drown out my thoughts. For a little while at least.

I'm the sixth person out, zopping when I should have zapped. When Anton bests Phoebe to secure the win, I join in on chanting his name and I don't think about Priya. Not at all.

Not when Twee allows us to grab our first costumes and my hand brushes the ball gown.

Not when Etan tosses an uneaten sandwich crust in the garbage.

And not when I hear someone ask why all the silverware on the dining table is glued face down.

I haven't seen Priya in an hour and—now that all the set pieces are loaded onto dollies and the backdrops are in order—I can't even convince myself that she's messing with last-minute adjustments. She really isn't here. She isn't here, and we go on in thirty minutes.

The seats have begun filling up, indecipherable snippets of conversation straining at the thin wall near the dressing tables.

Crowds don't bother me. They never have. I remember peeking around the heavy velvet curtain at my first Little Star Search, seeing the enormous shadow of an audience, and feeling nothing but anticipation. But this time, it's not an anonymous crowd; those faces are familiar. These people know me.

I fumble the buttons on my bodice and the dress slips off my shoulders. A hand steadies the garment before it drops too far.

I turn, expecting Priya's hands, marred with needle pricks from last-minute costume adjustments. Instead, the hands belong to Gia, Lucy beside him with a small bouquet of wild-flowers. As Lucy passes me the flowers (mostly grass), Gia deftly buttons up my dress.

"Nervous?" he asks kindly. One of my favorite things about Gia is the way he lives on the line between silliness and serious-ness. I've never seen him choose the wrong side of that divide. He always knows exactly where to step to navigate a situation.

Lucy reads the answer on my face and pulls me into a hug.

"You're Juliette Barrera-freaking-Wright," she practically threatens. "You'll crush it."

I try to focus on my incredible friends who always show up for me when I need them, but I find my attention pulled to the nearby cast.

Maris, the Beast, stands in the wings, looking like an eighteenth-century thirst trap for the opening scene where the enchantress curses him. His royal-blue waistcoat is thrown wide, exposing a white button-down, half tucked into linen trousers that Priya rehemmed three times. Using his hand mirror—a prop with an elaborate rose painted on the back—he checks the mass of gelled curls atop his head. He runs a hand along his fade, winking at his reflection.

Etan, Gaston, paces the back wall, wireless earbuds in. His mouth moves silently as he adjusts a prop shotgun over his shoulder. The gaggle of "Silly Girls," as the script calls them, sit on milk crates and compare Color War bruises. Twee is a pinball. She bounces from person to person, barely making contact before her nervous kinetic energy carries her along to the next.

"Clear the stage, please," she singsongs at my friends without slowing.

Lucy and Gia kiss me on each cheek and tell me to break both my legs before scurrying off to their seats in the front row.

Twee calls out, "Curtain in fifteen!" and we all chorus back, "Thank you, fifteen!" to let her know we heard her.

After laying the flowers down, I apply an ungodly amount of blush across my cheeks and the tip of my nose. The chair squeaks when I sit back at "Thank you, five!"

I look like myself, but I don't. It's like the scene in *The Princess Diaries* where they detangle Mia's hair, then act shocked that she's been Anne Hathaway all along. While I was helping the production team earlier, Frankie took a curling wand to my hair and transformed my natural curls into old Hollywood beachy waves. The entire look gives me an air of soft innocence that I've never had before.

"Places in two!"

"Thank you, two!" I say, grabbing the card from Lucy and Gia's bouquet. In sloppy handwriting (Lucy's), it declares *You may be Belle, but you're still a beast :)—Lucy and Gia.*

Nearly stabbing myself in the eye, I position the card under my lower lashes and scrape the mascara brush against it. When

I'm done, my friends' names are partially obscured by black streaks. Knowing it'll find a place on the nostalgia corkboard in my room, I slide it between the pages of my script on the vanity.

My two minutes are almost up. I should've been ready thirty minutes ago, but every time I reminded myself of that fact, I found another task that might lead me to Priya and I couldn't help but take it. Hands shaking, I crimp the eyelash curler along my upper lid. My lashes stick to the metal. A light tug frees the lashes of my left eye, but when the same thing happens on the right side, a light tug isn't enough.

*Don't cry*, I caution my tear ducts, ripping the curler free and losing a few lashes.

I run my fingers beneath my eyes like windshield wipers, and freeze, staring at my reflection. I learned that from Priya.

"Places!" Twee calls, voice cracking slightly.

"Thank you, places," I cry, gathering my skirts and sprinting to stand beside Maris.

A hush rolls through the theater at the lights flickering on and off three times. Maris takes a deep breath, the lights go down, and with his head held high, he strides through the curtain.

On the stage, the lights are so bright that the audience is merely a dark void. It's a relief. I can picture what I want to see: Pat nodding proudly and Priya mouthing my words like a stage mom. I wish I could look Galahad in the eye as I option up—singing an octave higher than the song calls for—at the end of my introduction song and prove that this is *my* part.

Even Gaston, harassing me, breaks character with a wide-eyed eyebrow raise when I hit a high D. The cast backstage goes berserk, mobbing me after I exit.

"Money note," Maris proclaims, whacking my shoulder with his magic mirror.

"Watch the props!" Frankie hisses at him.

The mood backstage is largely relaxed as the scenes zing by. Etan twerks slowly to the orchestral soundtrack and Maris does the Macarena to a song about the death of my mother.

Only I, preoccupied with Priya's disappearance, can't find an ounce of calm. Every moment in the wings, I wait for her to push through the curtain with a breathless explanation.

I know my jitters are worsening as the ballroom scene approaches, because Maris places a comforting paw on my shoulder just before our cue.

I look away from the emergency exit, finding Maris's eyes through the holes in his mask.

"We got this," he whispers, comforting me for the wrong reason. He offers me a furry fist bump, then leads me onstage.

I follow, with childlike wonder. "I've never attended a ball before," I marvel.

Maris stops suddenly. I slam into his back a little too forcefully and the audience laughs.

"Never attended a ball?" the Beast exclaims, incredulous. "Missus Tops!"

At his bellow, Missus Tops runs onto the stage in a gray maid's costume that I helped Priya distress using a knife. She drops into a dramatic curtsy. "Yes, m'lord?"

"How could you not notice that this poor wretch has never

attended a ball? Make haste," he snaps. "Take the lady to her quarters and prepare her for a ball."

"This very moment, m'lord? You mean to have a ball . . . now?" she asks tentatively.

"Yes, this very moment! Yes, now!" Maris projects his voice so strongly that it echoes off the walls. "What is the point of servants if they don't listen?" he asks the audience with a disappointed headshake.

"Very good, sire." She nods quickly and takes my hand, dragging me to the other half of the stage.

We hit our mark and all the lights go dark except for one, focused on Gaston, standing atop a table in the tavern set. His mob song starts alone, low and sinister, before it's joined by the backing string instruments, a steady drum, and, eventually, the other villagers.

With the audience enraptured by Gaston's voice, I slip behind the wardrobe and go from graceful to harried. I whip my vest off and spin, hands outstretched, ready to slide into the glittering ball gown being held up by a stagehand.

But when I come face-to-face with Priya, all the hurry goes out of me in a whoomph. She offers me a luminous smile, whispering, "You're doing great."

I barely move as she pushes the sleeves up my arms and reaches around me in a hug to secure the magnets down the side.

Priya steps back to fluff up the skirt, and I distantly register Etan's solo coming to an end. She plucks at the dress. Her smile turns shy, knowing. "I never did finish this."

I breathe out a laugh. "Good."

She wears all black. Everything, from her head scarf to her chunky shoes, is black. Raven feathers, queen of spades black. I knew she wouldn't be backstage in stark, noticeable white, but it still feels weirdly like a miracle to see her like this.

I'm transfixed. Etan's syrupy baritone and my adrenaline were already mixing to form a drug in my veins. And then I saw Priya, dressed like a starless sky.

Before I step out with a flourish, I look back at her and say the first thing that comes to mind, "You look gorgeous. Wear black to your wedding."

All the color drains from her face.

It's the last thing I see when I take the stage in her dress, to thunderous applause.

# THE GIFT OF THE MAGI

After I give my final bow, my blood is thrumming in my veins. For the last few hours, everything has been so loud: the music, the microphone-amplified voices, the crowd. Now silence ricochets around in my skull, setting off a massive headache.

People pull me into hugs, with whispered congratulations, even though we don't have to whisper backstage anymore. The core cast does one last group cheer of Twee's name. Tonight, there will be a camp-sanctioned party for the cast and crew, but, while I've developed friendships with them, I would trade one hundred wrap parties for Senior Twilight.

I catch sight of the clock while removing my ten billionth bobby pin. The Senior Twilighters are probably gathering their supplies and meeting with Pat right about now.

This will be the first time I don't watch the seniors leave camp. I can't face ten years of wanting, hoping. I'd imagined it so clearly. My eyes blindfolded by the stiff fabric of a black bandana with SENIOR TWILIGHT printed on the front. The weight of my backpack clutched on my lap. The crunch and rumble of Pat's Jeep off-roading on the forest trails, bouncing me against my seat belt. The woods, the night sky. Me, finally breaking the tree line as Pat announces my name.

Now, I'll never know what it's like.

I'll. Never. Know.

A handful of bobby pins slips from my fist and clatters to the floor. The few cast members still milling about backstage don't seem to notice me careening into the hallway.

When I cry, it's not pretty or subtle. Full, body-racking sobs weaken my knees and drop me to the floor, where I curl up and weep into the neckline of Priya's unfinished ball gown.

I cry for all the past selves I've let down. I grieve the things I'll never have. The Senior Twilight bandana that'll never hang on my corkboard. The story I never get to tell. The proof that I could've done it.

I cry for the person I've become that I don't even recognize, the one who does plays and gave up Senior Twilight to help Priya goddamn Pendley. I cry for the person who *cares* that Priya Pendley missed three-fourths of the play we both worked so hard on. I cry for all of it.

A joyful voice bursts through the curtain. "Juliette! Are you— Holy shit!"

Lucy trips over my body and lands hard on top of me, rolling so we're face-to-face. Swiping her ginger hair out of her eyes, she props herself up on an elbow and grins. "Didn't see you there."

I duck, sure the makeup on my face has become an unflattering Jackson Pollock painting.

Lucy falters, registering the state I'm in. "Who did this? I'll kill them."

That wrenches a watery laugh from me. "I, I—" Choking on the words, I cover my face.

"Hey, what's going on?" Lucy pulls me into a horizontal hug.

"Everything—" I shudder. "It's—"

She shushes me, smoothing down my hair. Instead of being comforting, it tugs at the bobby pins still stuck there, causing sharp twinges of pain with each stroke.

"I screwed everything up," I whisper into her shoulder.

Gently, she pushes my hands aside so she can see my face. "What are you talking about?"

Shrugging helplessly, I cover my face again. Waves of tears break against my palms.

"Breathe," Lucy commands. "Slow breaths." She demonstrates loudly. I struggle at first, but slowly gain control of myself.

I lean my forehead against hers and repeat, "I screwed everything up."

She pulls back in disbelief. "What? You did fine. I mean, you fumbled that one line, but Etan covered it well. I wouldn't have even noticed if I didn't rehearse with you!"

I swipe at my face with my sleeve, staining it with mascara. "Not that. Life. Camp. I think I—Priya—" I whine, my voice turning up at the edges, "I want to do Senior Twilight."

Lucy throws her head back and laughs. "Oh my God. Problem solved. Pat sent me to get you. He said if Nurse Mari approves it, he'll let you go tonight."

The shock stops me cold. "What?"

She nods. "He'll explain. We should head over." Her gaze travels my body. "After we get you into different clothes. Although, a ball gown would be a badass look tomorrow morning."

"Wait. Wait, he just . . . ? What did he say exactly?"

"Let me think." Climbing to her feet, Lucy offers me a hand and scrubs at my face with the cuff of her gray Henley. It comes away covered in black blotches. "He said"—she drops her voice into a lower register—"'Miss Swentek, if you cause any trouble tonight, I'm pre-firing you.' And I said, 'Patty, if I don't cause trouble tonight, it's because a panther got me.' And he said, 'Miss Swentek, there are no panthers in California.' And I said—"

"Luce," I say, following her onto the stage and up the aisle. The seats, which had been empty for so long, are now covered in playbills and forgotten water bottles. Contraband gum wrappers litter the space between rows.

She sighs. "For someone who was just the lead in a play, you have no patience for drama. He should be the one to tell you. I don't know exactly what happened. But apparently, if Mari says you're good to do Twilight, you're good."

We push through the doors of the theater, and I'm startled by how bright it still is outside.

"Do you want my advice as Fogridge's resident trickster god?" Lucy asks with a sidelong glance.

I sigh. "Probably not."

"I love you, so I'll say it anyway." Lucy laughs before dropping her voice to a near-whisper. "If I were you, I would do whatever it took to make Mari say you're good."

———

"Welcome to Senior Twilight."

About thirty of us gather at the base of the pavilion, looking up at Pat on the top step.

I cross my hiking-pants-clad legs, kicking the small bag sitting at my feet. I packed it while Lucy cleaned my face with the diligence of a mom whose toddler got into the chocolate fountain at a Golden Corral.

I haven't visited Nurse Mari for assessment yet. The fact that I might see this send-off and still be denied the chance to participate is very close to sending me back into hysterics. And a bothersome voice in the back of my mind points out that nothing has changed about the promise I made to Galahad. I shouldn't be here. If I get in that Jeep and walk back to camp tomorrow to Pat announcing my name, I'll just be the exact person she thinks I am.

"I'm glad we have such a good turnout this year." Despite his words, Pat's mouth is set in a firm line. "Now, there may be rain tonight. We know that; we've been watching the radar. Rain is okay. I've camped in the rain many times. As have many of you, I'm sure."

Some campers in the crowd groan-laugh knowingly, Lucy included.

"What isn't okay is lightning." He surveys us each in turn. "If I hear a hint of thunder—Lord, if a suspicious-sounding *truck* drives by too loudly—I am personally going into the forest and pulling each and every one of you out."

There's a soft murmur of objection from the group.

Pat holds up a steadying hand. "I know, I know. I get how important Senior Twilight is to you all. *Some* of you have been asking to do it for years." He shoots a pointed look at Lucy. Unbothered, she finger-guns back at him. "But do you know what's more important than Senior Twilight? My kids' safety."

I'm starting to get warm, fuzzy feelings. He's never been the touchy-feely type, but Pat makes it clear that the campers at Fogridge, especially those of us who have been around for a while, are like children to him. And, unlike other adults who say that just to get us to shut up and follow instructions, I know that Pat truly means it.

He continues, "Plus, with what a summer camp makes in this day and age, I couldn't afford that many hospital bills."

Ah. Just like that, Pat goes from protective dad back to camp director.

"Like I said, though, I know that Senior Twilight means something. Not only to you, but to your siblings and friends. To your former counselors and peers who decided not to take part. I would never take that away from any of you. If we do end up having to evacuate tonight, you can camp in my garage, and I'll drop you back off a few hundred feet up the trail in the morning. We'll pretend it never happened. You'll all still get to walk into camp in the morning having conquered the Senior Twilight."

I don't know who hugs him first, but soon we're all squished together. TK, the only counselor among a handful of specialists, watches from beside a pile of sleeping bags. She beams proudly at her father.

At first, he resists our embrace, shouting, "Side hugs only! This is not camp appropriate!" Eventually he gives in, though he holds his hands straight up so as not to touch any of us.

Priya sidles up next to me, elbowing my ribs. She is wearing a crisp white jumpsuit. On a scale of Red-Carpet Event to Very Clean Car Mechanic, this outfit falls squarely in the middle. It's an absurd choice for a night of camping, but she looks stunning. "Decided to show up, huh?"

My eyebrows draw together involuntarily. I'm caught off guard by her . . . accusing me of something? I don't know, but it leaves me with a weird taste in my mouth.

Before I can answer, Pat escapes the fray. He catches my eyes, indicating an empty spot off the path. "Juliette, a word?"

I approach him slowly because I've never seen Pat looking so solemn. He leads me beneath a blooming jacaranda tree, away from the busy throng of campers moving bags. We're still in view of everyone, but far enough away that they can't hear us. The camp's owner origamis his long limbs into a sitting position and gestures for me to join him.

"I won't beat around the bush," he starts, his voice low. "Priya spoke to me about what's been going on with you and Galahad. You should've come to me, Juliette."

I dart a glance over to the steps. Lucy sees me looking and waves enthusiastically. Priya glances away the second we make eye contact. I drop my gaze to the ground.

"No, no, no," Pat protests quickly. "I'm not blaming you. The way Galahad has been acting, at least according to Priya, Lucy, and Gia, has been completely inappropriate. *Completely* inappropriate. Now, I've spoken to her and she's packing her bags as we speak."

My head shoots up. "I didn't want to get her fired! Did she—" I stop myself, feeling both pathetic and disappointed that my first thought was to ask whether or not she watched the play.

He claps. "Juliette, you *didn't* get her fired. It's very important to me that you understand that. Her own actions got her fired. No matter her reasons, she's the adult and you're a child."

I balk a little at being called a child, but I know what Pat means.

"She should've discussed her problems with a staff member. It wasn't your responsibility to manage her emotions. It was your responsibility to enjoy your last year at camp." He sighs, looking up at the periwinkle jacaranda flowers. "And now I'm afraid that you haven't."

My automatic reaction is to tell him that he's wrong, but before I say it, I think—actually think—about whether it's true. It hasn't been a normal summer, but I'd be lying if I pretended that a few bad experiences ruined the entire thing. "Twilight would help make it better," I hedge.

"Wonderful." Pat slaps his hands on his lap and stands, offering me a hand. "I do want to make sure your ankle is properly healed before I send you off, but I think you and Miss Pendley are going to enjoy your Senior Twilight."

I nod gratefully, then the words register. "Me *and* Miss Pendley?"

Pat's long legs have already carried him a few feet away from me by the time he notices I've stopped. He backtracks to meet me. "Yes, you can thank her for this, actually. She came to see me just before the play and explained everything. She was the one who suggested I have Mari take a look at you, and she promised she would keep an eye on you for the night."

Priya agreed to . . . babysit me?

"Miss Pendley is a born leader." His tone is teasing, but his next words strike straight through me. "If she were here last year, you would've had stiff competition for North Star."

# IF A TREE FALLS IN THE FOREST

Nurse Mari gave the official okay after I lied through my teeth in the med center, feigning indifference when she torqued my foot this way and that. I managed not to flinch when she asked me to jump up and down. It wasn't my brightest idea, but once the hype of the Twilighters enveloped me, I knew the only thing that would stop me from going would be sudden death.

Pat clapped me on the back in congratulations, then set to organizing. Each Twilighter was assigned a number in case of an emergency head count. I'm five. Specialists shoved a makeshift bag together for me while Pat carted everyone else into the forest. Now I'm here.

It's happening.

"It'll take longer to drop you all off with one less seat available," Pat explains as he loads the first packs into the trunk bed. "But nobody wants you kids blindfolded alone in the woods with an old man."

"We trust you, Pat!" a senior named Nick yells.

"Why?" Pat responds, all seriousness. "I love all you kids like family, but that doesn't mean you should trust me. It's safer for everyone if Euphrates tags along as my lawsuit shield."

Groans rise from the crowd. Pat telling us not to trust him—

and sincerely meaning it—is precisely the reason we do trust him. He doesn't react to the protestations, just watches us from his pedestal of paternal indulgence.

"Stop trying to teach us things and just murder us already," Nick jeers half-heartedly.

In an obvious attempt to defuse tension, Euphrates peers at us through binoculars made from his hands. "Don't worry, you're safe with me. I got y'all."

"I wish," Lucy says under her breath, slumping into my side.

"Engaged," I remind her quietly.

"Hot," she reminds me.

Even after the hiking specialist ties the Senior Twilight bandana around my eyes, checks my seat belt buckle, and confirms that I know how to use the emergency walkie-talkie, I still don't believe this is happening. The car rocks, Euphrates climbing in shotgun.

The Jeep takes each bump of the upward slope with graceless speed. I breathe in the rich smell of dirt and ponderosa pines while the wind whips my hair around my face.

While Pat drops off a different senior, we sit in total silence. It's a rule; once you set foot in the car, you are alone.

Except, I'm not alone, am I? Priya sits beside me, having saved the day yet again. Logically, I know I should praise her. Wasn't I *just* crying on the floor over not doing this? I should be thankful that she told Pat about Galahad, that she read me like a book when I lied about being fine. I should be happy I'm spending the night with someone I like being around.

But the only emotion boiling inside me during the sensory-deprived trip up the mountain is anger, the kind I haven't felt since I saw Priya Pendley emerge from Polaris's bathroom on the first day of camp.

The vehicle slows to another stop and Pat taps our shoulders, the signal that it's our turn to exit. He guides us by our arms away from the Jeep's path. I don't know how long we walk before he spins us a few times, releases us, and leaves without saying a word.

I wait until Pat's footsteps are far enough that I can't hear their crunch on the leaves anymore. Within seconds of taking my blindfold off, I am stalking away from Priya.

"I'm not staying with you," I announce.

"Juliette—" Priya starts, ripping off her bandana.

I sigh loudly, cutting her off. My eyes follow the tree line. There isn't a footpath, wherever we are, but a narrow animal trail branches away from the summit. "I'm so tired, dude." I don't clarify. Even if I wanted to, I couldn't. The exhaustion I feel is too huge for words.

She wraps her arms around herself. "I wanted to help. You . . . wanted this."

"I did," I say, crumpling up the bandana, fist tightening around it. "But I didn't give up Senior Twilight so you could miss the play."

Yes, I wanted Senior Twilight, but I didn't want it like this. I didn't want to get Galahad fired, even if Pat says it wasn't my fault. I didn't want the only people I cared about seeing my performance to miss it. I wanted to prove I was good for something, for sticking to my word, for committing. Not doing the Twilight was a crappy decision, but it was *my* crappy decision.

"I didn't miss the whole play," Priya protests. "I only missed half! It was worth it."

"You can't just choose! You don't get to trade your thing in for mine." I wring the bandana, nearly tearing it in half. "This isn't . . . I didn't want Galahad to get fired."

She exhales a laugh. "You might be too stubborn to see this Juliette, but it's not just about you. How do you know you were the only one she was being unjust to?"

"Can you do anything without being a martyr?" I clutch at shallow breaths, my heart fluttering riotously. "I don't need justice from knight-in-shining-armor Priya Pendley and her ridiculous white pantsuit."

"Oh my God!" Priya fists her hair, throwing her head back as far as it will go. "Chill. It's no big deal if you need help! I need help all the time—"

"I. Don't. Care," I spit, my voice rising. The forest is deadly silent around us. "I do not care what you do or what you need. I am so tired of being handed things because you—"

Priya's green eyes flash. In one swift motion, she's standing in front of me, jaw clenched. "You know what, I'd be tired too if I spent every moment of every *fucking* day inventing new ways the world is against me!"

I bite the inside of my lower lip so hard I'm afraid I'll draw blood. "Back off, Pendley."

She raises her chin and says, "Or what? You're gonna hit me for helping you?"

I shove my fists in the pockets of my hoodie. The collar bites into the back of my neck. I inhale violently, saying nothing.

"Then hit me." She angles her head to the side and taps her jawline with her forefinger. "Right here. Do it."

"Screw you," I say, turning my back on her.

As I walk away down the animal trail, she calls after me, "Don't die tonight, asshole!"

I flip her the middle finger over my shoulder, turning down the path and out of her sight.


Dusk comes and goes quickly, as it always does in the forest. I didn't notice when the light started to fade, but now the sky is that special blue, deep yet bright, that you only find on a summer evening. I switch my flashlight on, trying to outrun the sense of dread that stalks me.

I haven't found a place to set up camp. I don't need anywhere fancy, just a spot where I won't be crushed to death by a widow-maker—a dead tree limb poised to fall on an ill-prepared camper. Normally, the worst-case scenario would be to have to cowboy-camp in just my sleeping bag, but with the rain coming, that's not an option.

It was silly to let my annoyance fuel me as I walked. I argued with an imaginary Priya for twenty minutes instead of looking for shelter. I was so deep in a tantrum of my own making that I'm surprised I didn't walk right off a cliff.

There's a tiny clearing with two thick trees to hang my tarp between. Before I get my hopes up, I point my flashlight up, checking for loose branches that might dislodge and kill me in my sleep. I make a full, careful circuit to ensure the area is safe.

And that is why I am looking up, instead of at the ground, when my foot lands directly inside a burrow. I drop suddenly, injured ankle deep in the dirt. The weight of my pack tips me forward, but I drop to my left knee quickly to keep from face-planting. Despite the strum of pain running up the back of my leg and hip, I am okay. I wiggle my foot back and forth, evaluating my ankle. It's a little sore, but not unbearable.

I sigh a hymn of relief.

I'm okay.

With a twist, I lower myself onto my butt. That's the mistake. I'm wedged in the hole such that when I turn my entire body around, my foot stays where it is.

There is no snap this time.

The only sound I make is a quiet, desperate whimper.

# 3 4

## THE TRUCK AND THE SNAKE PIT

I take a deep breath and urge my body out of flight mode. It's so peaceful here—my flashlight illuminating the trees and the birds singing sweetly—that I feel like my ankle and my mind are in two different planes of reality. I tilt my head up to see the canopy above while I slowly rotate my foot to gauge how bad the injury is.

It's not as bad as the first fall. Not even close. But I haven't set up my tarp or my tent. I still have a rain-slicked night ahead of me. If anything goes wrong . . . I shake my head. My fingers automatically go to the yellow-and-black walkie-talkie clipped into my waistband.

If I tap out, I won't walk into camp tomorrow morning and hear Pat call my name. Worse, he'll know I lied to Nurse Mari. Even if he believes whatever harebrained story I make up, he'll know I didn't stay with Priya like I told him I would. It would disappoint him. And I can't. I can't do that tonight. Not my last summer. Not on Senior Twilight.

I don't have to survive out here forever—just 'til morning. I ease my foot out of the hole, stabilizing my ankle with both hands. It doesn't feel swollen, and I think that's a good sign. Slowly, I slide the straps of my backpack off and unzip it. Right at the top rests a small first aid kit in a white box. I dig through it until I find the compression wrap.

While I'm wrapping my ankle, flashlight in my mouth, I think. I could set up here. I was lucky enough to find a safe place before I did the exact thing Pat warned me not to do, so at least one thing has gone right. I could do most of the tent assembly sitting down. As I think this, I'm struck with a premonition of dropping one of the metal tent poles on my ankle. I recoil.

I don't want to stay here, alone and hurt. But the alternatives— crawling (literally) back to Priya or calling for an evacuation—give me a stomachache. I soothe the anger at my own carelessness. Time's not on my side; I can't waste it. Pat was very clear that it *would* rain tonight.

I need to choose. Now.

I tuck my pack under my right calf, elevating my foot off the ground. The aching throb of my ankle marginally subsides, leaving my thoughts a little clearer. I swing my flashlight in a wide arc, toward the trail I just left behind.

*Think, Juliette.*

But I'm distracted, reminded of a conversation I had with Priya at the beginning of camp, which feels like years ago. She was on a *Survivor* diatribe while we lay on our respective beds during rest hour.

*"In every episode of* Survivor, *someone gets voted out,"* she was saying. *"But sometimes, people have things called idols that keep them from going home, even if they get the most votes. This is important. Are you listening? Pay attention."* She looked over.

I gave an unenthusiastic *"Mm-hmm."*

*"They have to play the idol before they know what the votes are."*

Despite my bored front, I was interested. *"How do they know when to play it?"*

Her eyes went wide with excitement. Through the balustrades, she appeared to be trapped in one of those magician boxes, body cut into strips. The slats obscured her mouth, so I scooted up in bed in order to see her as she spoke. *"They don't. That's what makes it exciting. People burn them all the time unnecessarily. And, one season, a guy went home with two idols in his pocket."*

*"Ouch."*

She hummed in agreement. *"Here's what I think is most interesting. Listen. Do you know about the truck and the snake pit?"*

*"If it's a* Survivor *thing, I don't know about it,"* I responded, point-blank.

Priya gave a warm laugh. *"It's not* just Survivor. *But okay, imagine you're standing in the middle of a mountain road."*

*"All right."*

*"And suddenly, around a bend, a truck comes barreling toward you. You look for somewhere to go, but the side of the road with grass is too far. On the side closer to you, there's a ditch you can jump into. But!"* She sat up, bouncing with excitement. *"The ditch is full of snakes. And you're afraid of snakes. Like, deathly, deathly afraid."* She raised her eyebrows.

*"Okay?"* I prompted.

"So, now you've made the decision about the snakes. Snakes versus no snakes. You've forgotten that the bigger problem is 'get hit by a truck or don't get hit by a truck.' The snakes are irrelevant. People don't play their idols because they want to save them for the future. They turn it into 'play the idol or save the idol' when, actually, it's 'potentially go home versus stay.'"

In the quiet of the forest clearing, I try to decide what the truck and snake pit are.

Priya was right. This isn't me versus her, or even me versus Senior Twilight. This is safety versus danger. My options are simple: find Priya and finish the night with her help or call Pat and tap out. Setting up a subpar camp, in the dark, with an injury, racing a storm, is nothing more than standing in the road because I'm afraid of snakes.

My pride is not worth my life. Although, it does kind of feel like it is.

I haul myself to my feet, grabbing a nearby fallen branch to use as a walking stick, and head back the way I came.

Sweat stings my eyes as I struggle my way back to my drop-off point. This is foolish, goes my mantra. This is foolish. This is foolish.

No matter how much my rational side tries to convince me, I don't stop. The palms of my hands quickly blister, then bleed, against the rough bark of my makeshift walking stick.

The pain doesn't improve. I guess I've seen enough movies that I thought sheer grit and determination could hold the pain at bay. Like, if I wanted to finish the Senior Twilight bad enough, it would just happen.

My ankle would wait to be injured.

Mind over matter.

That is not how it works. The pain gets worse. Every time I think I've adjusted to it, I put my foot down on uneven ground and an electric shock shoots up my leg. By the time I reach the drop-off point, I could collapse. If I sit down, though, I won't get up again.

I pause, weighing the different directions Priya could have gone in. She didn't follow me, that's for sure. That leaves downhill, which is back toward Fogridge, uphill toward the summit, or straight ahead. I look up the hill. I know, deep in my gut, that she went up that animal trail.

I try to convince myself that I'm wrong, because if I am wrong, I'll have chosen the most painful option for no reason. But my eyes find a human-size break in the bush. I'm right.

I cling to the walking stick while my free hand worries at the button of the walkie-talkie. I even press it, just to hear the crackle over the speaker. Just to make sure it's still working.

Then I start up the hill.

Ten more steps and then I'll call, I tell myself.

Step, clunk, step, clunk.

Ten steps later, I say it again. Ten more steps. Then I'll call.

Twigs crack under my sneakers. Remaining upright takes all my focus. These feet have run miles. Broken records. They have always landed underneath me. Ten more steps.

This pain will end, I coach myself. People have been through worse than this. I channel my inner Barry and his PAIN IS WEAKNESS LEAVING THE BODY tattoo.

This is not the worst thing to ever happen.

What about that man whose brain was impaled by a railroad spike? He survived. I once heard a podcast about a woman whose husband tried to murder her by cutting her parachute lines before she skydived. She jumped out of a plane, fell forty thousand feet to Earth, and survived.

My ankle probably isn't even broken. Ten more steps.

I'm holding down the walkie button now, tapping it out like a heartbeat. Soon this will be too difficult. I can't hold the walking stick and my flashlight and navigate rain at the same time. But for now, it's only ten more steps.

This is foolish.

Every time I top a crest, I hope to see Priya. After this ridge, the trees will part and she'll be sitting there. But no. After one crest, there's just another crest. After one tree, there's just another tree. After one step, there's just another step.

Ten more steps. One more crest. Ten more steps. This pain will end.

And then it starts to rain.

In the way that all California storms are born, it starts as a faint drizzle—light enough to make me think I imagined it, that a squirrel is shaking dew loose overhead. Seconds later, fat drops are landing directly in my eyes, and I realize that I am not meant to walk triumphantly out of Senior Twilight tomorrow morning.

This is as good a spot as any.

I plop down on the ground, taking a moment to lie flat on my back in the mud. Maybe if it rains enough, a mudslide will carry me back down the hill, all the way to Polaris. And I'll hide there in shame until I can get back in my car and drive away on Sunday morning.

The words play over and over in my head. *Pat, this is Juliette Barrera-Wright. I'm officially tapping out. I'm* officially tapping out. I am.

I can't believe this is how my last summer at Fogridge ends. The rain falls faster, in cold sharp spikes that get caught on my closed eyelashes before pouring down my face like tears. Turning my head to the side so I don't waterboard myself before I'm rescued, I bring the walkie to my mouth and click the button.

"Pat," I say. Removing my finger from the button, I loose a shaky breath. This is so silly. A rod didn't impale me through the skull. I didn't fall forty thousand feet from a plane. People are dying, Kim. I cannot be upset about this. "This is Juliette Barrera-Wright." I cannot be upset. I can't. "I am officially tapping out."

I cradle the walkie to my chest. I think I'll just lie here and pretend to be dead until someone rescues me.

A voice crackles over the walkie, staticky and distant. Pat says, "Please repeat. I didn't read that."

Oh my God. Maybe I won't have to pretend. Maybe I will truly die here before someone comes. How fast does pneumonia set in? I think I feel a cough coming on.

I lift the walkie to my mouth, but before I can speak, the

low hum of someone pressing the button vibrates through the speaker. I wait for the noise to end so I can shamefully repeat myself, but it keeps going.

The rain is so, so loud.

And I am so, so dramatic.

I toggle the button, but the staticky noise doesn't go away. The walkie won't pick up my message until the channel is clear. Great. I tilt my head back again and lay spread eagle in the mud with my eyes closed.

Then I hear a voice. Not over the walkie but from somewhere close to me, and from someone who is very out of breath. "You look like crap."

# 3 5

## SAVIOR COMPLEX

I futilely try to wipe the rain away. A beam shines right into my eyes like a police flashlight. I reach out to push it to the side.

Above me, Priya leans into her knees, breathing heavily. She clips her walkie onto her belt, extending a hand in my direction.

"You hurt your ankle again," she pants. It's not a question.

"How do you know?" I turn my head enough to watch her through the corner of one eye.

"I knew the second you walkie'd. So, can I help you yet?" She practically screams in order to be heard over the roar of rain.

I laugh, looking down at my soaked clothing. "Yeah. I'll allow it." I slide my muddy hand into hers and let her pull me to my feet. I wince, my weight shifting back onto my injured ankle.

She lifts my pack off my shoulders in one fluid motion as I stand. Then she slaps me on the back of the head lightly. "You stubborn doofus. I can't believe you actually called."

"I wasn't going to!" I yell. "But I thought about the truck—"

"The truck and the snake pit," she finishes, smiling broadly. "Jeff would be so proud."

She takes my hand, hauling me toward the summit, exactly in the direction I'd been heading. I fall in step with her. I want to ask a million questions, but it takes all my energy to plant my feet in such a way that I won't fall.

"Pat to Senior Twilighters." His voice comes in a loud ear-splitting blast over both of our walkies at once. Priya twists the dial to turn hers down. "Confirming I did not hear an evac call. Please check in by number."

Priya watches me, as if she half expects me to say I still want Pat to pull me. "Tell me you aren't going," she says.

"One, Rayshawn Allen," crackles the speaker. "No problems here."

"Juliette," Priya presses.

I look down at my ankle as the next call comes in from Max Atkinson, two. Maybe a wiser person would leave. I might have Priya to help me now, but I am still hurt.

"Three, Laura Averdick. I didn't call, Pat."

I open my mouth as Priya meets my gaze. The pouring rain separates us like a curtain. We both stop as the fourth name comes through.

"Sarah Badree. All good here. Oh, whoops. Sorry, I'm number four."

"Stay," Priya says.

I want to. I don't know why I'm hesitating.

"Number five?" Pat calls after a minute.

Priya comes to a stop, swinging me around to face her. "Please."

I take a deep breath, hold the walkie up, and say, "Five. Juliette Barrera-Wright." I release the talk button and shoot Priya the biggest smile I can manage through the ankle pain. "I'm having the time of my life. No evac needed."

Priya's face melts into a soft smile. She slings an arm around my shoulder and continues leading us up the mountain. On her turn, she answers in definitive staccato sentences. "Hey, Pat. It's Priya Pendley. Twelve. I'm good."

I don't know what was worrying me, but after I hear her report in, muscles I didn't notice I'd been tensing suddenly relax. It's not far to her tent, sheltered beneath a tarp. We both laugh with relief when we step out of the rain.

Voices continue to check in. We hear Lucy, her voice bouncing up and down with characteristic cockiness, "Seventeen, Lucy Swentek. I'm gucci, Patty-o. See you in the morning."

Priya and I laugh. Once the check-ins are complete, she nods at the tent, indicating that I should enter.

I sigh at the idea of warmth and dryness. But then I pause at the entrance. My pack is sopping wet. Which means my tent, my clothes, my everything is unusable.

Priya notices my silent debate as she slings my pack onto the dry ground beside one of the trees. "I have clothes you can wear." Then she tilts her head. "Kind of. We'll figure something out. And don't worry, it's not the ridiculous white pantsuit."

I cringe, letting my head fall back. "I'm an asshole," I tell the tarp above.

"Sure are," Priya says with a smile. She still doesn't enter the tent, and it finally registers that her clothes are soaked, too.

"Tell me your pack is within reach," I say hopefully.

"Nope. Back corner." She twirls a finger, directing me to spin while she undresses and enters the tent. She takes long enough that I give up and collapse onto the ground, bringing my ankle into my lap and massaging it.

She comes back out in a white tank top and overalls. One strap is over her shoulder and the other dangles at her waist. She holds a bundle of white clothes out toward me.

"You can't sleep in overalls," I tell her, realizing she's handing me her sleep clothes.

She shakes the bundle at me again, and I finally take it. "Either I sleep in overalls or you sleep in overalls, pumpkin," she says, overly sweet. She points at the tent. "I'll be inside when you're finished getting dressed."

The flap falls behind her, and I hear the zipper close with a whoosh.

Alone, soaked, and sitting on the ground, I falter. There's a fluttering in my chest as I quickly undress, trying to repress the inherent weirdness of being almost totally naked outdoors. I toss my hastily chosen Senior Twilight outfit in a pile on the ground and change into Priya's white shirt and terry cloth shorts. The clothes are soft—and, more importantly, dry. Once they're on, a cloud of sweet, citrusy lemongrass surrounds me and sends my stomach plummeting.

I unzip the tent flap and crawl in, glad to be off my feet for the foreseeable future. Priya lazily scrolls whatever feed she has open. On the lowest setting, her phone's flashlight casts a soft glow over the interior of the tent, and okay, I admit it. I was wrong to make fun of her for bringing the phone.

She looks up, jiggling her phone at me. "See? Signal every-where."

The tent is a lot smaller than it looked from the outside. My sleeping bag is out of commission, so Priya's pristine white one lies fully unzipped across the center of the tent. I make no attempt at poise, toppling right onto the down-filled nylon. It rustles sweetly beneath me, and I think it's my new favorite sound.

"I can't believe you actually called," she says again, patting her walkie, which is now lying silent next to her pack, like it's a good dog.

I don't lift my cheek from the sleeping bag, so my voice comes out muffled. "I couldn't believe I did it either."

"I figured everything had to have gone to shit for you to tap out." She shrugs. The metal closures of her overalls clink at the movement. "That's why I came to find you before you could finish the call."

I flash back to the moment I first saw her in the rain, with her hand on her walkie. My mouth drops open. "Oh my God. You were the one keeping me from getting through to Pat."

"It was for a worthy cause."

"You have a savior complex," I say into the sleeping bag.

"It's an affliction." She drops her head, grinning.

I run a finger along one seam of the sleeping bag, tracing it back and forth so my nail catches on the stitches. "How did you know where to find me?"

"Uh," Priya pauses. Her eyes flick to her walkie again and she runs a hand through her wet hair. Whereas I'm sure my curls have clumped into a shapeless mass, her hair still somehow looks good wet—more influencer at the Met Gala than drowning

Shetland puppy. "I didn't know. I figured I'd run around and try to spot your flashlight. And would ya look at that? I did."

I close my eyes. I argue with her because that's who I am, but the words are sleepy and flat. "I needed help. I could have died. What if you slipped and fell while running and you tumbled down the mountain and got knocked unconscious and landed on top of your walkie's call button and Pat never heard me."

Priya's voice sounds like she's holding back a smile. "Well, in that situation, I'd have bigger problems than your ankle, to be honest. But that was never going to happen. I told you, I'm lucky."

I let my eyelids flutter open until I'm looking at her through half-lidded, skeptical eyes. "First of all, nobody is lucky. Luck happens *to* people. Second, you can't call yourself lucky for having to run in the rain, carry my pack, give up half your tent, and sleep in overalls."

Priya tucks her legs under herself and meets my eyes. There's a mischievous quirk to her eyebrows when she says, "Why not?"

I smile sleepily. "I have it on pretty good authority that all of those things suck."

"Maybe you're the lucky one, then."

I snort and flip over onto my back, resting my hands on my stomach. "Unlikely."

"Maybe we've spent so much time together that all my luck has left me and transferred over to you."

I snap my fingers, a foiled Scooby-Doo villain. "If only I'd known all along that that would happen. I would've worked hard to convince you not to hate me sooner."

"I never hated you." She looks down at me, face pinched. "Did you think I hated you? If anything, I've always been jealous of you."

I make an incredulous noise. "What?"

Priya sighs and tucks her hands behind her head. "You're only ever yourself. You do what you want. You say what you mean." Her mouth twists to one side, like she's not sure if she should continue, but she does anyway. "I know it's not fair for me to complain about this, but you don't know what my life is like."

The old resentment flares inside me for a moment, though I manage to stay silent and focus on her words.

"People are always looking at me. And judging me. All of the time. I have to be on, constantly. Fogridge is the first place I've gone where I can actually step out of the spotlight, and even here . . . I mean, you said it yourself. On a trip where the point was for me to be alone in the woods, for nobody to see me for twelve hours, I wore a custom white jumpsuit. That fabric was eighty dollars a yard." At my blank stare, she adds, "That's a lot."

"Okay," I say.

"I know how fortunate I am, but I'm, like, trapped in a zoo. I can be the best version of myself all the time. I can be pretty, with perfectly done hair and makeup on point. I can be kind and friendly and gracious, not cry when people DM me death threats and essays about how disgusting and ugly I am. If I try to be real about how I'm feeling, people call me privileged and ungrateful. If I try to show appreciation, they call me fake and shallow. Even if I do everything right all the time, they find something vicious and hateful to say. I can't even be seen in another color because preteen me decided to make white her 'brand.'

"I mean, I love my parents, right? But even they feed into it. I *know*—logically—they would still love me if I decided I didn't want to get my hair and nails done every two weeks, but it doesn't always feel like it." Her eyes flash to me, glistening with unshed tears. "And I'm happy with my life. I really am. I love Priyatopia and my clothes and my car and the fact that I never have to worry about money. I wouldn't trade it. But sometimes I just . . ." She stops and takes a deep breath. Her eyes close. Complete stillness. The silence stretches, not like a rubber band but like slime, drooping under its own weight.

"Want to dig a hole in the ground and stand in it for a year?" I suggest softly.

Priya barks a laugh, shaking her head. "Yeah. Exactly." She turns to me, her face sobering. "Sorry. I know this is all very 'annoying first-world problems,' but—"

"Oh my God," I interrupt dramatically. "Even when you're talking about your problems, you do it perfectly. Stop apologizing. You know, sometimes you can just be upset. That's okay."

When she doesn't react right away, I'm worried that I've overstepped. I was joking, but what if Priya thought I was just being a jerk. Before I can take it back, she stands and mimes elbow-dropping me, like a wrestler. She misses me by a wide margin, giggling as she lands.

There's something so charmingly un-Priya about the move. It disarms me, and I can't help but stare at her with a puzzled expression.

"The first person I ever saw do that was Carlos from third grade. Remember him?"

I nod, conjuring a mental image of Carlos's curly dark hair and round cheeks.

"I saw him do it off a slide to his little brother at the playground across from school. I think he broke his nose, but I thought it was so cool. I spent all weekend practicing it, but when my mom saw me doing it, she laughed at me."

"Deepika, no!" I gasp.

Priya waves it off with a laugh. "I'm sure it was very cute. I was such a tame child and suddenly I'm suplexing Bucket Bin the teddy bear in the sunroom."

"I just . . ." My voice catches in my throat. "I don't know what I should focus on first: the fact that I don't think that's what a suplex is or that you had a teddy bear named Bucket Bin."

"I was a very lonely child, okay?" she snaps good-naturedly. "Anyway, I never did it again after that. I was too embarrassed that everyone would laugh at me the way my mom did."

"Well," I say slowly. "If you somehow got the impression that I wouldn't laugh at you, you were wrong."

An ineffectual swat grazes my arm. "No, I knew you would laugh at me." Her eyes twinkle. "But I don't mind when it's you."

## WELL AFTER THE
## RAIN SUBSIDES

Priya pulls her hair back into a messy ponytail, but it isn't long enough to stay in place. Stray pieces of black and white escape around the nape of her neck, and I can't stop looking at them.

She sees me looking and pushes her hair back self-consciously. "I know, I look like I have a mullet."

"No, it looks . . ." There's another word on the tip of my tongue, but instead I say, "cool."

"Well, you are the authority on cool," Priya jokes, rolling her eyes and smiling. She turns her phone over and our source of light wings in a wide 360. "Did you ever learn any shadow puppets?"

I hold my flat palm sideways and move my pinky up and down. "Just the dog."

Priya places her phone face down on the sleeping bag between us, so the light is shining up at the ceiling. Then she drags her mostly empty backpack over to use as a pillow and lies down beside me.

My stomach twists, forcing me to suck in a deep breath. *All right, Juliette,* I tell myself. *Chill.*

"Okay," she says, making a big show of getting ready.

"Please don't tell me that you can do shadow puppets on top of everything else," I say.

Priya turns in my direction, but because of the bag underneath her head, she ends up looking down at me. Her green eyes sparkle wildly in the flashlight's glow.

Sophomore year, in chemistry, Mr. Tejas started the oxidation unit by holding different metal compounds over a flame. Copper turns fire green. That's what her eyes remind me of now.

"No, I have no idea how to do shadow puppets," she admits.

I laugh. "Thank God. If you did, I'd . . ." I trail off.

"You'd what?" she teases, squinting through the beam of light at me.

I take an anchoring breath. *Okay, Juliette. Relax. Think of something funny.* But I can't think of anything.

She starts to speak, but the sky chooses that moment to open up like a trapdoor. The rain, which had been constant and steady, buffets the tent's walls. The phone's light bounces off the vibrating canvas, scattering the shadows. Priya jolts, and I'm transfixed on the O her mouth forms.

"You would have been so screwed," she says of the sudden downpour, letting her head fall back on the backpack.

"Are you kidding?" I chuckle. "I would've been back to Polaris by now. And you wouldn't have to sleep in denim."

Priya laughs. "Yeah, but would that really be better?"

I peer over at her, and we lock eyes for a moment before I look away. Suddenly, I'm glad for the phone between us. It feels like a physical barrier, taking up much more space than it actually does.

"Yeah, good point." I flex and extend my hand over the flashlight, watching the enormous projection copy my movements overhead.

"This is kind of nice," I say, staring pointedly at my shadow, my hand—basically anywhere but at Priya.

"Yeah. It is." Her voice, pitched deeper than usual, surprises me enough that I glance over. She meets my eyes and blinks deliberately as her teeth scrape slowly back over her full lower lip.

My breath hitches, and I automatically sit up, reaching for my water bottle. I'm not thirsty, but I take my time unscrewing the top and taking a long sip. I feel like every possible emotion has taken up residence in my chest. I am Pandora's box. I want to run my hands over my face in frustration. I want to find a spot at the root of a tree where I can sit until moss covers my entire body and nature reclaims me. I want to lie back down and act like a normal human being. I want . . . I don't know what I want.

I take another sip.

Actually, I do know what I want. And that's worse.

I fall back, gripping my water bottle like it's a door, I'm Rose, and the *Titanic* is sinking.

"Well," Priya says so quietly that I have to lean a little closer to hear. "We have an early day tomorrow. Maybe we should go to sleep."

I want to protest. *No, I'm having a good time. No, talk more. No, let me keep looking at you.* But, of course, I don't say anything.

Without a rebuttal from me, Priya seems to shrink into herself. I wonder if she misread my nerves as something else. Rejection? As if I could reject Priya Pendley? Or am I the one misreading her? Maybe there's not even anything to reject in the first place and I'm one of those people who finds out their friend is queer and immediately thinks everything is flirting.

The tilt-a-whirl of thoughts comes screeching to a halt when Priya reaches for her phone.

"Wait," I say without having prepared a follow-up.

"What's up?" she asks, her hand hovering over the phone and casting a five-fingered shadow above us.

"I actually know one more shadow puppet."

A look of amusement crosses her face. "Oh yeah?"

I laugh. "Yeah." I point to her left hand, the one reaching for the phone. "Make the dog with that one."

She rolls her eyes but does as she's told, holding her flat palm with a thumb up over the light. "Oh, wow," she says sarcastically. "Never seen that before."

Before I can second-guess myself, I set down my water bottle, letting it roll off to the side. Making a thumbs-up with my right hand, I hold it against her palm, our thumbs crossing. "Look it's a different dog. Cool, huh?"

Priya chuckles. "I've seen cooler."

I turn my body so I'm facing her and fix her with a serious look. "Who is the authority on cool here?" I ask, throwing her words back at her. "You have to move the mouth to fully under-stand it, obviously."

Priya smiles, running her tongue over her top teeth. "Obviously." She moves the dog's mouth, then nods in appreciation. "Oh I get it now; it's a totally different dog."

"There you go," I say approvingly.

Now that the moment is over, I begin to pull my fist back, but Priya's fingers close over mine. A sharp inhale escapes me before I can stop it. With my eyes glued to our hands, I straighten my fingers and Priya loosens her hold just enough so that my fingers can curl over her hand.

My eyes track down her arm and settle on her face. Shadows dance across it, catching the golden highlighter on her cheekbones. And I don't look away. I can't look away.

I can't look away as she fluidly shifts her weight until she's over me and our hands are clasped beside my right shoulder.

The rain bounces off the tent rhythmically, and I've never been more thankful for a sound in my life. I'm sure it's the only reason my heartbeat isn't audible right now.

Priya lowers herself onto her forearms, one of her hips pinning me down. She drops her face close enough that her long lashes brush my cheek, and my chest tightens with a mix of pain and pleasure.

Is this happening? I feel half-asleep.

Her breath tickles my ear. "Have you ever . . .?"

I'm not sure what Priya is asking. Have I ever . . . kissed someone? Have I ever hooked up with someone? Have I ever done either of those things with a girl? To be honest, it really doesn't matter exactly what she's asking because the answer to all of them is a shy headshake. Which I give, and then immediately ask myself since when does Priya Pendley make me feel shy? Since when does she make me want to do things I've never done before? Never *wanted* to do before she looked at me like that?

"Then . . . is it okay?" Priya asks, her voice low and gentle.

"Oh my God. Yes," I breathe, my head spinning. My eyelids flutter closed.

Her laugh is a warm huff of air in my ear that sends goose bumps over my whole body. "Huh. I just don't know if you want it enough . . ." Priya's tone turns playful.

My eyes fly open to find her biting her tongue and smirking. Annoyed, I roll my head to the side, my body still trapped beneath her. "Why are you such a d—"

Priya's lips settle on mine, and I gasp. Her mouth is warm, soft, and salty-sweet, like gorp. She moans, a deep rumble that echoes through my entire body.

Wow. Priya. Goddamn. Pendley.

My fingers twine into her damp hair, easily shaking it loose from its ponytail and showering us both in the smell of lemongrass.

She pulls back for a second, and I miss her weight the moment it's gone. Instinctively, one of my hands hooks into the belt loops of her overalls and pulls her down closer. Instead of kissing me, though, she rests a hand on my cheek, gives me the sweetest smile, and says, "Sorry, you were saying?"

A zing of want hums through me. Without permission from

my brain, my body arches, but her mouth still hovers just out of my reach. I groan, "You're the worst."

Priya's laugh has never sounded so beautiful or melodic. "That's just one of the many, many, many—"

I incline my head so that my forehead presses into her lips. Grinning, I play along. "Many."

"Many reasons you like me," she finishes, finally relaxing into my arms.

I get to kiss Priya again. And again. I kiss her deeply and desperately and don't stop kissing her until well after the rain subsides.

# THE FOSBURY FLOP

"Remember when I told you that my mom dragged me to all your Little Star Search competitions because she was obsessed?" Priya asks, twining her fingers in with mine.

"Uh-huh," I say. We lie on our backs, looking up at the roof of the tent.

"It *may* have been the other way around."

I face her, tracing her profile in the dim light of dawn.

She continues, "I may have been the one dragging her to them."

"Oh my God," I say with a soft gasp. "That is so . . ."

"Cute?" she supplies.

"Embarrassing for you," I finish.

She untwines our hands suddenly, shoving at me. "Be nice!"

With a laugh, I push up from her sleeping bag and stretch. I say through a yawn, "We should get a move on. Pat will be calling for us any minute."

Priya doesn't respond, just stares at the skin that my stretch exposed. I tug my shirt (really, her shirt) back down and cross my arms. That gets her attention.

She looks up, blinking like a newborn baby. "Hmm?"

I shake my head and nudge her off the sleeping bag with

my knee, then I roll it up into my lap. "Oh, stop."

I'm glad to have something to occupy my hands and mind, because Priya says, "We gonna talk about last night?"

Biting back my knee-jerk reaction to make a joke, I say, "Sure."

She looks at me expectantly, but when I don't say anything, she speaks instead. "I, for one, had a delightful time."

"Oh, yeah. Me too." The sleeping bag is finally secured inside its elastic cords, and my hands are once again empty. I squirm, desperate to not sit in this discomfort.

Priya laughs. "I'm going to ask you this once and you need to be honest. Did you not enjoy last night, or are you just acting weird because you're you?"

I can't help but snort. I love that she knew to ask me that. It makes my stomach hurt. "I enjoyed it. I'm just being me."

She rolls her eyes, though her smile is understanding. "Classic. We'll work on that."

I follow her out of the tent. My ankle is tender but not excruciating. Without the added pressure of last night, the pain is much more manageable.

Priya gathers the mud-laden piles that are our clothes and stuffs them first into a plastic bag and then into her pack. The job of disassembling the tent has fallen to me.

I break the contented silence by abruptly blurting, "Why did you say I hate women?"

Her mouth drops open. "What?"

"You said I hate women," I repeat.

"I said that?"

"Yes," I answer, staring at the tent.

"Last night?"

"No. Earlier."

With confusion in her voice, Priya says, "I don't know why I'd say that. I love women."

I pause, furrowing my brow. Then I realize what she means. "No, *you* said *I*"—I jab a finger into my own chest—"hate women."

Priya suddenly bursts into laughter, and I'm so startled that my hand slips. A spring-loaded tent pole snaps closed, pinching the flesh between my thumb and forefinger. I yelp and drop the metal pole with a clatter.

"Oh! Are you okay?" Priya is at my side instantly, helping to pick up all the things I dropped. "Yeah, yes, yeah. No, I did say that. Not my finest moment."

Our hands brush as she helps me gather the poles. "Do you really think I hate women?"

Priya looks sheepish. "Um. No, I don't. I was actually trying to get you to tell me if you were queer . . . ?"

"What?" I nearly drop everything again, but Priya steadies the collection with both hands.

"Yeah, like I was hoping you would say, 'No, Priya, I don't hate women! I love women! I want to kiss a woman!' Something like that."

Staggered, I gape at her. "In what world would I have said that? In what world would any human being respond like that?" I gently push her shoulder. "I had a whole identity crisis because of you!"

Together, we roll the rods up in the canvas of the tent.

"What identity crisis?" Priya asks, securing one of the Velcro straps.

"I thought I hated women!"

Priya stops what she's doing, sits back on her heels, and gapes at me. "Huh?"

I shrug sharply, palms up.

"Juliette. You live in your brain. You know whether you hate women or not." She smirks and slips the tent into its designated spot on her pack. "And based on what I've seen . . . I mean . . . Not to sound too presumptuous, but—"

"Oh my God," I exclaim exaggeratedly, failing to keep the smile off my face.

Priya throws her hands up, carefree. She swings her pack over one shoulder and then mine over the other. I make a move like I'm going to protest, but she rolls her eyes and takes off down the mountain.

"Juliette and Priya, sitting in a tree," she sings gleefully. "K-I-S-S-I-N-G."

There are many things that don't live up to expectations. The morning after Senior Twilight isn't one of those things. Pat radios for everyone to start heading back into camp, with instructions to call out our numbers on the walkie as we approach the tree line. Priya and I arrive early and set up a picnic just out of sight of the crowd. I think to some degree she knew my ankle would need a break before parading myself in front of camp.

We sit on my tarp and eat the peanut butter tortillas that Pat tucked away into our packs. Soon, stippled predawn light filters between the trees. Priya is weaving a daisy crown when Lucy crashes through the brush.

She stumbles to a halt, bracing a hand against a nearby tree. "Morning, pals. What are we doing?"

"Waiting for the sun to come up," Priya replies, placing her completed daisy crown on her head. "Wanna wait with us?"

Lucy smiles, looking back and forth between us. "Absolutely not. I got my eyes on the prize: bacon." She gives us a salute and radios Pat that she's about to step out.

"Hold on a minute, seventeen. I have a situation," comes his reply.

Turning back to us and rolling her eyes, she says, "Well, I'm glad you two finally hooked up."

Priya's mouth drops open. "Wait, how—"

At the same time, I blurt, "When did—"

Amusement fills Lucy's face. "I have a Spidey-sense for these things." She points at Priya. "You, I've known about your thing for Baby J since day one. Well, maybe day three." She raises her eyebrows at me. "I was on the fence about Juliette, though. Gia and I couldn't figure out your whole . . . deal. Ya know, sexuality and whatnot."

I breathe a laugh. Them and me both, I guess.

"Okay, seventeen. Ready?"

"Hell yeah," she says into the walkie.

"Lucy! Language," Pat snaps, despite his own rule of exclusively using our numbers for this part.

Lucy gives us a salute again, then frowns. "Man, that was so much cooler the first time. Damn you, Pat." She shakes her fist at the sky.

"Lucy Swentek!" Pat's voice booms over the makeshift sound system. "Fogridge camper for six years and awarded this year's Adventurer of the Summer."

In a single, explosive exhale, Lucy says, "Ohbytheway, I'm totally telling Gia about you two the second I see him." I expect her to walk away at that, but she stares at us expectantly, clearly waiting for our okay.

"Whatever," I sigh.

Priya gives her a thumbs-up. "Do your thing."

Lucy throws up a satisfied shaka and swaggers out past the tree line, arms raised like a champion gladiator. Priya and I cheer at the top of our lungs.

"Do we all get an award?" Priya asks, beaming at Lucy's back. "Everybody has so far."

"Yeah, but they're not real; the staff makes them up for the campers who complete Senior Twilight. It's part of the whole"—I circle my wrist—"thing." I pause, nervous to ask my next question. But I want to try. I want Priya to know I'm trying. "Are you okay with . . . them knowing?"

She gives me a genuine smile. "Juliette Barrera-Wright, do you think I'm embarrassed of you?"

I laugh and pop my last bite of peanut butter tortilla in my mouth. "Well, you are *the* Priya Pendley."

Her expression flattens a little. "Yeah."

A bird chirps above us, catching her attention momentarily. She tilts her chin to look up, and I'm struck by how stunning she is. In profile, straight on. At dawn, lit up by a phone flashlight. Covered in paint and sawdust. Framed by rain-drenched strands of hair. I will never get tired of looking at that face.

"You still think of me like that?" she asks, playing with the laces of her muddy hiking boots.

"Huh?"

"Like . . ." She squints out at the grassy field. "Someone who . . ."

She doesn't finish, but she doesn't have to. Someone who would be embarrassed of me. She's asking if I still think of her as the person I've always said she was. Spoiled. Shallow. Social media Priya. Priyatopia Priya.

A lump forms in my throat. "No, I—" My voice cuts off, and I have the same petrified feeling I had the night she asked about my siblings, a fossilization of every muscle in my body.

I'm intense. Pugnacious. I always say what I mean. So why can't I speak now, at the moment it feels like I need to most? As the seconds stretch by in never-ending eternities, I drown in humiliation. Unable to meet Priya's eyes, I zone out into the forest, and center on the sensation of tapping my canines together.

Priya's hand lands on my cheek with painful softness. I finally look up to find her head tilted and her expression thoughtful. "It's not me, is it? It's you."

"What?"

Her thumb strokes my cheekbone. "Yes or no: you think people will think you aren't good enough for me."

My stomach clenches. I make a noncommittal noise, but she continues to silently hold my gaze. Her hand drifts to the crook of my neck, and I instinctually press deeper into it.

Voice gentle, she says, "I can wait all day if you need me to. But I want you to answer. With words."

A chill runs down my spine. I close my eyes, take a deep breath, and whisper, "Yes."

My back hits the ground with a thump, knocking all the air out of me. Priya, having just tackled me into the dirt, rolls off my chest and rises to her knees like she's about to elbow-drop me again.

"You silly, beautiful, ridiculous, perfect buffoon." She shakes her head, jaw clenched. "You knock this off right now. You're amazing, you know that? Your singing voice could cause a hundred Grecian shipwrecks. You light up when you accomplish things. Do you remember that away meet you guys had last year at that high school where the track was on the roof?"

Of course I remember that. It wasn't just a meet. That meet was the qualifier for regionals. I hit my PR in the prelims but missed each of my attempts in the final round. I can still feel my heel clipping the crossbar on my third jump. I knew I'd been eliminated before I even hit the crash pad.

I nod.

"I went to that meet." She waves a hand. "For Barry. And I cannot describe to you how sexy the grin on your face was

when you landed your last jump in that first round. Oh my God."
Her fingers tangle into her hair, bunching it up. "I can picture it.
You were wearing your cute tank top team jersey and these *tiny*
athletic shorts, and you did that little backward jumpy thing you
guys do, you know?"

I nod, amused by her description of the Fosbury Flop.

"And you were upside down." Her mouth quirks up on one
side. "And I swear to God, you smiled right at me. Just this huge
shit-eating grin, like, 'Screw you, look what I can do.' I remember
watching you stretch on the track after and thinking that a girl
like you could ruin my whole goddamn life."

I can feel my face turning tomato red. "Did you swear this
much before you started hanging out with Lucy?" I deflect.

"Obviously not. But don't try to distract me, Barrera-Wright."
Her face wrinkles at my mouthful of a last name. "You are
smart and funny and, despite how often you're a pain in my
ass, you are one of my favorite people. So, if anyone thinks I'm
'too good'"—Priya puts air quotes around the words—"for you,
screw them. And screw you if you believe them."

"Promise?" I joke, but my heart feels like it's going to burst out
of my chest.

She narrows her eyes and ignores me. "You are more than
enough. For anyone, not just me. And if you need me to prove
that shit, I will. Over and over and over again until you believe it."

I stare up at the trees, the shadows shifting across the leaves.
"Oh my God," I breathe. "Pendley, are you obsessed with me?"

"Oh, stop." A hazy ray of sunlight falls across her face and

Priya shields her eyes, chuckling. I love her laugh. How could I ever think I didn't love her laugh?

With all the sincerity I can muster, I say, "Thank you."

"Any time," she says, rocking back on her heels. "If we don't go soon, Pat's gonna come looking for us."

I watch her grab the empty sandwich baggies from break-fast, stuffing them into the outermost pocket of her bag. How can this be so easy for her? The fact that she can jump from that conversation to cleaning up is mystifying.

"You planning to help me or what?" she asks, nodding her head toward the tarp laid out on the ground.

Together, we roll up our makeshift picnic blanket and tuck it into the straps beneath my pack. Every time our hands brush, she shoots me a smirk.

Once we confirm we've LNT'd (left no trace), I turn to her. "Ready?"

"Ready." She offers me an arm. I don't know if it's for moral support, to show affection, or to keep me from limping across the field. I appreciate it no matter what the reason.

I click the button on my walkie and say, "Five and twelve, Pat."

"Copy."

The crackle of Pat turning on the microphone sends silence rippling through the crowd.

"Priya Pendley, Fogridge camper for one year and awarded Rookie of the Year. Juliette Barrera-Wright, Fogridge camper for ten years, reigning North Star, and this year's Best Future Staff Member."

I can't wipe the smile off my face as we step out of the woods.

# EFFIGY

On the last night of camp, they burn the effigy.

Priya and I spend the whole morning packing (her stuff, obviously, because mine only takes two seconds to shove into my duffel bags). After we finally get everything loaded into our cars, we head back to Polaris to change into this year's camper shirts.

"A lot of people like her," Priya is saying as we climb Polaris's steps. "But I don't think she should have won. I went into that season's finale sure she was just being dragged along like a lamb to the slaughter."

I step into our cabin and am finally hit with that sun-warmed cedar scent I spent all summer missing. But now I miss the smell of lemongrass and roses. The room is empty, except for my backpack and one of Priya's suitcases. I imagine next year's North Star moving in, no evidence of Priya or me ever having lived here. Glancing up at my loft, I realize this is the last night I'll ever sleep in this tree house, and the nostalgia punches me in the stomach.

"I'm just saying that there's a difference between a good social game and being friendly." The end of Priya's tirade is muffled as she pulls this year's sky-blue Fogridge shirt over her white tank top. She turns to me with a serious expression. "We've got to watch *Survivor*."

I chuckle, pulling on my shirt as well. "I don't know about that."

"Juliette. This is a hard boundary for me. If you don't watch *Survivor*, I *will* break up with you." She shrugs as if she hadn't just spoken such monumental words.

What?

I'm afraid to move and shatter the moment, which feels as fragile as my ankle. "Can you . . . Are we . . . in a . . . position for you to break up with me?"

*Oof. Go ahead, make this sound more like a business transaction, Juliette.*

Priya looks unfazed as she flits around the room in search of the permanent markers she put aside while we were packing. "Are we not?"

"Uh. G—Um, I—" The little people who live in my brain are preparing to slam the self-destruct button when Priya spins around, holding two black Sharpies up in the air like they're winning lottery tickets.

Her smile softens when she sees my panic. She approaches slowly, the way you'd approach a stray cat hiding in your wheel well. One hand holds a marker out toward me. When I reach out to take it, she doesn't let go.

"I don't want anyone else." Her voice is steady and assured.

A wave of dizzying warmth floods my body. "Me neither."

She releases the marker and flashes me a million-watt grin before spinning around and exposing her back. "Good. Then, we'll start with season thirty-seven; there's a guy who calls himself 'the Mayor of Slamtown.' Now sign my shirt."

I laugh, uncap the marker, and write the first five words that come to mind. Priya doesn't criticize me for the brevity of the message. She simply proceeds to pen an entire novel across my left shoulder blade.

"Done!" she finally declares with a flourish.

"What does it say?" I ask, tugging my shirt forward but still unable to see.

"Oh, it's a list of the first ten dates I'm going to take you on when we get home."

My breath catches.

"What did you write?" she asks, and I'm once again impressed by her ability to make earth-shattering comments as easily as reporting the weather.

I shrug. "You'll just have to wait and see."

She doesn't protest or try to read it backward in the mirror, just says, "Okay. Can't wait."

"Come on." I gesture at the door. We only have a little while before the effigy ceremony starts and entire shirts to fill with messages.

"Age before beauty," Priya asserts, pushing past me. She skips out the door, and I catch sight of the sentence I messily scrawled along the collar.

*I'm glad it was you.*


"Tonight, we say goodbye to a wonderful summer." Pat scans the crowd. In the waning daylight, he's barely more than a silhouette, but he still manages to drip with gravitas. "It is a tradition here at Fogridge that while the effigy burns, nobody speaks. Out of respect for your friends, your counselors, and the memories you've made, I hope you will all honor that tradition. This is a time for reflection. To think about the things you are grateful for and the challenges you've overcome this year. When you feel it's time, when you're ready, you may head back to your cabins in silence."

Someone on the edge of the crowd holds up an unlit torch, which Pat takes with a flourish.

"To light the fire this year, I'd like to call up our winning Color War captain and MVP staff member, Flagstaff." There's a subdued applause, as most people have already fallen under the spell of Effigy Silence, but I can't help letting out a small whoop. "And also, next year's North Star, Amer Pierce!"

It's not a name I recognize, but the claps and cheers are louder this time as a brown-skinned boy with a bright smile moves through the crowd. The dark outlines of his tightly coiled hair bounce the entire length of his jog up to Pat. Flagstaff claps the boy on the back, and together they dip the torch into the campfire, igniting the end with a whoosh. Carefully, they approach the effigy—ten-foot-tall wooden letters spelling out FOGRIDGE—and hold the torch to the base of each letter until it catches.

The fire grows, tendrils reaching for the stars, and I can feel the heat even from this far back. By the time the last of the untouched straw goes up in flames, I have to take a few steps away from the warmth. A flickering glow illuminates the audience, enraptured by the inferno.

My eyes roam the upturned faces. Lucy and Gia each stand with their group. When I find Lucy, she's already looking at me. I expect an irreverent wink or finger gun, but she just gives me a small, genuine smile before turning back to the effigy. From my spot, I can only make out Gia's profile, not his whole handsome face, but it's enough to see him wipe silent tears from his jaw.

It's easy for me to think of camp as something that belongs to me. This ceremony always reminds me that my two best friends feel the exact same way. Everyone here feels the exact same way.

TK—the frizz of her hair glowing and creating a halo around her head—stands near the front. Even in seriousness, her face is soft and kind. Pat, beside her, crosses his arms and sets his feet wide apart. It feels silly to love the Zimmermans the way I do. Lucy would tell me that Pat is simply a capitalist pawn doing his job, but I know she secretly loves him. How can you not love the people who gave you a space to be the person you've always wanted to be?

Flagstaff grins up at the fire, one hand holding the torch and the other resting atop Amer's head. My heart feels like breaking just thinking about not seeing his face again. People always say not to meet your heroes, but I think that Flagstaff is a hero worth meeting. I try to psychically communicate my gratitude to him, hoping he can somehow sense it. In fact, I send gratitude to ten years of counselors and specialists. At Strat and her endless enthusiasm. At the long-haired boating specialist, Gamble, who wore jeans that always ended up soaked. At Zebra, the stylish craft specialist everyone had a crush on a few years ago. At Barto and Drell and Seafoam and Twee and Euphrates. At Galahad for bringing Priya and me closer.

Gratitude for Fogridge courses through me. My entire being is a love letter to it, the good and the bad. The sprained ankles and the opening nights. The losses and the wins. Every time the Lazlots stormed the field at Color War. The slight chill of the morning air. Kicking up dew from the grass and feeling it sprinkle the backs of my legs. Every painful and boring moment of a hike, but also the view from the summit.

All at once, finality runs like a chill from my head to my toes. Never again. I never get to come back and do those things the same way. Maybe I never get to come back. Period. I don't know what my summers will look like. If I'm at Yale, will I give up internships or better pay just to fly back to the West Coast and work here? And after I graduate college, will I get a real job that takes up my summers? Will I even live in California?

One way or another, there will come a day that I drive past the arch, down the dirt road, and never come back.

The thought settles like a lump in my throat, and then I'm crying. Not Gia's silent tears. Not dignified sniffles. Full-on sobs. I'm not the only one. The people nearby give me sympathetic pats on the back, but it only makes me cry more. How can I say goodbye to this community and this place? How could I have packed up all my things not knowing whether I'll get to unpack them here again?

I can't. I can't.

I can't.

I can't.

A soothing hand settles over mine.

Priya stands in front of me. The concern is plain on her face as she pulls me into her, shushing me softly.

"I don't want to go," I whisper into her shoulder. Not even her familiar smell is comforting right now.

"We don't have to go yet," she tells me, smoothing my hair.

If it's possible, I cry even harder. My tears soak her shirt, but Priya just continues holding me. People trickle out of the crowd and back to their cabins, but we stay where we are. We are the eye of the storm.

When my weeping slows to the occasional miserable hiccup, Priya steps back. She takes my tearful face in her hands, using her thumbs like windshield wipers. Her eyes sparkle, reflecting the blaze. I can't believe she's always been this beautiful and this kind and I thought I hated her.

I'm a fool.

Quietly, she recites an A. A. Milne quote I've seen before on social media posts and promotional materials for vacations: "How lucky you are to have something that makes saying goodbye so hard."

Those words have never meant much to me, but hearing

them spoken by Priya Pendley in the glow of the Fogridge effigy changes that.

I breathe in. Lucky for Senior Twilight, for Polaris, for *Beauty and the Beast*.

I breathe out. Lucky for s'mores, dancing in the firelight, and cozy sleeping bags.

Lucky to have Gia and Lucy.

Lucky to have Priya.

I am standing on my own, not crying. I hold Priya's hand as the fire goes from inferno to ember. Lucky.

When the fire finally burns itself out, we are two of the last people to walk back to our cabin in total silence, under the watchful stars of the Southern California sky.

And the whole time, I do feel lucky.

# EPILOGUE

## *THREE YEARS LATER*

It's dark inside the flimsy paper box. Where the sun manages to cut through the thick coating of crayon on the outside, it casts a dim purple glow.

My body hurts. I've been crouched in this same position for hours, but Pat warned me that if I broke the box early and ruined the surprise, he would publicly guillotine me on the last day of camp. *And, Juliette, camp does not bring in enough money to pay for years of therapy after these kids see you beheaded.*

So, here I am, dutifully motionless, deeply uncomfortable and soaked in sweat as my brain cooks like a scrambled egg.

Still. My heart is racing so fast that I can't keep the delirious grin off my face.

About thirty minutes ago, the growing ruckus of children arriving at the soccer field began. The noise seems to have passed its zenith and is leveling out to a steady hum. Occasionally, that hum is punctuated by a shriek as the kids spot the paper boxes.

"What is that?" they squeal futilely. "What's going on? What are those?"

I imagine Lucy recounting the moment later: *They kept asking what was going on. Like I knew anything! I know just as much as they do at all times; Pat doesn't tell us shit.*

Suddenly, the sound drops ten decibels. There is a profound silence from the crowd as I hear Pat take the mic. From my position inside the box, his voice is muffled. I worry I won't be able to hear my entrance line, but there it is, loud and clear:

"Help me welcome this summer's Lazlot captain—"

I don't hear him say my name over the adrenaline pumping in my ears as I burst through the paper triumphantly, silently thanking God that I broke the box in one go. There were no test runs and I was afraid I'd end up pathetically trying to claw my way out in front of the entire camp.

I must black out briefly, because the next thing I know, I'm across the soccer field. I seek out my group and, when I find them, scoop up my favorite camper. Arno is a precocious ten-year-old, tiny for his age, except for his abnormally large head. He asks more questions than anyone in the world has answers, and he wears little khakis (often backward) with a button-down every day. I swing him around while he shrieks.

"What the heck?" he demands in a tiny little screech.

"Surprise!" I say, setting his shiny little oxfords gently back down on the grass.

I run to Pat's side. Now that I'm stationary, my brain catches up to my ears. The thrum of my own pulse fades and I can hear the kids and counselors screaming for me. Strat jumps approximately twenty feet in the air, leading a chant of my nonsense name.

"LUCKY, LUCKY, LUCKY!"

I skim the faces until I find her standing among the specialists. Lucy's eyes have gone as wide as the mess hall plates. Both hands cover her lower face in shock. Then, she cups her hands around her mouth and screams, "Hell yes!"

I look between her and Pat as he gives her a disapproving headshake. She gives him her favorite *Eh, what're you gonna do? Fire me?* shrug. To be fair to her, much worse could have come out of her mouth.

Lucy catches my gaze and ever-so-subtly brings the tip of her index finger to her ear. It's been a long time since I saw her do that, and it startles a laugh out of me. According to Pat, we can't play Get Down, Mr. President anymore. Lucy complies, not because she cares about whether it's camp appropriate, but because Pat warned us that if we do it and the campers injure themselves copying us, Lucy will have to file the incident reports. If there's one thing she hates more than rules, it's paperwork.

I give her a little salute, then she points a finger straight at me, and bellows, "THAT'S MY CAPTAIN!" She draws the last word out, pumping her fist in the air. Tears stream down her face. I look away before I get too emotional. Lucy hasn't been a captain yet, but I know her time is coming. Pat told me that both of our names have been on the short list since we graduated from campers to staff.

I hope when she gets it, she doesn't tell me either. It's the only way I'll be able to live this down. I can already feel her punching me in the shoulder, demanding to know how I could've kept it a secret from her. She'll be even more livid when she finds out that I texted Gia the second Pat approached me for the position.

Gia wasn't at camp this summer. Not for the first time, I badly wish he could be here to see my reveal, but when he got an internship offer at one of the biggest architecture firms in LA, he couldn't turn it down. I look for TK, holding up a phone, and wave fervently at the camera. I'd bet good money that Gia is hiding in his office bathroom, glued to that livestream right now.

I'm doing that cornball grin again as Pat uses both hands to signal for silence. He announces the Mariket captain, Howl, who's new this year and already a BNOC. I'm happy for him, but I can't take my eyes off the green box. I didn't think I could be more nervous than I was about my entrance, but as Pat quiets the crowd for the last captain, I am overcome with nausea.

"And our captain for the Dondos, Romeo!"

In one smooth motion, the paper of the box tears, and Priya jumps out. And now I really am crying—just a little bit—as she screams a Dondo chant at the top of her lungs, running back and forth in front of her campers.

She's dressed head-to-toe in green. Green cat ears, green feather boa, green shirt and shorts under a green tutu. Even the bottom half of her hair, the part that's normally white, is dyed green. We had to sneak out of our bunks last night (with Pat's permission, of course) and drive to Party City for cheap spray dye. In classic Priya fashion, she did buy an exorbitantly expensive fancy holographic dye online, but she accidentally shipped it to our apartment in New Haven instead of to the camp office. By the time she realized, not even a rush order would have arrived in time.

She still looks amazing though, because of and not despite the emerald stain on her neck from hours sweating her hair dye off. She sprints toward us, beaming the brightest smile I've ever seen from her, setting butterflies aflutter in my stomach. Even after three years.

By the time Priya takes her spot beside me in our lineup, the entire camp is on their feet. I grab Howl's hand with my right and Priya's hand with my left. It's clammy. With her palm pressed against mine, I can feel her heart beating rapidly. She squeezes my hand, and I look in her direction, breathing hard.

She scrunches her nose at me happily, and seeing her like this brings me back to our first summer together. I can barely remember seeing her enormous smile and not loving it with everything I have. I was a different person back then, before I woke up next to her every day in our king-size bed that she somehow manages to take up ninety percent of. Before we opened our letters from Yale and she waited to celebrate until she was sure mine also started with "Congratulations!"

There was a time when I couldn't have imagined the way Deepika screeched when Priya introduced me as her girlfriend. She had whacked Priya on the shoulder and said, *Dear God. If you're lying, just kill me now. I refuse to live in a world where this is a joke.* Once Priya and I confirmed that it was actually true, Deepika hugged me and whispered, *I'm so glad you're finally part of this family, my beautiful girl. She doesn't deserve you. If you break up, I'm coming with you.*

My camp nonsense name started as a joke, but I do feel lucky. I feel lucky for every incredible moment I've gotten to spend with my favorite person at my side. I feel lucky that we got to jump out of these silly little boxes together and that we ever got the chance to share this place I love. Maybe it's my old age (nineteen) turning me into a sap or maybe I'm going mad with the power of being a Color War captain, but I'm confident that no one in the history of the world has ever been as lucky as I am.

I lean in so Priya can hear me over the noise. "I love you," I whisper.

Instead of answering, she presses into my side and briefly rests her head on my shoulder. She flashes me a heart-melting smile, the kind she saves just for me, before turning back to her adoring fans in the crowd. Priya's told me she loves me enough times that I could forgive one transgression.

But I won't. I'm going to give her so much shit for this tonight.

"Fogridge," Pat says in his deep, booming voice. "I present to you, this year's Color War captains!"

The three of us raise our interlocked hands and, cheering wildly, race forward into the crowd.

# ACKNOWLEDGMENTS

I didn't grow up going to summer camp (I was waaay too poor; we didn't even have electricity most summers), but I always wanted to. Then, when I was in college, I was summarily fired from a retail position—unfairly, might I add—and in my desperation for a new job, I stumbled upon camp.

It changed my life. I worked at that same camp for the next seven years, even quitting full-time hospital gigs and driving three thousand miles just to relive that magic.

*Wish You Weren't Here* is a love letter about home-away-from-homes, inner children, and the wonder of summer. And this love letter is addressed to my entire camp fam (including but not limited to: Josh, Max, and the Clique; Janet; my ropes crew; the icons of Powerhouse; and the Senior Chip girlies). If I tried to list everyone, I wouldn't have time to write my second book. But if you've ever gotten me through a heat wave, done my riddles, or listened to me complain about an authority figure (you know the one) while I belayed, this is for you.

Secondly, this book is not for Elon Musk, but it is for pre-X Twitter. For the writing community that I wouldn't be published without. For #LGBTNpit, the friends in my circles who celebrated and commiserated with me, the haters and gossipmongers (affectionate) in my DMs, and my incredible beta readers/CPs. It's for all the authors in the 2024 debut group, who I am so lucky to be on this journey with.

Lastly, I'd like to tell you little stories about some specific people, because to simply list their names out of context wouldn't do them justice:

Laura is my most wholesome friend. One time, I asked her, "Do you know what Tinder is?" and she said, "Of course I know what tinder is. I used to start the fires on the farm every morning." She's a librarian, a ladder-master, and a good egg.

Sarah is braver and more adventurous than I'll ever be. We went caving in Budapest while she was pregnant. She did great. I concussed myself. I've done karaoke exactly once, with her, in Amsterdam. She sang "Bohemian Rhapsody" with me, even though she didn't know the words, and brought me bread the next morning while I vomited into an American Standard toilet.

Sam was, and still is, this book's biggest champion. But I don't think he would like it if I told you a story about him, so I won't. You can learn about him when he wins the sixtieth season of *Survivor: Nerds vs. Geeks vs. Dorks.*

Dean and I met in a creative writing class, and to this day he remains the writer I'm most jealous of. Many of my best phrases are stolen from him. Priyatopia is based on Beantopia, a going-away party he threw for himself.

Theresa and I exchanged notes in middle school by tucking them behind the front flaps of Lemony Snicket books. I've eaten ten times my weight from her family's fridge, lost every game of DDR, and spilled a full glass of wine on her bed the weekend *Lemonade* came out, but she still talks to me through some miracle. If you're trying to blackmail me, she's got some good dirt.

In 2009, Gabby and I wrote a children's book called *Tom Matt Otto* about a sentient tomato. A blurb on the back says, *"Best book I ever wrote!" —Erin Baldwin*, and that's true to this day. When she visited me in Arizona, she'd wake up, put on her shoes, and just head toward the mountains until she got tired of walking.

Clare Edge and I send approximately one hundred voice notes a day to each other. Approximately ninety-nine of them are us asking, "What was I just saying?" She is a master of the craft and I am lucky to share a singular brain cell with her.

Lauren Spieller was always my dream agent, and I'm so lucky to be working with her now. She advocates for me when I won't advocate for myself, and her brainstorming makes me feel like my mind just ran a marathon.

My editor, Aneeka Kalia, helped give voices to my silly little camp goofballs, and I am eternally grateful to her and the rest of the team at Viking who lent their genius to this book.

And, of course, for my little buddy. Leave your oxygen on. 🩶